THAT WAS THE YEAR

I0460761

JENNY BRAVO

Book Layout ©2016 BookDesignTemplates.com

Cover Design by Alloco Designs:

Edited by Tanya Gold and Mary Bravo

That Was the Year/ Jenny Bravo. -- 1st ed.
ISBN 978-0-9963011-2-1

To the girl who knew me first

ONE

She knew this bed.

Or, at least, she thought she did.

Waking up, Reese felt like she was prying her eyes open from a coma, the lids heavier than they'd ever been in her life, her head aching in a way that felt less like a migraine and more like an axe through her skull. She willed herself to pick up her head. She insisted that she open her eyes.

Nothing.

That's when she remembered the alcohol. And as soon as she remembered it, she felt it. Sloshing around in the pit of her stomach like a fish in its bowl.

She remembered the party. *Her* party. Turning twenty-six had been a pretty big deal, so throwing the party had been a pretty big deal, too. Bottles had filled the trash can. Shots had caked their throats. And God, had they thrown them back.

Open your eyes, Reese, she told herself. *Open your stupid, alcoholic eyes.*

And by some miracle, her left pupil graced the world again.

But this was not her room.

That was not her vintage dresser.

That was not her rose-colored wall.

Lift your head, Reese. Lift your morally-questionable head.

Again, the pep talk worked. Slowly and painfully, she dragged her body upright, which was covered up by a fluffy gray comforter that was also, coincidentally, not hers.

This was not her room, but she did know it. She knew the sheer, golden curtains. She knew the ornate mirror next to the closet door.

This was Sophie's room.

If she was here, then where was Sophie?

"What the—"

That's when she saw him. Beside her, a tan back with broad, man shoulders tucked into the comforter beside her. A nest of black hair on his head and beneath his armpits. And he was snoring, she noticed now, lightly.

"*Holy shit,*" she whispered. She could save this. If she acted fast. She placed her hands on his skin, very tentatively, shaking him awake. "Lane. Lane, get up. *Lane—*"

He didn't get up.

So, she decided to bolt.

If she could just find her clothes.

Scattered around Sophie's room, her clothes fell like evidence. She tugged her pants over her legs, shoving her underwear into her pocket. She slipped the shirt over her head, her bra nowhere to be found. Probably under the bed. She'd need to get it later.

Get out, get out, get out.

Reese opened the door.

And Sophie did, too.

Sophie's face, normally sunny and disgustingly kind, had a warranted look of confusion caked over it.

Reese thought fast. "Morning! Man, what a night, huh?"

"What the... did you two..." Sophie connected the dots, seeing her boyfriend lying naked in the bed. Then yelled, "*LANE!*"

"Sophie, it's not what you think," Reese said.

Because really, who knew for sure?

Yes, Reese had been naked in bed with Sophie's boyfriend.

Yes, they'd both consumed enough alcohol to stock a liquor store.

But did that necessarily mean that Reese had hooked up with Lane? No, it did not.

Lane sat up. "Oh my God, Sophie."

"Let's all just take a breath here," Reese said.

She hadn't seen it coming.

She hadn't seen the fist until it connected with her face.

She hadn't seen the punch until she felt the sting of her cheek.

"*Get out of my house!*" Sophie yelled again.

Reese pressed her hand against her cheek, buckled over, not knowing if Sophie was yelling at her or Lane.

"Okay, okay," Reese said, backing up, surrendering. "I'm just going to go to my room and—"

"*Get out, get out, get out!*"

That one was definitely directed at Reese. "What about him? He cheated on you, not me."

The fire in Sophie's eyes could burn a village.

Reese ducked the next swing of Sophie's arm, and charged into the living room and out of the house, calling back, "Okay, but I want my bra back!"

Wendy answered the phone on the first ring. "What's the damage?"

"Well, I screwed up. And it's all *your* fault. Where did you go last night?"

Driving away, Reese knew that she'd crossed more lines than normal. She could feel the faintest bit of guilt settling into her stomach.

Sophie's my friend, she thought. *She's my friend... right?*

"I'm at Vivian's," Wendy said. "Are we talking bail-me-out-of-jail bad or pregnancy-test bad?"

Reese gritted her teeth. "That is one messed up scale. You see, what happened is—"

Reese didn't sugarcoat it.

She spread out every detail like food at a picnic.

This always went the same way: Reese would tell her story and Wendy wouldn't judge. That's why Reese loved her. Wendy always listened intently before she doled out her advice. Sometimes, Reese would even take it.

"Oh God," Wendy said. "You really did screw up."

"Ya think? Now, I'm kicked out of my place in last night's clothes and all I want in this world is a mountain of ice cream. Or maybe a breakfast taco. I'm too exhausted to decipher my own taste buds."

"Here's what you're going to do. You're not going to like it."

Reese tapped her foot on the brake, crawling to a stop at the red light. "I swear to God if you tell me to come to Vivian's—"

"You need a place to crash. Plus, I'm here until tomorrow. We can have a good old fashioned slumber party."

Reese was almost sold. "Just let me get through this work day first."

They were filing soon.

And she was already so late.

Not to mention un-showered.

"Hey, it's better than your mom's house," Wendy reasoned.

"I hate it when you make sense," Reese said, groaning.

Reese let her head fall against the steering wheel.

Rita.

She'd completely forgotten about her family birthday dinner tonight.

"Okay, I'll see you tonight after my birthday dinner from hell," Reese said, sighing. "I'll be the one with the melodrama."

"See you later, little home-wrecker."

Out of all the bad things Reese had done, which was a rapidly growing list, somewhere near Bible-length at this point, sleeping with another girl's boyfriend had never been one of them.

And it kind of made her sick.

More accurately? It made her sick how much it *didn't* make her sick.

TWO

"Latelatelate. I know. I'm so sorry. You wouldn't *believe* the morning I had."

Reese threw her body down into her desk chair and kicked out her heels in front of her. She tossed her tote bag onto the floor and leaned her head back as far as her chair would recline.

No one in this office was a stranger to her being late. In fact, if she ever *was* on time, they usually looked at her funny and asked if she was sick or something.

It's a good thing I'm so damn good at this job, Reese thought.

It was the only reason she got away with anything.

Like the hair color and the tardiness and the occasional mid-afternoon naps on her keyboard.

"What happened?" Jessica asked, her head rising from the cubicle beside Reese.

"Got kicked out of my apartment."

"So an average weekend for you, then?" Jessica asked, laughing.

"More or less. But this time I'm thinking it's on the serious side. And since I don't have a lease..."

"You don't have a lease?"

"I didn't think I needed one!"

"Forget all that," Reese had said. *"We're friends. We don't need contracts."*

Reese shook her head thinking back on it.

Please be more dumb, I dare you.

Jessica leaned in closer over the cubicle wall. "Okay, well, not to change the subject, but Dean looked *pissed* when he walked in this morning. So, heads up."

"Great," Reese said, straightening up in her chair. "Of all the freaking days."

Ever since Dean had taken over as President of their oh-so-illustrious accounting firm, he'd been acting like the sky was falling at every twist and turn. He liked her. Hell, he'd been the one to hire her. But, still.

Reese waved off Jessica's comment. "Whatever. I can handle Dean."

"Weller," Dean's voice called, as if on cue. It practically reverberated through the walls.

Or maybe not, Reese thought.

Jessica's eyes widened. Then she waved it off. "He's just in a mood."

"Like I said," Reese said, swallowing a cheek full of air. "I can handle it."

Rita once told Reese that her entire life was happening just two inches in front of her face. Showed her, actually.

Rita had held her crooked finger out in front of Reese's face and said, *"You see this? Right in the center my fingertip? That's your life."*

And she'd never understood that, until right now.

When your life is two inches in front of your face, you can't see the shit-storm brewing just a few feet ahead of you.

Not until it's right there, ready to bowl you over.

Lucky I've got catlike reflexes, Reese thought.

"Hey, boss," Reese said casually, as she strode into his office. *Yes, casual, like it's your name on this office, not his.* "How's it going?"

He did not look amused. "Sit."

"I know what you're going to say." She melted into the chair. The more comfortable she appeared, the less threatened he'd feel.

"Oh, do you?"

"The tardiness," she offered.

Get ahead of the situation, Reese. Professional. Proactive.

"I know, I know," she continued. "It's not my strength. But, if you look at my record, I'm sure you can see that I stay later than anyone else. I can't tell you how many times the lights have turned off on me."

"Three times, Reese." His lips curled upward. "*These* are your regular work hours."

He pointed to a report that he shoved across his desk. It listed every time she swiped her card to get into the building.

March 22nd: first swipe at 9:30 a.m.

March 22nd: last swipe at 4:30 p.m.

March 23rd: first swipe at 10:00 a.m.

March 23rd: last swipe at 4:00 p.m.

It went on and on, much the same way. The evidence was incriminating.

She created a dozen excuses in her head, but none of them made any sense:

Chronic ear infections that flare up on Mondays.

A diagnosed, biological clock that is always one hour late.

Poor circulation.

"Okay, well, I don't take lunch breaks. And I don't drink coffee, so no wasted time there," Reese said, throwing out her best. She leaned back from his desk. "What's this really about, Dean? I'm good at my job. You know that."

"I don't need good, Reese. Not during busy season. You signed a contract to devote sixty hours during tax season, and you're barely making thirty-five."

Reese could see it on his face.

The words were already there on his lips.

"I can do better," Reese said.

"I'm sorry, Reese," Dean said. And he genuinely looked it now. "We're going to have to let you go."

There was an angry, screaming voice in the back of Reese's brain.

It's not fair, the voice cried. *I'm a freaking good accountant!*

But mostly, she wanted to laugh. She hated this part of herself, but it was what it was.

When bad things happened, Reese would burst into a fit of laughter, like her body couldn't handle the gravity of the situation. So, it counteracted.

People cried.

People yelled.

People hurt.

And she launched into laughter.

"Are you... okay?" Dean asked her.

She was laughing now, and she hadn't even realized it. "Ignore me. This is my weird reaction to hard conversations."

"Oh," he said. He took the box of tissues he'd had ready, and placed it back up on his shelf. "Take your time."

Her side felt like it was splitting. Most people might feel embarrassed, but Reese just felt exhausted. She felt like she could lie down on Dean's floor and pass out for forty years, Rip Van Winkle-style.

She took a deep breath.

"I think I'm ready to go now," she said.

He said more to her then about severance and benefits and stuff that her brain could not absorb properly. He promised to send her an email about it later.

She walked back to her desk with a cool, commandeering stride. She imagined that she was Marilyn Monroe. How would Marilyn Monroe have acted if she'd just gotten fired?

Like a freakin' star.

Jessica was there, looking sincerely concerned. "How did it go?"

"This desk is too small for someone as magnanimous as I," Reese said, flicking her hair behind her back.

"Huh?"

Reese sloped over the desk that was no longer hers, and she couldn't remember if she was sad or not.

I love my job. I love my job... right?

"Oh, God," Jessica said, realization spreading over her face. "They fired you?"

Reese didn't say much else as she threw everything from her desk into a box. Photos of her friends. Her slightly inappropriate, firefighter desk calendar.

She wiped everything clean.

THREE

Bras dangled from the trees.

Bright pink, zebra-striped bras. Black, lacy bras.

Bras with enough padding to stuff a prize-winning, carnival teddy bear.

This was the sight that greeted Reese as she pulled into her driveway. But it wasn't just the bras that made her do a double-take. The lawn was littered with clothing. Thongs on the shrubs. Sweaters on the roof. Dresses carpeting the grass like a quilt.

What. The. Hell.

Now, she was officially angry.

Reese screamed. Reese screamed so loudly that the neighbor's cat went running away in a panic. She screamed so loudly that by the time it was over, her tonsils kept vibrating in the back of her throat, and it felt like they may never stop.

She slammed the car door so hard that she almost threw her back out.

She went to check the door.

The key wouldn't even fit into the lock.

"Sophie!" she yelled.

Sophie was definitely inside, her car parked mockingly outside, as if to say, "*You think you still live here? How cute.*"

"I know you're in there, Sophie," Reese barked.

She could wrap her fist in a sweater and break in the window. She could throw a rock through it. She could knock and knock until a neighbor called the cops.

Sophie's angel face appeared from behind the sheer curtain. "Go. Away. Reese."

"Sure, let me just go to my room. Oh wait, you locked me out."

"This is my house," Sophie said, trying to take a stand. "And you're... you're not welcome anymore."

Her voice was soft and unsteady. Her face was pale and her eyes were rubbed raw.

All at once, Reese felt like the worst person on the entire planet. Sophie was a good person. One of the best Reese knew, probably. And Sophie just stood there broken, like a baby bird fallen from a tree, while Reese took her big ugly foot and stepped right on top of her.

What am I doing?

This wasn't Reese.

She was the loyal defender.

Not the atomic bomb.

"Okay," Reese said, retreating. "I'm going now."

Walking back to her car, Reese went through the checklist in her mind.

Slept with your roommate's boyfriend? Check.

Lost your job? Check.

Got kicked out of your house? Check.

She picked up her clothes that were lumped together in a pile of pity and shame.

She held them to her chest as she looked up at her house.

No, not my house.

Reese loved the sweet, sunny yellow paint of the walls. The way it was the only house on the street that had any color to it at all.

She fit there.

She belonged there.

She *had* belonged.

2006

Sixteen was supposed to be sweet. But this birthday made Reese think about death again.

She could practically picture her cold, blue body six feet below the soil. She could see it in a morgue, too, like on *Law and Order*. But she didn't say any of these things to Wendy. Wendy wouldn't get it.

"Do you think we'll be married?" Wendy asked.

"To each other? Never say never." Reese said.

"Seriously, I'm sure we'll be married by twenty-five."

"I'd rather not."

Marriage is legal slavery, Reese thought.

She wouldn't say that either.

"So you think you'll marry Simon?" Reese asked.

Wendy's face muffled a soft glow. "He's going to college soon. We'll see."

Right, sore subject, Reese thought. Simon and Wendy had been a hairline fracture away from breaking up *for real this time* for months. They were on the week-on, week-off schedule, and this week? They were off.

"You need a distraction," Reese said. She ran over to her desk and grabbed a sheet of looseleaf and a pen. In big scribbled letters, she read aloud as she wrote, "Twenty-Five Things to Do Before You Turn 25."

"I don't know."

Reese knocked her over. "Oh, come on. This will be fun. I'll start."

She quickly wrote down her first item and set the paper in Wendy's lap.

"Number one," Wendy read. She laughed when she read, "Have a one night stand."

"See? You're having fun already," Reese said. "Now you go."

Wendy waved the paper in her hand. "I'm not having a one night stand. I just feel like that needs to be said."

"Whatever, just write."

Back and forth, they wrote their dreams.

From the generic, like *get a job.*

To the specific, like *stop seeing your ex-boyfriend.*

Twenty-five might as well have been a thousand years away, sheltered on a distant planet, the way that they talked about it. They could barely comprehend college, let alone their *twenties.*

They still had movie nights.

They still ate cookie dough out of the tub.

It still had no effects on their bodies whatsoever.

"If you could *really* do anything," Wendy said, lying on her bed, her arm linked through Reese's, "like soul-changing, life-altering anything, what would that be?"

Reese watched the ceiling fan spin.

The answer came to her nearly instantly.

And, it was completely unexpected.

"I think..." she started, letting the thought trickle down from her brain to her teeth, "I think I'd like to maybe meet my dad."

Wendy rolled over toward Reese. "You never talk about your dad."

Dad was a strange word. Finding her dad would be like sifting through change in a dirty mall fountain. A whole lot of pennies. A whole lot of possibilities.

"Yeah, I know. It's just something I know I should probably think about eventually. You know, before either of us die."

Wendy laughed. "You're not going to die."

"Any of us can die at any moment at any second of the day. That's why you have to live like a crazy person, Wendy. You have to dance naked in the eye of the hurricane. You have to make every day one that you remember because if you don't, then you'll just end up with a string of Thursdays that don't mean anything at all."

Wendy closed her eyes, letting her head curl into the pillow. "I like Thursdays."

"Of course you do."

Wendy was always so *content*. More than that, she was *happy*.

Reese didn't get that gene.

She was restless. Even when she was content or happy-adjacent, there was a small piece of her that wanted, needed, craved something different.

"So, are you going to ask Rita about your dad?"

Reese got nauseous just thinking about how that conversation might go. "Maybe. I'll figure that out when I get there."

"Be careful, Reese. Any of us can die at any moment at any second of the day."

Wendy was teasing her, but the words were still true.

If she never asked, she'd never know.

And if she never knew, then she'd only be half.
Half a history.
Half a gene pool.
Half a Reese.

FOUR

Sophie would cool down eventually.

Her boyfriend was an asshole, but at least she knew about it now.

Thinking about it now, Reese had actually done Sophie a favor. She'd given her a chance to find someone else. Someone decent.

You're welcome.

Her childhood home was a two-story brick house that had a yard filled with every kind of plant you could imagine. In the front, there was a solitary, sullen oak that the Homeowner's Association tried to uproot every year. Rita always gave them hell about it, until they, quite literally, drove the issue into the ground. (And let that damn tree stay there.)

Reese hung out in her car. She always had to psyche herself up to deal with Rita. If it weren't for Wally, she may not come around at all.

She turned the volume up on her radio as Joan Jett's raspy voice hammered through the speakers. Reese closed her eyes and sang, a punch in her syllables, her head flailing from side to side.

The knock on the window nearly barreled her over.

"Jesus," she said to her mother through the window.

"I thought Catholics didn't take God's name in vain," Rita said, with a self-important grin. "Come on inside. The teapot's on."

Reese turned her car off with the dramatic force of a Shakespearean monologue. She waited until Rita was in the house before following after her.

The house smelled like fertilizer. Every room in Rita's house came equipped with at least five potted plants, ranging in color and size. Reese's personal favorite was the cactus in the living room. The same one she used to terrorize houseguests with as a kid.

Wally turned the corner before she could even shut the door, his hands masked in garden gloves and dirt. "Grease Bucket!"

"Whale-y!" She laughed and launched herself into a hug. He towered over her at 6'6", but still his long mane of hair came spilling over her back.

"Twenty-six," he said plainly. "What happened to the toddler making mud pies in the backyard? Ah, I remember it like it was yesterday."

She followed behind him as he headed for the back of the house. "Ha. Ha. Classic step-dad joke."

Reese could still remember the first time she'd met Wally, the only boyfriend of Rita's that she'd ever actually liked. She was ten, and to her, Wally looked like a bear with all that hair toppling off his head and face. Three months later, he'd married Rita in their own backyard, with Reese as Best Man and Maid of Honor combined.

"Um, what's that?"

In the middle of the backyard, just beyond the pool, there was what looked like a large stack of bright yellow moving boxes.

Wally turned his head to look, but it was Rita who answered. "The bees?"

"Bees? You have bees?"

"Of course," Rita said, setting the teacups on the table. "Bees are essential to the sustainability of our environment."

Wally laughed at Reese's face. "We break ground on the chicken coop next week."

"It's sad that I can't tell if you're kidding right now."

"Hashtag dad jokes." Wally gave her two finger guns to show just how *cool* he really was.

Rita set the steaming pot of tea on the table. A floral, hand-painted set of cups and saucers that Reese's great-great-super-great grandmother had made. It wasn't her taste or Rita's, but it was ancestral.

God knows how important *family is to us,* Reese thought sarcastically.

"Come sit," Rita said, motioning Reese to the table. "And clear your mind."

Reese had never been open to the idea of having her tea leaves read, even after all these years. In reality, she was just humoring Rita. Reese's birthday was her favorite day of the year, and if she had to be considerate of the woman whose cervix had pushed her into being, well, she'd go ahead and deal.

Wally tried to stay serious. He didn't believe in this hoodoo much either. So he stared down into his cup, trying his best not to meet Reese's eyes.

"Drink your tea, Reese," Rita said, her voice in a forced softness, her eyes just barely shut. "Think of a question for which you'd like an answer. Anything you'd like to know. Anything you wish to seek."

Wally suppressed a laugh with a cough.

Reese focused harder on her cup. She usually asked the tea leaves if she would become rich and famous. It usually responded with an indecipherable image. Rita would ask Reese what she saw, and she'd always say something like a star or an arrow or a cloud. Rita would then tell her that there was *great success* in her future.

Success was clearly not in her future this time.

Maybe she would ask if Sophie would ever forgive her.

Maybe she would ask when she'd find another job.

But, if she were actually asking a question that she may actually like an answer to, she figured she should ask about what happens next.

She squeezed her eyes too tight. So tight that the muscles around her eyes shivered. *So, what now?*

She nearly choked as she chugged the last sip of tea.

"And now, flip," Rita guided her.

Reese flipped the cup upside-down onto the saucer, counted for three seconds, and flipped the cup back.

Inside was a mess of leaves.

Once again, it was nothing but a jumble of damp herbs.

"Now, Reese, what do you see?" Rita's hands cupped around her own mug, as she carefully rubbed the outside of the porcelain, like she expected a genie to pop out of it.

Reese turned to Wally. "It's way too serious in here. How about a hashtag dad joke to lighten the mood?"

Wally laughed, but tensed when he saw the look of hurt on Rita's face. "Sorry, dear."

"Can you please take this seriously?" Rita implored.

"Fine." Reese exhaled, sending the small strands of hair around her temples flying.

She glanced back into the cup, trying to remember what she told Rita last year. She really should start writing these down to avoid repeating herself.

Reese sighed, turning her cup toward Rita. "I see a person. Uh, maybe a man person. And, umm, a circle."

Rita carefully pried the cup out of Reese's hands. She nearly pressed her nose into it. "Interesting."

"So... what's it mean? Imminent death? Imminent death by solar flare? Imminent death by solar flare and a zombie apocalypse?"

"Maybe it means you're going to meet a dance partner and y'all will compete in a famous competition, where you'll make so much money that you can buy us the chickens for our coop," Wally suggested.

Rita couldn't take her eyes off the ashes of leaves. From this angle, Reese could almost swear that she was crying. No, not crying. Misting. But Rita didn't mist or cry.

Maybe Reese really was dying.

"Uhh, Rita?" she asked cautiously. "Penny for your thoughts?"

"How about a grand?" Wally said. "You are a soon-to-be billionaire, after all."

Rita nearly slammed the cup onto the table.

"Woah, it was just a joke," Reese said.

Rita hovered over the table. She looked like a mad scientist, her never-brushed hair spilling over her shoulders, sticking up every which way. But it was her face that really completed the look. The crazed eyes. The pinched forehead. It was spot-on.

"I need to uh... lie down..." She frantically grabbed at the cups and saucers around her, trying to carry them all to the kitchen at once, holding them tightly to her chest.

Wally intervened, grabbing the saucers away from her. "Here, let me help you."

"Am I going to die?" Reese spat out quickly and too loudly. "Because if I'm going to die, I'd like to know. For preparation's sake. I mean, there's a lot I haven't done yet."

She glanced outside. "I've never been stung by a bee, for example. If you tell me I'm going to die, I'll go out there right now and let that little buzzer shock the hell out of me. Unless of course, that's *how* I die..."

"You're not dying," Rita said. She placed a shaking, dramatic hand to her lips, before darting out of the kitchen and up the stairs.

Wally stood stark still in the kitchen. When he turned back to Reese, his smile was a construct of *let's pretend this never happened*.

He turned on the faucet. "So, kid, got any big plans for your birthday?"

Reese knew what her face must look like. Between the hangover and the Rita episode, she must look like she'd been hit by a truck. Square in the nose.

"What *was* that?" she asked.

Wally sighed, and it sounded like a bear's snore. He carefully washed Rita's abandoned china, which looked like a doll's toy in his giant hands. "Your mom's an iceberg, Reese."

"Been watching Titanic, have you?"

He sets the cup down, wiping the water off his hands. "Okay, let me see if I can make this make sense—"

"I get it. I get it. Mom's an iceberg. We only get about 10% of her. The rest is submerged under icy cold water."

He started to agree with her, then stopped short. "Your mom's not cold."

"No, she's just a free spirit."

"Like it or not, you've got to admit, Rita's never boring."

Reese sunk further into her chair. "Does this mean I can go now? I could really use a nap."

"Yeah, I don't think we'll be seeing her for a few hours. She's probably in the meditation room."

"Naturally." Reese threw her tote bag over her shoulder and crossed the room to hug Wally. "Love you, Wally. Thanks for making the trip worth it."

"Love you, kid. Come home more, okay?"

Reese saluted him, saying in her best French accent, "But of course."

She circled back to the Sophie topic with Wendy.

"She's overreacting," Reese said.

"You slept with her boyfriend."

"She has no proof of that. I hid the condom under my pillow!"

"There are so many things wrong with that statement."

"Hold on, Wendy. Wally's on the other line."

Reese accepted the call. "Hey Whale-y, did I forget something?"

"Got a pen, Grease Bucket?" he asked.

She hadn't carried a pen since college. Even then, it was borrowed, conveniently unreturned and lost a day later.

So, naturally, her answer was, "No, sure don't."

"Okay, how's your memory? Foggy, at best?"

"Something like that. What's with the mystery?"

Wally took a deep breath, releasing it out of his mouth into the receiver like a gust of wind. "Your dad."

Reese slammed on the break. Her heart flew forward into the steering wheel.

"I think that's who Rita thinks you saw in the leaves, Grease."

She couldn't say anything.

She couldn't move the car.

All she could do was hope that someone would crash into the back of her and send her flying into next week.

"But I made that up," she admitted.

A car sped past her with his middle finger raised in the air.

She should pull over to the shoulder.

But her feet were lead.

"Sometimes," Wally said solemnly, "things work out by accident."

"Wally, I don't know what that means."

"I've got a name. You want it, you got it."

What had she told Wendy all those years ago?

It's just something I know I should probably think about eventually.

"Okay," she said. "Okay."

"His name is Miles Russell."

Nothing happened.

No earthquake.

No flood.

Nothing.

FIVE

"This'll be good."

Owen laughed at her, which was a fair reaction, all things considered. Reese stood at the door with the pile of clothes in her hands. A neon pink thong beside her, fallen on the doorstep.

Call me classy, she thought.

"After you," Owen said, waving her in.

Owen and Vivian's house always smelled like a cross between baby powder, roses, and the inside of a spa.

Reese dumped the clothes on the floor.

She knew Vivian wouldn't like it.

She didn't care.

"Well, well, well," Wendy said from the couch, draped in the thinnest, most useless blanket in existence. "You've had quite the day."

Owen slid into the leather armchair. "Yes, please, tell us all about this day of yours."

"Tell Reese I'll be there in a second," Vivian called.

This house didn't feel like a home.

It was the kind of place where you had to take your shoes off at the front mat. The blankets were always folded neatly. The beds always made. Everything had a purpose and a place.

Even Owen.

There is no room for mistakes under this roof, Reese thought.

"I must say you look like absolutely radiant, Reese," Owen said.

Reese joined Wendy on the couch, tucking her feet under Wendy's side, pulling the blanket on top of her and wishing for more.

"Let me die here," she said.

"R.I.P." Owen lifted his water glass to her.

Reese heard Vivian's reaction before she saw her. A gasp sounded through the room when she saw Reese's clothes pile, but she didn't comment on it. Instead, she said, "Let me get y'all another blanket. How about dinner? Have you had dinner? Oh, I know. Homemade chocolate chip cookies. What do you think about that?"

"Hey Martha," Wendy said, "there's room for you here, too."

Reese hugged her knees into her chest, making space for Vivian.

Vivian wasn't always warm, but when she was, it had a magical, soothing effect on Reese.

She sat down in between them, placing her head on Reese's shins.

"You can stay here as long as you need to," Vivian said, at an almost whisper.

"Hey Owen," Reese said, "how about you get in that kitchen and make yourself useful?"

Thirty minutes and a dozen cookies later, the entirety of Reese's story was out on the table, rotting.

Owen had dismissed himself somewhere around the word *condom,* so it was the three of them, alone and together, the way Reese always preferred it.

She missed them.

She missed them just like this.

Everything seemed less complicated when they were all together.

I love my life. I love my life... right?

"I have an idea," Vivian said to Reese, slowly breathing air into her lungs. "But you have to be serious about it, okay? I have two conditions."

"Me? Serious? Always."

"I mean it..."

Wendy scrunched her face. "Yeah, Reese, be serious."

Reese kicked Wendy. To Vivian, she said, "Okay, okay, what's your best offer?"

"So you know how Owen's family owns a house in New Orleans?"

"I was not aware of that, no."

"They have a house in Lakeview that they rent out. The guy living there now has been there a while, but he's looking for a roommate for the spare bedroom."

A guy?

A spare room?

Reese felt like she'd just won the lottery.

"Yes." Reese planted her feet on the ground, suddenly bubbling up with energy. "Do I know him?"

Vivian evaded Reese's eyes, connecting with Wendy's instead. "Uh huh."

"No way," Wendy said. It was her turn to sit up.

"What's the catch?" Reese asked. "Why do y'all look like I did something wrong?"

"It's Liam."

Holy crap on a cracker.

Reese scowled. "Nope. Veto. I'd rather live in a bucket."

Vivian smiled softly. Almost like she was enjoying this.

Wendy, her face lit up like a Christmas tree, definitely was.

"Liam's an adult," Vivian said. "He won't be weird or anything. At least go talk to him."

"She won't go," Wendy said, assured. "Seriously, Viv, Reese is the get-out-quick girl. She's not going to circle back to scorched earth."

A switch went off inside Reese's brain.

That competitive, *I-can-do-whatever-I-want* switch.

The one that, when flipped on, landed her in perpetually awful situations and infinitely tragic patterns.

"You think I won't?" Reese answered.

"Are you kidding?" Wendy said, baiting her. "You wouldn't set foot within a mile of that place."

She had a choice.

She could ignore Wendy.

She could leave the bait on the hook.

Not a chance.

"Vivian," Reese ordered, "set it up."

Vivian dropped her head into her hands. "Two conditions."

"Blah. Okay."

"One: you have to start being an adult. Job-hunting. Tax-paying. Whatever."

Reese nodded with a complimentary eye roll.

"Two: leave Liam alone."

Another nod.

"Okay, repeat that last one back to me."

"That's ridiculous," Reese said. "I'm not a puppet."

Wendy shook her head. "No, but you're a dummy."

Reese blinked, confused.

"Ventriloquists talk through dummies," Wendy said, like Reese was supposed to know this. "You're a dummy."

Reese looked away. "You are full of useless information."

"Thank you," Wendy said, nodding.

"Reese," Vivian said, pulling them back to the conversation at hand. "I need to hear you say it."

Reese pulled the blankets back over her head. She mumbled, "I'll leave Liam alone."

"A little louder."

Reese growled, loud and gravelly.

"*I will leave Liam alone.*"

SIX

Liam had a real house like a real adult.

He had a yard for his lab, Cecil. He had a lawnmower that he probably used on Sunday afternoons. His car was clean and nestled into his grown up garage.

Reese rocked back and forth on her feet.

This is a mistake, she thought. *A colossal, life-undoing mistake.*

She thought back to when Liam was *only* Owen's college friend that he never brought around.

When he was *only* a stranger.

When he was *only* an idea.

"If Liam is even real," Reese would say.

"Which he is," Owen would counter.

"If he's as real as you say, then you should set me up."

Owen would pretend to cringe. "Eh. You're not his type."

Or so you thought.

Reese stopped thinking.

She climbed the steps to the front door.

No plan of action.

Don't answer the—

When Liam answered the door, she noticed his glasses first. Those ridiculously spectacular black rims that held his face together. The exact same face she fell in like with at Vivian's wedding.

"Oh, you opened it," she said. "The door, I mean."

Liam didn't look thrilled, but at least he didn't shut the door in her face.

Good sign.

"I'm sure you're wondering what I'm doing here," Reese said.

"Yeah, kind of."

"Kind of?"

He leaned his thin, toned body against the door frame. Like a freaking Greek statue. "You're not exactly predictable."

"True," she said. "Can I come in?"

He stepped aside, gesturing her into the house.

Liam's house looked like a Pottery Barn sprung to life. No, not a Pottery Barn. A real barn. All dark woods and fine furnishings.

He had good taste, plain and simple. He listened to the right music. He ate food he cooked himself, from real cookbooks. He even wore ties on dates.

Like a real adult.

You were always better than I was, she thought.

Seeing Liam again, she couldn't help but think back to the wedding. How he held out his hand to her, confident and assured.

"I'm Liam," he'd said. "Would you like to dance?"

No bullshit line.

No games.

Just an honest, straightforward question.

And for whatever reason, that was the scariest possible approach.

It was the right approach.

For the wrong girl.

"I, uh, like your place," Reese said. She sat on his couch, with its rich, leather smell.

"Thank you."

She should apologize or explain or something.

"If you're wondering why I'm here, which of course you are, since, my life is so clearly a riveting topic of thought, well I'll tell you. Turns out I'm homeless now. It's the nomad life for me."

Liam said nothing. He was opening drawers. Neat, organized drawers. He was fooling with a set of keys.

"Oh and bonus?" Reese continued. "I'm also jobless. Yeah, I got laid off. No big deal, though. I can always strip. Work my way up to one of those high-class escorts. I wonder how much they make. Hopefully enough to support my Chipotle habit."

"Sounds like a promising career choice," he mumbled.

He was going to make her say it.

He was going to make her *ask* it.

She tried one last time.

"So for now, I'll crash at Viv's. Which is totally great. I mean, aside from the fact that she follows me around picking up my crumbs. I could always move home, too. With my mother who reads auras and keeps bees for pets. All good. Yep. All good."

Liam walked back over to her. He walked like a baseball player, all lines, all focus.

"Here," he said.

He held out his hand.

A peace treaty.

A key.

"What is this?" she asked.

"You can stay here."

It's what she'd hoped he'd say. But now that he had, the reality slapped her in the face like a cold, dead hand.

I can't live with my ex-almost-boyfriend.

Reese's throat went dry. "Come again?"

"I've been looking for a roommate, but I'm sure you already knew that," he said, backing away from her. "You're just as good as any. You're clean, right?"

"Absolutely."

A total lie.

"You cook, maybe?"

"I'm Rachael Ray."

A total joke.

"Okay, so you want to live here, then?"

Reese turned the key around and around in her hands.

Liam.

Roommate Liam.

Every day Liam.

"I'm not one to question—" she started to say.

"Then don't," he said. "You'll move in next week. We're roommates. Don't make it a big deal."

He walked her to the door.

She didn't deserve it.

He knew it.

She knew it.

And yet, they'd just cracked open their quasi-relationship again in the sore spot that had never fully healed in the first place.

Here goes everything.

1997

"Tell your dad how old you are," Rita said.

The connection was bad. Reese could hear the buzz of static, the television in the background.

"Seven," she said softly. "I'm seven today."

There wasn't a party. Rita didn't believe in them. She told Reese that parties were vain. Parties were for little girls who couldn't be happy without the endless parade of attention.

"Seven? Oh, right. Seven," her dad said gruffly.

This wasn't her dad.

She'd known this for quite some time now.

Every birthday, every Christmas, every Earth Day, Rita would hand Reese the phone and tell her that it was her dad calling.

But it wasn't.

On the other end of the line was a phony. The mailman, Jerry. She'd figured it out a few months ago when Jerry asked about the telescope she'd received from her Aunt Mitzi for Christmas.

The voice.

The look on his face when he realized he'd slipped up.

It all fit.

"Tell your dad what kind of cake we got you," Rita prompted.

Reese sighed into the phone. "A vegan and gluten-free carrot cake."

"The hell kind of cake is that?" he mumbled.

Her mother knelt over her and mouthed, "What'd he say?"

Reese covered the receiver and said, "He says to save him a piece."

Rita's eyes widened before she took the phone away from Reese.

When Reese was younger, Rita used to tell her that her father was off fighting to cure world hunger. She liked that idea. Her father, the savior of the hungry. As she got older, Rita told Reese that her father was traipsing around Europe to find himself.

"How do you lose yourself?" Reese used to ask.

"It's easier than you think," Rita would answer.

For a full year, Reese lived in constant fear of losing herself. She'd check every mirror to make sure her reflection was still on the other side. She'd wake up in a panic, thinking that maybe her body had run away without her.

But now, she was seven.

Now, she was smarter.

"Say goodbye to your dad," Rita said, handing Reese the phone again. She'd taken it away and whispered in hushed, furious tones.

"Goodbye, Dad," Reese said convincingly. Then she added, to really hone in the effect, "I miss you."

"You too, Reba," her fake father said. "Maybe I'll make it in next year."

When he said this sort of thing, Reese imagined what it might be like to actually have a dad. The kind that came home after a day at work. Maybe he had a briefcase or maybe he had a guitar case. And he'd ask Rita what was for dinner and she'd tell him tofu and he'd tell her it was his favorite.

It was a nice idea.

"Okay," Reese said. "I'll see you next year."

She hung up the phone.

"Time for cake!" Rita said enthusiastically.

"Rita?" Reese asked. Her mother stopped at the kitchen table, her mess of hair swinging behind her. "Why doesn't Dad ever visit?"

Reese hoped that Rita knew what she really meant.

Not Jerry the mailman.

Not the list of fictional fathers Rita had concocted over the years.

The real dad who was somewhere out there in the world, living his life, away and apart from Reese.

Rita pressed a finger against the corner of her lip. "Well, Reese, be-cause you're seven, I will tell you the truth." She paused, gently lacing her fingers together, one at a time like a dance. "We don't need him. You have me. And I'm all the parent that you need. Understand?"

She didn't, but she nodded anyway.

"You are strong, Reese Weller. No man can ever add or subtract from that."

They had cake after that, and Reese pretended to like it. That night in her bed, Reese imagined what her father might be doing that very moment.

Something very important, she hoped.

SEVEN

He licked her leg.

"Well, hello to you, too," Reese said.

Cecil the labrador was a secondary roommate. He had big, padded paws that clicked as he ran around the house, and he never jumped on the couch. He was the politest dog she'd ever met.

"Cecil, bed." At Liam's command, he obeyed, clicking his way over to the pallet on the floor, and laying his body down noiselessly.

"So, uh, your room's this way," Liam said.

So far, he hadn't looked directly at her. His eyes landed in her general direction, but never actually met hers. She felt like jumping up and down, waving her arms and yelling, "*Notice me, damnit.*"

She didn't.

When he opened the door to her brand new room, she felt an instant love for the empty space. This little place didn't know of her messed-up life. It didn't have to hold all that drama that lived *out there.*

"Let's grab your stuff," Liam said, already aiming for the front door.

"Oh," Reese said, pulled out of her reverie of sorts, "I can get that. Don't waste your Sunday on me."

Liam nodded. "Okay, I won't."

Before she could even blink, he'd spread out on the couch, flipped on the TV and kicked off his shoes.

Reese stared at him.

Well, alright.

Her first matter of business was setting up the bed frame. She carried in the box with the smallest of smiles toward Liam, then got to work.

"Okay," she said out loud. "I can do this."

Reese didn't read instructions. She was a believer in the learn-as-you-go method. So she started assembling the parts according to the small, incongruous sketches on the paper.

Surprisingly, she managed to get the thing together. Apart from the clattering, it went relatively smoothly.

"How's it going in there?" Liam asked as she made her next trip to the car.

"Swimmingly."

She didn't need him to help her.

And, to be fair, he had offered.

But he was her *roommate*, not her... whatever.

She was still getting used to that distinction.

Reese dropped the last box in her new bedroom. The walls were light gray and empty, ready for her to customize and colorize. She planned to hang her poster of John Lennon and maybe her woven tapestry.

She dropped to the bed, looking up at the glow-in-the-dark stars she'd pasted to the ceiling.

Wally's words ran through her head, the way they did now, in the quiet moments.

"His name is Miles Russell."

Why did she care about this?

Why now?

Dads had nothing to offer her. If her dad walked through the door, here and now, what difference would it make?

Probably none.

Someone knocked on the door.

"Come in," she said.

Liam cracked the door. Even around the house, he wore button-up shirts. She wasn't sure if he actually owned any t-shirts. And *definitely* not sweatpants.

"Hey," he said, "I'm going to grill tonight. Do you want steak or chicken?"

Reese lifted her head. "Is this some kind of cruel joke?"

"Um... no?" he said.

Did he really just offer to make dinner?

Reese's stomach growled.

"Yes," she said. "Either. Both."

"Okay. I'll be back," he said, and closed the door again.

Reese collapsed back to the bed.

Liam was in her top ten best make outs.

Top five.

And now, she had to look at his lips. Every. Single. Day.

Should be interesting.

Half an hour later, he knocked on her door. "Dinner's ready."

The spread on the back porch was impressive. Not only was there steak and chicken, but there was corn on the cob, a bowl filled with salad, and a not-so-subtle bottle of wine.

"Wow, we could feed a village with this."

"I like leftovers," he said, sitting down.

She followed suit.

"Wine?" he asked her, holding up the bottle. She nodded. Maybe a little too eagerly. "Tell me when."

She let him fill that sucker up right to the top. "When."

"Okay," he said. She thought he might laugh, but he didn't.

He reached for the steak first. She commented, "Red meat? Excellent choice."

"I think we need to set a few ground rules," he said.

Right, she thought, *time to get down to business.*

"You've been talking to Vivian, haven't you?" she teased.

"Are you seeing anyone?" he asked.

"No, I'm seeing multiple someones."

An unmistakable shudder ran down his back.

"Kidding," she said, quickly, reaching for the wine. "I'm kidding."

He nodded.

"So, ground rules?"

He shook the hair out of his face. "Don't sit too close."

She had to laugh. It was too perfect *not* to laugh.

"Okay," she said, gathering a semblance of composure. "No touching either, then?"

"Correct. And no couple-like activities."

She raised an eyebrow. "What kind of *couple-like activities*?"

"No flirting," he said, pointing at her, accusingly.

She took a slip of wine. "Understood."

Reese knew how this worked.

When you're the *guilty one* in the relationship—the one who breaks the hearts, the one who dances on the graves of their dead dreams—it's your job to yield to the will of the *innocent*.

It's the circle of life.

"I won't cross any lines," Reese said, on a more serious note.

"Thank you," he said.

And that seemed to be enough.

EIGHT

When Reese woke up, she realized there was no place she had to be. Work wasn't a reality for her anymore. There were no friends to visit at 8:30 on a Monday morning. And in a brand new house, with a brand new room-mate, there wasn't anything to really do.

She shuffled into the kitchen in just a t-shirt and her underwear. That part felt good at least.

"Well," she said to the empty room, "it looks like it's just you and me today."

Toast.

She could make toast.

On the counter behind her, Liam had a loaf of sourdough tucked into a basket.

Fancy much?

A door behind her opened and shut. Reese jumped.

"Who's there?" She tried to sound menacing, dropping her voice to a low register.

From the drawer, she carefully withdrew a knife.

Footsteps fell from around the hall.

Reese held out the knife, her whole outstretched limb shaking. "You should know, I'm armed."

Then, Liam was standing in front of her. He looked at the knife, then looked at her bare legs, and veered away. "Jesus, Reese, you could at least wear pants."

Looking down, Reese realized that her t-shirt had risen up to the top of her underwear, her whole legs and *more* clearly in view.

"God, you scared me," she said, dropping the knife to the counter. "You can look now, I'm no longer, uhh, exposed."

"Err, right." He still didn't look directly at her as he went to the pantry, grabbing a protein bar. "What were you planning to do with that knife, anyway?"

"I hadn't thought that through exactly, but I watch zombie movies, so."

"Well, as long as you're qualified."

Reese nodded. The awkwardness felt like an ocean between them. He moved around her like she was a puddle and he was a fancy Italian shoe.

She hated it.

"So," she said, "I take it you don't work 8 to 5. See, I'm learning so much about you already."

"I have a meeting out of the office today. Normally, yes, 8 to 5." He grabbed his keys off of the coffee table. "See you tonight."

As he walked toward the foyer, she called after him, "See you then, darling."

He shut the door.

Admittedly, the *darling* might have been a poor joke.

The next few hours crawled by. She watched TV. She took Cecil on a walk. She even alphabetized Liam's movie collection. In a moment of pure liberation, she dyed her hair in the bathroom to a lavender, *live-in-the-moment* shade.

By noon, Reese found herself lying on the floor next to Cecil, staring up at the ceiling fan just to watch it spin.

"This is ridiculous," she said out loud. "I should be making myself at home. Getting acclimated."

She sat up. "Cecil. We have to get Liam to like me again. Tolerate me, at the very least. Otherwise, we'll both be miserable forever and then you'll be miserable and then what?"

Cecil's eyes bore up to her apprehensively. Not even a dog had faith in her.

"Cecil, we're going to bake an apology cake."

After a successful trip to the store, Reese returned with six bags of baking material, and one more hit to her ever-dwindling bank account. She didn't realize until she was inside her new house that maybe baking a cake wasn't the most practical way to spend her time and/or money.

But, she told herself, this would work.

As soon as she learned how to actually bake something.

Reese opened her laptop to the Pinterest recipe for red velvet cake, that used words like "easy" and "DIY" to really catch her attention.

There were several steps she realized now, but to her benefit, she had hours before Liam was bound to show.

"Okay, Cecil. Let's do this."

She set the oven for 350 degrees and spread all her ingredients out on the counter. She grabbed the mixer, an apron she'd found hanging in the pantry, and blared music through Liam's speakers.

Everything went better than expected, just like it had with the bed frame. She whisked and she mixed. She cracked eggs and she poured the ingredients perfectly into her new baking pan. She even made her own cream cheese icing, for God's sake.

Reese wiped her hands together, and carefully slid the cake-to-be in the oven, setting the timer for twenty-five minutes.

She texted Wendy and Vivian: "Domesticated status: I'm baking the best red velvet cake this world has ever seen. New career option: Naked Baker."

Wendy texted back first: "Are you cooking naked in your new cohabitation arrangement? Overachiever."

Vivian texted next: "Don't forget an apron!"

Reese took a much-needed break on the couch, with Cecil at her feet, wrapping herself up in the closest available blanket.

The sound of Cecil whining woke her first.

Then, the sound of the fire alarm.

"*What!*"

She flocked to the kitchen. Everything was up in big, black smoke. The timer clicked desperately, in symphony with the smoke alarm.

Her phone was ringing off the hook.

She opened the oven door, setting forth a billowing puff of smoke.

Bad idea.

Grabbing two potholders, she reached inside the oven and grabbed the blackened cake.

"*Damn!*"

She set it on the counter and ran to the back door. She opened it, then continued to open the back windows one at a time.

"What happened? Are y'all okay?"

His voice made her stomach flip.

And for good measure, Reese said a final, "*Damn!*"

There was Liam, making his way into the kitchen, waving his hands through the air.

"It's cake," Reese yelled over the chaos.

"What?"

"*It's cake!*"

Liam launched into full crisis mode right along with her. He grabbed the black brick of cake and carried it outside, setting it onto the lawn. They ripped open windows. They waved the smoke away from the alarms. They flipped on the fans.

Finally, everything went quiet.

"Well, that was dramatic," Reese said.

Liam was unshakeable. "Nice hair."

There was an unmistakable *something* hidden on his face.

She couldn't quite grasp it, but it looked like a laugh.

A smile, maybe.

A hidden smile.

Buried, but not gone.

NINE

"You got a plant?"

"Yeah," Wendy said, reaching for the succulent behind her. She was back in Nashville now. Life was back in session. "I like having something living in the house. Makes me feel less lonely."

"You should probably get a dog. They're friendlier."

Wendy looked smaller on screen. And a little tired, too. It was like someone stole all the color off her face.

"Plant is friendly, too. He's just less talkative."

"Speaking of talkative," Reese said, "my new roommate is anything but."

Wendy cradled Plant in her lap. "Are you being nice?"

"Yes, mom."

"Are you being *too* nice?"

"Oh, come on. Why is everyone acting like I have uncontrollable hormones? I nearly control them every single day."

"Who else? I mean, besides Vivian."

Reese explained the little sit-down she'd had with Liam. *The ground rules.* And the whole time, Wendy's face told stories with the rainbow of feelings on her face.

Confused.

Surprised.

And then, a moment of insight.

"I'm going to need a perpetual bucket of popcorn for these next few months," she said. "Things are about to get interesting."

"You lost me."

"Two exes living in close quarters? Come on. If someone doesn't fall in love with someone, I will be sorely disappointed."

"Love is disgusting. It's like a tumor. And not one of those benign ones."

Wendy tucked her knees under her chin. "You're such a romantic. It's really heartwarming."

"Thank you, it's genetic."

Maybe.

Rita was a romantic convert. Before Wally, she was a solo act, through and through. She used men like napkins. But with Wally? She fell hard and fast and never looked back.

But what about the second half of her DNA?

Maybe he was married somewhere, with a bushel of kids. Maybe he was old, surrounded by younger women. Maybe he'd been pining for Rita all these years.

"How did we get here?" Reese asked, folding back onto her bed. "I'm twenty-six with nothing to show for it but fabulous hair color and furniture I collected from dumpsters."

Wendy's eye twinged. "I don't know. I wish I did."

Reese reflected. She didn't do much of that. "Remember our life list. Those things we want to do before we turned twenty-five?"

"Yeah, of course! Did we ever do any of that stuff?"

"Well, we never got married."

Wendy high-fived the computer camera.

"And we never did anything illegal," Reese continued.

"Eh, speak for yourself," Wendy said.

Reese took a big swig of water, then carefully set the cup back on the table. "And we never found my dad."

Wendy stared directly at the camera now, so that her eyes were sinking into Reese's soul. No matter how inauthentic video chat was— the false sense of closeness, the sometimes pixelated image—at least Wendy's eyes were somewhere, miles and miles away, searching for hers.

"Do you want to find him?" Wendy asked.

"Well, I have a name now. So, that makes things easier, right?"

Wendy sighed. "It's never going to be easy."

"Miles Russell," Reese said.

Hearing it out loud felt like she was standing in a dark bathroom chanting Bloody Mary. Like any moment now she would summon him to her just by saying his name.

"Miles Russell," Wendy repeated.

Reese winced. "Bloody Mary."

"Huh?"

"Nothing."

"So... should we... internet stalk him?"

Reese laughed. It shook through her chest like a wave.

"Okay," Reese said. "Okay, but you do it."

"Popcorn break?"

"Meet you in five."

Reese kept a stash of popcorn in the bottom of the pantry. Liam didn't look like the kind of guy who ate popcorn—or anything with carbs for that matter—but still, she needed to take precautions.

"Hey," Liam said, a look of surprise over his face.

He was all dressed up, even more so than usual. He wore dress pants and a nice, work-appropriate shirt. He'd even put some kind of product in his hair.

She checked the clock on the microwave.

1:07 p.m.

"Where are you off to?" she asked. "Trying to get a jumpstart on your emails?"

"You walk like an elephant, by the way," he said, slipping on his shoes.

She unwrapped the popcorn packet, letting the plastic crinkle at will. "Are you calling me loud?"

"Never." Liam walked into the kitchen, grabbing his keys, with Cecil trailing at his heels.

"So really, where are you going?"

He ignored her. "What are you making?"

"This is called popcorn. You see there are kernels, and you place them in the microwave—"

"So you're cooking again."

"All I have to do is press Start. I can manage."

She pressed the button with an extra dose of bravado.

"I'm sorry," she said. "For the almost fire."

He nodded, a half-smile posed on his face. "Okay, then."

Liam lingered for a moment longer before heading out the door. Her mind went wild with suspicion.

He's a secret agent.

He's a drug pusher.

He's a male prostitute.

"I'm back," Reese announced, closing the door behind her. "With sustenance and a story. Where would a shy, homebody of a guy go on Sunday night at 1:07 in the morning, I ask you?"

Wendy sat quietly.

"What is it?" Reese asked. "Did the sky fall?"

Still quiet.

Wendy let her head hang.

"Is this screen frozen?" Reese asked, banging her hand against the computer.

"No, I'm here," Wendy said.

"Okay, then what?"

Wendy rounded her shoulders back. "I know where your dad is."

1999

She had a party.

Against her mother's better judgment, Reese had finally got her party, as long as she agreed to Rita's very particular terms. First, there had to be time for meditation. Second, no children climbing on the plants. Third, bed by ten, because circadian rhythms need not be disrupted.

Reese waited impatiently on the stairs near the front door. She'd bought a new dress, a pretty, lilac colored frock with two ribbons for straps. Rita hated it, but gave in eventually.

The first car pulled up to the curb. Her first friend, Alice, stepped onto the sidewalk, a large gift box with an even larger bow in hand.

Reese waved and yelled, "Rita, someone's here!"

Rita, barefoot, sauntered up to the door. "Is that Alice?"

"Yes." Reese couldn't hold her excitement inside of her.

This was her party. People were showing up.

They are all here. For me.

"She's maturing rather quickly, don't you think?" Rita asked. "Is that makeup on her face?"

Reese squinted. "No, Rita. I think that's chapstick."

"Hmm," Rita said, still fixating. "What kind of mother gives a child that death stick?"

There was the usual commotion when Reese threw open the door. Hello's and how-are-you's were exchanged. The girls hugged.

Reese shuffled Alice into the living room, begging to know what was in the gift box.

"Brownies, anyone?" Rita asked, a weird, too-big smile on her face.

Alice bounced in her seat on the couch. "Yes, oh, oh, yes!"

"They're eggless," Reese clarified.

"Huh?" Alice asked.

"And sugarless!" Rita said proudly.

Alice made a gagging noise, then pulled her manners together. "No, thank you."

"Alright then," Rita said, wrapping her hands around her waist. "I'll be in my room. You girls have a great time."

When Rita climbed up the stairs, Alice grinned as wide as her face would allow. "Your mom is so cool. We get to stay down here all by ourselves?"

Reese didn't know why this was cool, but she pretended like she did. "Yeah, she's the best."

Reese didn't have anything in common with Alice.

Alice liked pink. Reese liked black.

Alice liked Backstreet Boys. Reese liked Alanis Morissette.

Alice liked Barbie dolls. Reese liked VooDoo dolls.

Hey, Reese thought, *we both like dolls!*

Reese kept checking to make sure this was really happening. She would squeeze her eyes shut, then flip them back open. Alice was still there, and more were on their way.

This is what it feels like to have friends, she thought.

The doorbell rang.

Again.

And again.

And over again.

"I'll get it!" Reese leapt off the couch every time.

The sixth time it rang, Melissa and her mother waited patiently. Melissa's mom had a big, plastic smile on her face. She said sweetly, "Happy birthday, Reese! I love your dress."

"Thanks."

"Here you go," Melissa said, handing over her contribution to the gift pile.

"Thanks," Reese repeated.

"Where's your mom?" Melissa's mom asked. "I want to talk to her about Melissa's dietary restrictions before I head out."

"She's upstairs," Reese said.

"Okay, then, I'll wait."

Reese felt like she was in trouble. She didn't know why. She hadn't done anything wrong.

But she felt even worse when she told Melissa's mom, "She may be a while."

Melissa's mom had a twisty look on her face.

"Yeah!" Alice chimed in, poking her head around the corner. "I think I heard a snore a little while ago."

Reese wondered what it would be like to have a mom like Melissa's. The kind of mom who briefs other parents on your dietary restrictions. The kind of mom who knows your dietary restrictions.

Melissa's mom held onto Melissa's hand, peering inside. "And you girls are all by yourself down here?"

"Yes, ma'am," Reese said.

"Okay, Reese. I'm coming inside."

Reese didn't stop Melissa's mom. She didn't stop her from walking into the house. She didn't stop her from walking up the stairs. She certainly didn't stop her from raising her voice and yelling, *what kind of mother are you?*

She wished she had stopped Melissa's mom from taking the other girls home.

Alice left.

Melissa left.

And all that *was* left was Reese.

Alone.

Reese waited at the stairs, thinking about her father, wondering if he would let her have parties with friends who would actually stay.

"Should we have cake?" Rita sounded sad. Reese didn't care.

In her most powerful, angriest, earth-shaking voice, Reese said, "I hate you."

And then Rita left, too.

TEN

Reese could buy his friendship.

She wasn't proud of it.

But, drastic times called for *drastic* purchases.

When it came to buying expensive things, she had no idea what grand purchase would constitute spending her nearly nonexistent savings.

She considered something for the kitchen. An expensive blender? A juicer?

No, she wasn't that healthy. She needed a shared activity.

Plus, she was avoiding cooking ever since the *dead cake* debacle.

Maybe something for outside. A four wheeler? A kayak?

Yes. A kayak. Boys liked kayaks.

There was this place in downtown Baton Rouge that sold outdoor gear.

She grabbed her bag.

She almost ignored her phone ringing, but at the last second, answered unthinkingly. "Reese here."

"That's how you answer the phone?"

Reese almost bit her tongue at the sound of Vivian's voice. "May I help you?"

"I'm on your side of the lake today. Can I stop by? See how you've wrecked the place?"

Reese threw her head back. Stomped her feet a bit. All the mature reactions she could muster.

"Kidding," Vivian said. "I'm completely kidding."

She had an out.

She should take it.

But, to her detriment, Reese hated driving alone. And Baton Rouge was an hour away.

"Are you up for an adventure?" Reese asked.

"Always," Vivian said. Truthfully, it was a bit shocking. "I mean, not always, just so we're clear, but for now, yes."

That was more like it.

"I think... I should have been the one to drive." Vivian braced herself against the seat. Her face was pinched and puckered, like she could control the car with the force of her face muscles.

"Relax, will you? I swear, I don't know how you live with all that stress in your body. Have you tried medication?"

Vivian released her face. "I can relax. I can be cool."

Reese shook her head. "Can you repeat that one more time? I'd like to record it for posterity."

"So why are we buying a kayak, again? You're not exactly outdoorsy," Vivian said, slowly placing her feet back on the ground.

"Like you're one to talk."

Vivian laughed. "I go hunting every year... my family owns a lease in Alabama... and I shot a massive six-point last year. Do you ever listen to me when I talk?"

"What's that?"

Vivian turned her head to the window.

"Kidding," Reese said, dropping her hand on Vivian's leg. "I'm completely kidding."

"You always give me such a hard time," Vivian said. "Sometimes, I wish you wouldn't."

Reese didn't know how to answer that.

So, she didn't.

The store clerk, a bearish guy with cool, tribal tattoos, asked if they needed any help.

"Yes," Reese said, "is there something I should know about kayaking before I just up and buy one?"

He stared back at her. "Uh, wear a life jacket?"

"Cool," Reese said. "I'll take one kayak and two life vests, please."

"Better get a couple'a oars while you're at it," the man said.

"Sure, throw in two of those, too," Reese said.

When the man walked away, Reese grabbed Vivian's arms. "He's kind of attractive, don't you think?"

Vivian pinched her face again. "He looks like he has fleas and eats take-out every night."

"Mmm," Reese said, licking her lips. "Just my type."

They wandered around the store together, pretending to be athletic and sporty. They came to the conclusion that Reese would make an excellent rock climber, while Vivian was better suited for synchronized swimming. Wendy, not to be left out, would be a professional parasailer.

"The tattoos," Vivian said.

"The tattoos?"

"Yes," Vivian said. "You always fall for guys with tattoos. That's your type."

"I don't have a type. I have many types."

Vivian picked up a basketball, dribbling it lightly on the ground. "Name one non-tattooed guy that you've dated."

"Dated? That's a short list."

"Fine. Dated. Hooked up with. Pick your slang. Name your men."

"Men?"

"Or women. Good lord, you make this difficult."

"And you make it so easy," Reese said, laughing. She stole the ball from Vivian, mid-dribble. "Liam, by the way."

Vivian thought it over. "Okay, you win."

They bounced the basketball through the aisles, passing it back and forth. Reese would never have put herself and Vivian in an outdoor store together, but here they were. And it wasn't as bad as she imagined it might be.

At the end of the aisle, Reese spotted it.

"Oh, wait," she said, stopping short. "Oh, that's it."

"But the kayak..."

"Screw the kayak," Reese said. "We're not outdoorsy."

"Well, as I said, I—"

"We're big kids. And we need a big kid, big dollar purchase. You with me?"

Vivian grinned. "I'm with you."

Liam came through the door like a strong wind. The door hit the wall, the bag hit the floor and the shoes flopped across the room.

"Reese, you here?"

She could hear him yelling from outside. He was in the kitchen now, nose-first into the fridge. He would kill her for this. Probably. Definitely.

"I'm going to get food. Need anything?"

"Um," she yelled, tucking her toes into the grass, "can you come here for a second?"

"Where are you?"

"Um, outside."

Screen slid open. Jaw hit cement. *What is that?*"

"A backyard?" she asked sarcastically.

It was the photo that really sold her. An ad, to be more specific. There were two kids in the backyard, a sprinkler spraying over the image, while the kids, happy and carefree, jumped on their trampoline.

Like she said, *screw kayaks.*

Liam didn't say anything. He chose to stare at her, to stare the truth right out of her, and that somehow felt worse.

"A tramp...o...line?" She stretched the word thin, so it was less of a word and more of a collection of syllables.

Liam kept staring. No indication of amusement. No hidden smile.

"A trampoline," she repeated. "I bought a trampoline."

"Question," Liam said. "What strange, Reese-like impulse made you go out and buy a trampoline for our shared backyard? Just curious."

Reese considered telling him the truth.

I'm tragically trying to make you like me again.

Then immediately ignored the impulse. He'd think she was crazy. Crazier than usual, at least.

"I thought it... looked nice."

Liam nodded. "Okay."

"Why don't you just try it?" Reese asked as Liam walked away. He stepped into the house. "Can't you just *try* to *pretend* I'm actually a person living in this house with you?"

"I'm going out."

And just like that, the shoes were back on, the bag was off the floor, and the door was slammed back.

It might as well have been in her face.

ELEVEN

Four a.m.

She didn't know why, but by some cruel twist of insomniac fate, this was the hour of unsleep.

She sat up in her new bed, closed in by her new room, with her new boy roommate just doors away.

Pros of a boy roommate:

1. Someone who can fix and break things all at once. Tools.

2. Someone to protect the household. And clean it, too.

3. Someone with hot guy friends. (Remained to be seen.)

Cons of a boy roommate:

1. Weird boy items. Boxers. Video game paraphernalia.

2. Mood swings.

3. Awkward non-vocal conversations.

Overall, it had been okay. He'd leave for work, and she... wouldn't. He cooked his dinner while she melted into the couch cushions. He'd shower and sleep.

She wouldn't.

And here she was.

One dead cake and one trampoline later, and Liam was only getting farther and farther away from acknowledging her existence.

Four a.m.

In the bathroom, she felt the lurch of her lower stomach. Her period. And without fail, her ice cream craving followed.

She tiptoed over the cold wooden floor to the kitchen and opened the freezer door.

Nothing.

Maybe candy?

She raided the pantry. Nothing but energy bars and canned vegetables.

Why did he have to be so annoyingly healthy?

"Need something?"

A low, sleep-ridden voice croaked from behind her.

"Oh," Reese said, jumping. "God, you scared me."

"Sorry." He circled around the the counter. He wore night slippers, she noticed. She wondered if he smoked cigars and read the newspaper, too.

"Do you have anything in the house that isn't good for me?"

He laughed, secretive, pointedly.

"What?" she asked.

"You'll have to be more specific."

She propped her elbows on the counter and glared at him.

Was that flirty? Did exhaustion make him flirty?

"Let me break this down for you. My lady parts —"

He recoiled. "Gross."

"Excuse you," she said. "I'm going to put this delicately. If I don't get some chocolate in the next ten minutes, my hormones will rage into the night, causing no sleep for either of us. Now. Where's the chocolate?"

He didn't say anything. He sat there, expressionless, his thick eyebrows carved into place.

"You're serious?" he asked.

"Cancer-serious."

He shook his head. "Don't ever say that again."

She could tell he was amused as he grabbed his car keys.

"You should know," she said, "that I'd drive myself. If, you know, I hadn't just had two glasses of wine."

He rolled his eyes. "You can never just say thank you, can you?"

Reese trudged outside into the humid aid, uterus aching, head reeling.

It wasn't until she sat in his passenger seat that she realized she wasn't wearing a bra.

"Oh God," she whispered, too loudly.

"What's wrong now?"

"Nothing," she said, hunching her shoulders forward, letting her shirt spill forward, trying her best to hide herself.

He noticed. "What are you doing?"

"Don't look at me," she said, shoving her hand in her face.

He started the car. "You're odd."

They drove past City Park. The streetlights cast a dull, hazy glow over the road, and Liam drove like a man on the run, shadily looking from side to side.

Maybe he just wanted to get this over with.

Maybe he *really* hated her that much.

"Where are you heading?" he asked her.

"A drive-thru, please."

"For chocolate?"

She shrugged. Small, not too dramatic. "Chocolate ice cream? Chocolate milkshake? Get creative here, Liam."

There was a flash of a smile on his face. A hidden smile come to life, a bunching of his cheek that was close enough to count.

They settled on McDonald's, their car the only one in the nonexistent line.

"An M&M McFlurry, please," Reese whispered.

A few minutes later, Reese was in chocolate heaven.

"Do you need anything... else... while we're out?" he asked.

"Like what?" she said, her mouth full of ice cream.

"I don't know," he said, trailing off. "Medicine? Umm, girl stuff..."

"I've got tampons, thanks."

He rolled his forehead through his hand. "Okay."

"It's just a period, Liam," she said. "I'm not rabid."

He didn't look at her. His eyes hovered over the steering wheel, following the ticks of white lines on the road.

"Hey, Liam?" she asked. "You never told me. Are you dating? You know, girls?"

He laughed. "Where'd that come from?"

"I'm curious. You know, the ground rules. We're roommates. *Just* roommates. I feel like I should get the lay of the land."

"I'm dating in the most casual of senses."

"So you're hooking up?"

He turned his head, looking at her in a questioning, *are-you-serious* kind of way. She liked when he looked at her like this. Like he couldn't handle her words. Like she'd won the upper hand.

"Can we just skip this conversation?" he asked.

"If you want me to follow the rules, then we need a code," she insisted. "You know, if you have a girl over. Or if I have guys over."

"I'm going to ignore the plurality of that last sentence."

She raised one, judgmental eyebrow. "So, what do you say?"

"Fine. If it'll get you to shut up."

"I can't promise that."

"The kitchen dish towel."

"Umm..."

"If it's hanging on the fridge door, then you'll know. For your late night snack trips."

"I resent that."

Liam was attractive. Objectively, Reese could admit that. As a girl who dated him and broke his heart, those thoughts were off limits.

She wouldn't be jealous if she found that he'd slipped the dish towel through the fridge door handle.

But, she might be weirded out.

Liam slowed at the red light. He looked at her through those stupidly adorable glasses. And for the first time since she'd moved in, Reese could see them being friends.

Maybe.

"We shake on it, then," Reese said, extending her hand. "A gentleman's agreement."

Liam didn't flinch. He reached over and hooked his hand in hers. "A gentleman's agreement."

When they got back home, the spell was broken.

Liam shuffled around her like she was gum on the sidewalk.

And Reese just shook it off, saying goodnight to the back of his unresponsive head.

She took the melty leftovers of her McFlurry out to the trampoline and sat straight up, her eyes on the stars.

Wendy would think this was majestic or something.

Vivian would study the dark spaces between them.

Reese wouldn't do either of those things.

She just sat there, sipping melted ice cream, her head a clear and empty pool.

She leaned back all the way in a corpse pose, imagining that this was how she might spend eternity. Staring up at the stars, while the rest of the world walked on top of her, doing whatever they wanted and living however they wanted, not noticing everything she was underneath.

Empty.

Clear.

Terrified.

Some things never change.

TWELVE

Friday night.

Her saving grace.

Reese was finally getting into the groove of things, but once the weekend came around, all she wanted to do was break free of the house.

As it happened, she wasn't so great at being cooped up in a house alone all day. She needed people.

Their horrible coffee breath.

Their awful tantrums in the grocery aisle.

Their awkward elevator exchanges.

She needed people. Bright, brazen, and anyone in between.

"I will mow your lawn," Reese negotiated. She was laying naked on her bed, the entirety of her closet sprawled out on the floor beside her.

"No," Vivian answered.

"I will babysit your child."

"I'll try and remember that in seven years."

"Seven? Really?" Reese said, then keyed back into her point. "What's it going to take to get you out tonight?"

"A miracle."

"I see your miracle and raise you a fancy dinner. Which, if you think about it, will kind of be a miracle if I actually find the money to pay for it."

Vivian was caving. Slowly, one rock at a time, but still. "Let me see if Owen is up to it."

"I'll wait."

She'd wear the black dress. The one that hugged her tightly and made her legs look runway long. And heels. Even if they made her look like a giantess.

She couldn't *wait* to put makeup on her face again. She was starting to forget what that felt like.

And brushing her teeth. Oh God, that would be nice.

Kidding, she thought.

She wasn't.

"Okay, we're in," Vivian said.

Reese punched the air with her fists. "You've just earned so many friend points."

"On one condition."

Reese sunk back to the mattress. What was with Vivian and all her conditions lately? "Of course."

"Liam has to come."

She wasn't nervous. She wasn't even sure if she got nervous, in the traditional sense. Actually, that anxious-worried feeling usually excited her in a thrill-seeking kind of way.

This was different.

This was selfish.

The thread wove threw her wind in this way: if Liam came tonight, then she couldn't hook up with anyone. That was too weird. Like she was openly cheating.

And if he didn't come, then no one else would either.

Vivian was good. Her manipulation still worked like a charm. She was the master of setting circumstances up in a way that favored her desired outcome.

It's what she did with Simon and Wendy.

And now Reese and Liam.

"Hey there," Reese said, rocking her body on and off the counter. Liam was reading again. "Long day? You tired? I'm making coffee for no particular reason. Want some?"

He looked over the couch. "You don't like coffee."

"The smell is... nice."

"What do you want?" he asked her.

He had his slippers on, too. The odds of getting him into a pair of Chino pants at this point was nothing short of—as Vivian would put it—a miracle.

"It's Friday night."

"Brilliant observation, Sherlock."

Reese laughed. She liked bringing the sarcasm out of his cool guy demeanor. It was a little, but mighty victory.

"I need to go out tonight," she said, spreading herself over the counter. "If you don't come, neither will Owen. If Owen doesn't come, neither will Vivian. And then, I'll be forced to go solo and you'll get a call in the middle of the night that somebody found me passed out in a ditch and either way, you're coming out eventually."

Liam just started at her blankly. "You done now?"

"No, one more thing," she said, picking up her head. "I'll be your best friend. And I'll cook you dinner."

"How about you never cook ever again, and you've got a deal."

She twirled. A stupid, girly twirl that made her feel like the fanciest damn ballerina in the show. "What about the best friend part?"

"We'll see."

THIRTEEN

They call it a hurricane.

Rum, passion fruit juice, orange juice, grenadine.

A hellish storm of sugar and alcohol.

"Let's go to the piano bar," Vivian said.

Reese violently shook her head. "No ma'am. Patio, all the way."

"Don't you want to listen to the music?" Vivian asked in her little-lost-lamb voice.

"No, I want to meet hot guys, make out with them in dark hallways, then leave and pass out in my bed."

"And why exactly did you need me to drive all the way across the lake for this?"

Reese scooped Vivian's shoulder up with her hand. "Because you're *pretty.*"

Owen sauntered up with Liam in tow. They had beers, like normal, non-touristy men.

"How's the living-together thing going?" Owen whispered in Reese's direction. "Sexual tension high?"

"How's the married life going? Libido still low?" Reese countered.

"Good to see you're still pleasant."

"Babe," Vivian said. Reese cringed. "Let's go listen to the piano."

Owen swigged the beer around in his mouth. "I'm good here, thanks."

Vivian watched her feet. She shifted her weight from one heel to the other.

Reese was about to say something, but Liam got to it first. "Dude, go listen to the piano with your wife."

Impressive, Reese thought, *chivalry is still on life support, after all.*

"Oh, before you go," Reese said, forking her camera over to Owen. "Take a picture of me and Vivian."

He did.

They smiled.

Hands on hips, forward bend, best features forward.

"Perfect," Reese said. "That's for Wendy. Want her to feel included."

"Speaking of that, did you invite Simon?" Vivian asked Owen.

Reese groaned. "Seriously?"

"Nah, he's traveling."

Simon was the mud under everybody's tires. Every time Wendy tried to get her car started again, he rose up from the earth and held her back.

She was so much better off in Nashville.

Far, far away from him.

Am I better off?

She was thinking about her father again. Miles Russell. Miles. Russell. The name that played on a loop in her brain, around and around and around.

"Do you want to know?" Wendy had asked her.

"Yes," Reese had said, not even waiting a beat. "I want to know everything."

He lived right here in New Orleans.

He owned a coffee shop.

He existed.

"I need a drink," Reese said.

Owen handed her a beer.

"No," she said. "A real drink."

Reese took a walk, looking for vodka and a familiar face. No, not vodka. Tequila.

Calm down, Reese, she told herself.

She felt uneasy. Restless. Like she couldn't wait another moment for the curtain to rise.

"Reese?"

She turned. Liam, rising like a phoenix from the crowd, closed in on her. Nearly instantly, she felt calm again. And all the racing thoughts parading through her mind seemed to stop.

Don't stare at him, Reese. She looked away.

"What's up?" she asked.

"Everything okay?"

"Just looking for some liquor."

He rested his hand on the bar. "Oh. Here, I'll get you something."

"No it's —"

"Are you turning down a free drink?" he said.

She shook her head. "Hell no."

Drink up, Reese. Drink and don't stop until you see stars.

Reese watched as Owen followed Vivian toward the piano bar. She was alone with Liam once again. He was like a wall. The perfectly unfortunate divider between her and the dozens of hot guys on the other side.

"You seem off," he said.

She looked up at him. "Please. I'm so on. I'm a party waiting to happen."

He sighed, like a balloon deflating. "Come on. I know you well enough to know when you're bullshitting me."

"Are you admitting that you actually know me beyond a roommate relationship? Well, well, well."

"I know we dated, Reese," he said plainly. "You don't need to remind me."

She suddenly felt underwater. Like she was looking up at him through a clear, rippling surface.

"Can I tell you a secret?" she asked.

She didn't know why she said it.

She tried to figure it out as she lifted her drink from the bar.

"Go for it."

Reese stuck the tiny straw through her teeth. "Never mind."

"Okay," he said.

"I found my father," she admitted. The words felt bitter on her tongue. "Father. Such a weird word. I mean, it's not like I'd call him Dad. Hell, I don't even call Rita by anything other than her name. So, I guess, I found my... Miles."

Liam's face softened. And then he did something stupid. He put his hand on her arm, and the feeling of it sent sparks through her like pop rocks on the inside of her cheek.

"Are you okay?"

Reese choked. She rolled her arm out from under his pity hand. "Yeah, I'm okay. I just don't know what to do. What would you do? If you were me?"

Liam lowered his chin to his chest. "I can't tell you what to do. But knowing you, I think you already know what you want to do."

"Drink more tequila?"

He laughed, openly this time.

Like he didn't want to hide it from her.

"Something like that."

After their fair share of alcohol, all four of them shared a cab home. Owen sang a medley of Frank Sinatra songs *very* poorly while Vivian passed out on Reese's shoulder.

It was out there now.

Her dirty little secret.

What would Liam do with that information now? Hopefully, pretend that it never happened. Hopefully, keep his opinions to himself.

They all toppled out of the car.

"Y'all can take my bed," Reese offered to Owen and Vivian.

"When's the last time you washed your sheets?" Owen asked.

Reese jabbed him in the back with her key. "You can sleep outside."

"Yeah," Vivian said sleepily. "You can sleep outside."

"Keep your bed, Reese," Liam offered. "I'll take the couch."

Vivian set her head back on Reese's shoulder. Reese fiddled with her key in the door. "What is this? Musical beds?"

"I know someone who could make your bed sing," Vivian giggled, then looked back at Liam.

The door finally opened. Reese looked down at Vivian. "Who the hell are you?"

Everyone scattered.

Owen to Liam's bed. Vivian to Reese's room. Liam and Reese were left staring at each other like idiots.

"So, what's the trampoline like?" Liam asked.

Reese smiled. "Cold. Infested with bugs. You'll hate it."

"Bet I can count more stars than you can."

Alcohol.

The great unifier.

It had once again worked its magic, freeing up Liam to actually treat her like a human being again, not just a cockroach making a home in his spare bedroom.

"Race you," she said.

On their backs, gazing up at the stars, someone might mistake this for romantic. But it wasn't that at all, Reese realized. This was an olive branch accepted.

"So, what are we?" Reese asked. "Best friends or something?"

The question was out there now.

She couldn't take it back.

I forgot how much you could miss a person you were just getting to know.

"Close enough," Liam said. "Close enough."

2004

His name was Andrew.

She wrote his name on her notebook. She sang his syllables through the school hallway. And he had the most adorable dimples that didn't belong to this world.

They'd been dating for two whole months.

"Are you coming to my party?" she'd asked him a week ago, as they cut class to make out in his car.

He was older, nearly seventeen.

"I wouldn't miss it," he'd said. "I got the best gift for you. I can't wait for you to see it."

"Is it a puppy?" she asked. "I won't settle for anything less."

"It's a pony. Does that work for you?"

Her friends were jealous of her new boyfriend. Her newest group of friends was on the shy side: some brainy, some dancers, some just plain awkward. They didn't like how comfortable Reese was around boys.

"I can teach you," she'd told them once. "You just have to stick your chest out. Like this." She'd roll her shoulders back and tug the front of her shirt down.

No one was very amused by this. They definitely never tried it.

That Was the Year

Her party would be the best one this year, she was sure of it. They were going to have a party on the lakefront, at night, with alcohol, maybe. Andrew's older brother had a fake ID, and his dad was on the police force, so they'd go easy on the underage drinking thing.

Fourteen was a big year.

Next year, she'd be heading to high school.

And if she could throw one, killer party as a way to impress the older classes, then she'd be set.

She'd have a name and a face and a reputation.

Maybe even a chance for a group of friends she actually liked.

They had an ice chest filled with "soda." Andrew's brother, the engineer-to-be, figured out how to cut open a soda can and use it as a cover to hide their beer.

It wasn't a perfect solution, but it would work.

"Happy birthday," Andrew said, kissing her as she slid into the passenger seat of his car.

"Let's make it a good one," she said, kissing him back.

As he drove her to the party, she wondered what it must be like to be in love. Like real, over-the-top in love. She liked Andrew a lot, but she didn't feel like they were steering toward the direction of love.

If love was North, they were East.

And that was okay.

She was only fourteen, after all.

The party was a huge success so far.

"Can I steal you away for a second?" Andrew asked. She didn't want to leave, but she didn't want to be a bad girlfriend, either.

They're all here.

It seemed like almost everyone in their class had shown up, plus more from grades above them. Freshman. Sophomores. Even some seniors were there, drinking from the dwindling pile of beer.

They're all here for me.

Reese passed on drinking.

She wanted to remember every moment of this.

"Of course," Reese said.

He walked her over to the swing set. His hands were all shaky and his forehead was sweating. It was pretty gross, but she tried to find it endearing.

"Reese," he said, starting off his speech. "You are the best girlfriend I've ever had."

Because you've had so many, she said sarcastically in her head.

"And I wanted to get you something really special, because I think you're special. At least, you're special to me."

She wanted this to be over.

And she felt guilty for it.

Andrew took a deep breath and handed her a velvety box. Reese held it in her hands, rocking back and forth. She imagined him walking through the store with his mom, picking out the perfect present.

And it made her feel sick.

"I can't accept this," she said.

"But you haven't even opened it," he said, laughing.

Presents like these came with strings. Maybe not now, but later. She knew enough about this to know that. He'd want an I-love-you. He'd want a story with her.

She couldn't give him that.

"No, I can't accept this," she told him. She had big, crocodile tears in her eyes. "I'm going to break your heart."

After that, it all snowballed.

Reese went back to the party.

Andrew did not.

She found herself with a senior boy, her back against a tree, his tongue down her throat.

And then, the sirens came.

Reese watched from the background as the cops descended on her party like flies on a picnic. One by one, they took her friends away.

And she felt like her skin was on fire.

Another party.

Another destruction.

Alone again.

FOURTEEN

They were watching Saturday morning cartoons. All four of them, knee to knee on the couch, watching cartoons and drinking chocolate milk. Except Vivian, who had recently declared herself lactose intolerant.

"I need a job," Reese said, arm-deep in a bag of popcorn.

Liam looked up from his phone. "Not your worst plan."

"Let's brainstorm," Reese said. "I need something low committal, just until I figure out the whole self-fulfilling, life-purpose kind of career."

"And you'll have to dye your hair," Owen said, chomping on kernels.

"Hell no," Reese said, clutching onto her lavender braid. "There are jobs for cool-haired people such as myself. Hmm. Let's think. An accepting, low commitment job. A work environment that accepts freedom of expression."

"Non-corporate," Vivian said.

"Non-boring," Owen added.

Liam patted Cecil's belly with his socked feet. "A theater, maybe?"

"That... or... you know... a coffee shop." Reese casually glanced at Liam, hoping he'd take her hint.

They'd talked it over last night.

Really talked.

And Reese slept better than she had in months.

He curled his lips into his mouth, then released them into a smile. A real one. "You're kidding, right?"

"Before you get all preachy on me—"

"I'm not getting preachy." Reese could see him tossing the idea around in his brain. "In fact, I'm impressed."

Vivian sighed. "I feel like I'm missing something."

"What's that?" Owen shoved more popcorn in his mouth.

Liam kept smiling.

This is what it feels like to have best friends.

"So what's the plan?"

Once Owen and Vivian headed back to Covington, Liam and Reese took Cecil to the dog park. City Park was a short walk from their house, and because it was unseasonably cool out, they strolled their way over with Bloody Mary's in tow.

Reese cracked her knuckles, one by one, hand by hand. "Don't know. Apply, I guess. Land the job. Meet Miles and show up to work somewhat on time."

"Good to know you've thought out the important details."

Liam threw the frisbee for Cecil. His back stretched tight in his t-shirt and Reese had to actively look away. Cecil, for his part, was excellent at fetch.

"Forethought is one of my best qualities," Reese said into the palm of her hand.

"Without a doubt."

"Just as long as you know what you're doing," Liam said. He threw the frisbee again, shading his eyes to watch it fly. "It's one thing to be a customer. Being on the payroll is a completely different story."

"You're right," she said, matching his seriousness for a fake, predetermined beat. "One costs you money, and the other earns it."

"Insightful," he said.

"I wish Wendy were here," Reese said, drawing circles in the dirt with her toe. "She'd go with me on my dadventure. She'd probably give me stupid, encouraging advice and lame words of wisdom." She stared off into the park. "God, I miss her."

"Here," Liam said, handing her the frisbee. "It'll make you feel better."

"Are you sure you want me to show you up?" Reese asked, flicking her wrist back and forth in preparation.

"Be my guest," he said.

Reese smiled at Cecil, who looked up at her with pure joy. "You ready, boy?"

She sent the frisbee flying. It sailed through the air effortlessly, as Reese gave Liam the smuggest smile she could.

Cecil was back in a flash, sitting patiently at her feet with a dopey happiness on his face.

"We get it," Reese said. "You're cute."

"He likes you," Liam said. "I didn't know if he would."

She threw the frisbee again. "What's not to like?"

"Can't think of anything."

Reese couldn't tell if he was being sarcastic or not.

"I'll go with you," Liam said.

"Go with me... where?"

"Your dadventure. I'll be your Wendy."

Reese laughed. "First of all, there's only one Wendy. Second of all, thank you."

Liam had every reason to not like her.

And yet, he'd somehow managed to find a way around that.

Or maybe, through it.

FIFTEEN

Monday.

Reese decided it would be Monday.

On Sunday morning, Reese woke up to the sound of jazz music filtering through her walls. Not the soft, soul kind. The loud, clamoring kind. Lots of trumpet.

"*What is that?*" Reese growled.

She tried to blink it away.

The music howled on.

Reese threw on a robe and stumbled out into the kitchen. Liam was in the living room, bent over the sofa, reaching the hose of the vacuum cleaner underneath. There was a mop propped up against the fridge. On the mantle, there were rags and dusting spray.

"What is this?" Reese growled again. She could feel the sleep caked on her face.

Liam poked his head over the couch cushions. "Morning. Grab a rag."

"It's 7 a.m. It's Sunday," Reese whispered. "I'm not grabbing a rag. I'm grabbing a pillow. And smothering you."

"Every other Sunday, we do a full cleaning. You wanna live here? You wanna burn down this kitchen? Grab a rag, Weller."

Reese counted in her head all the ways she could get revenge:

1. Rearrange his sock drawer.
2. Feed Cecil a laxative.
3. Slash his tires.

"Need bra first," Reese grumbled.

She took her time getting ready for cleaning day. Brushing her hair and teeth. Washing her face. Picking out what t-shirt she wanted to wear.

She texted Wendy: "Meeting Miles tomorrow. What should I wear?"

Wendy texted back immediately: "A dress and your game face."

Reese sighed.

Here goes everything.

Again.

Reese didn't help Liam clean. Instead, she locked the door to her bedroom and considered her options.

Maybe she would go back to sleep and life would fast forward to Monday.

No, she was too jittery for that.

This must be what coffee feels like.

Maybe she would take a shower. She should take a shower.

She was still thinking this over as she cracked open her bedroom window. It was a bad idea. And yet...

She crawled out.

It was not graceful by any means.

It was more like she rolled out of the window and splattered onto the grass, possibly bruising her elbow, possibly breaking her arm.

"God," Reese whispered under her breath, wincing, careful not to catch Liam's attention.

She crawled away, out the gate, to the front yard.

As she walked down the street, she picked up her phone and called Wendy.

"So what dress?" Reese asked. "I need you to be specific."

"I changed my mind. No one wears dresses to a coffee shop. You'll look too suspicious. How about yoga pants and a nice t-shirt? Not a sorority t-shirt. And not one of those t-shirts that say *breathe* or any kind of inspirational message."

"You literally just eliminated all of my t-shirts."

Wendy sighed. "You don't have a plain, relaxed-but-still-trying t-shirt?"

"No, that doesn't even make sense to me."

"Take a picture of your closet and send it to me," Wendy said. "Don't leave anything out."

Reese turned the corner. "I, uh, can't right now."

"Why? Where are you?"

"Running from my problems."

Wendy laughed. "How new and different for you."

It was true.

She wasn't great at handling problems.

But she was truly great at creating them.

Reese found herself outside a coffee shop with a sign in the window that read, BEIGNET, in big bold letters. "I'm going to have to call you back."

Four a.m.

Back like an old friend.

She liked the way the world looked at night. Dark, shrouded. Everything that happened at night was so much more forgivable than what happened in the light.

Reese tiptoed through her new home.

She liked it here.

She liked Cecil.

She liked Liam.

Reese opened the fridge and reached for the milk. From the cabinet, she pulled out her favorite mug. The chipped maroon one she bought from the flea market. She filled it to the top.

Microwave. Thirty seconds.

The plate spun, and the cup twirled around inside.

"Are you drinking warm milk?"

Reese turned to see Liam. His hair perfectly unslept in. Oddly fixed for someone who'd just rolled out of bed.

"Sorry. Did I wake you up?"

He shrugged. "Guess I'm on your schedule now."

"Careful. Our cycles may sync soon."

He squinted. "Huh?"

"Never mind," she said, taking the cup out of the microwave. "Want some?"

"No thanks, I'm not a cat."

"Hey," she said, "Don't knock it till you try it."

Liam shrugged and rested his forehead on the counter.

"I never could sleep properly," Reese said. "My mom used to wake up with me and she'd make me warm milk. Then we'd watch an episode of the Flintstones and I'd pass out."

"I always liked the Jetsons better," Liam said.

"Figures," Reese said, stirring her finger in the mug. "You'd never survive in the Stone Age."

He picked his head up. "You don't know."

"A sabertooth would rip through your pretty little bedtime slippers and you'd run away screaming. That's your life in the Stone Age."

"Good to know my masculinity is still intact," Liam said. He wiped his eyes with the back of his hands.

"Can I tell you another secret?" Reese said, pushing her warm milk toward him.

Who am I right now?

She always considered herself an honest person, but she usually picked her moments better.

He made her just come right out and say it.

"I'm scared shitless right now," she told him.

Liam laughed at her, an outright, full-throated laugh. "You're going to be just fine. You're Reese Weller."

She straightened up her shoulders.

She was Reese Weller.

Friend defender.

Ass kicker.

Life ruiner.

"You're right," she said, smiling. "I'm going to be just fine."

SIXTEEN

Bean There.

Clever name.

Ideal location for a dadventure.

The sun beat down on the bare skin at the back of Reese's neck. Beads of sweat pricked up as she dialed Liam's number.

"Where are you?" she barked, when she heard him pick up.

"Reese, I'm so sorry..." he trailed off.

"Sorry? Sorry for what? Where are you?"

She felt panicky in her stomach.

On the other end of the line, he took a heavy breath. "I'm at work. I can't get away. I know I said I'd be there for you, but I..."

"So you're saying you're *not* coming, then." She shifted from heel to heel, her free hand perched on the handle to her car door.

Bean There.

It was so close.

"No, I can't come, but I've sent reinforcements."

She squinted at the parking lot around her, getting an increasingly bad feeling. "What kind of reinforcements?"

He paused, then said, "*That* kind of reinforcement."

She looked around.

Nothing.

"What are you talking about?"

"Oh, that was supposed to be dramatic effect. Guess she's not there yet."

"Is this twenty questions? Liam. Tell me what you're talking about."

A small Mazda zoomed into the parking spot beside her, the front tire missing her foot by inches. She prepared her middle finger and her indignant-rage-voice, but the driver interrupted her. The window rolled down and the perky voice beneath the platinum hair rang out, "I'm ready for the stake-out!"

Reese turned away and said into the receiver, "No."

"Yes."

"Are you *freaking* kidding me?" Reese turned to see Vivian slipping on a pair of dark sunglasses. "You called Vivian?"

"Almost ready," Vivian said, setting her purse on the hood of her car as she pulled her chopped hair back into a nub of a ponytail.

Reese spoke to Liam again, "Are you crazy? Vivian is the last person who should be here right now. She is not chill at all."

"She's your friend, Reese. Give her a chance."

"I hate you. I'm going to set all of your clothes on fire."

He hung up before she could threaten him more.

"So," Vivian said, now standing at Reese's side. "We're on a paternity mission. I watch a *lot* of Jerry Springer, so you really should have called me first with this one."

Reese folded her back against the car. "You watch Jerry Springer?"

"It's surprisingly entertaining."

"Let's get this over with."

Bean There looked like it had evaporated out of an old, sepia-tinted photograph. It was as if you could pick the entire thing up like an old shawl, shake it, and watch as the clouds of dust flew from underneath it.

There were beat-up armchairs of every pattern, scattered around the store. The cups, used by a cast of characters, were a mix of hard ceramic, painted in wacky styles and shapes.

And then, there were the people.

Every kind of person, all shoved under one roof. There were men in suits, newspapers tucked under their arms, and phones glued to their hands. There was a group of women, all dressed in their Sunday best, an Easter egg assortment of bonnets on their heads.

Behind the counter, a black woman about Reese's age, with buzzed hair and tattoos crawling up her arms, fooled with the cash register. She wore a cobalt blue tank top and a collection of small black bracelets on her arm. When she returned the change back to the customers, she gave them a cheeky, condescending smile.

Reese liked her already.

Reese waited patiently behind the customers until it was her moment.

"Where do you think he is?" Vivian whispered, her eyes darting around the room.

"I don't know," Reese said. "Can you relax? You're freaking me out."

"Yeah, sure." Vivian bent her knees a little and crossed her arms. "I'll grab us a table. You focus."

Reese threw her thumbs-up at Vivian and scrunched her face in fake enthusiasm.

"What can I get you?" the barista asked, not looking at Reese.

"I'm looking for Miles," Reese said. "I'm here for an interview."

The girl, whose name tag read Trish, met Reese's eyes. She seemed to be taking a long, hard look at Reese, sizing up her potential coworker. Then she yelled, "Miles, another purple-haired girl out here for you."

"Thanks," Reese said. "It's lavender, but you know, same difference. I like your tattoos. Is that a wolf?"

Reese pointed to the bold design on the girl's shoulder. The teeth looked so realistic that they could launch right off her skin and tear into Reese's jugular.

"Never seen a tattoo before?" the girl said, flatly.

A door opened to the left of them. An incredibly tall man walked out with a rag draped over his stained t-shirt. He had a thick beard and a wild head of curls, his thin lips forming the straightest of lines.

Miles Russell.

Did he look like her? A little.

Did he recognize her? Not at all.

Did he change her life? Not yet.

"Reese?" His voice was deep and coarse, the kind of voice that would sound perfect for the radio.

He said my name.

Miles started to collect dirty dishes from the sink, and rinsed them. They moved like each other, she thought. All over the place. Taking up space. Un-Rita-like.

Reese said, "Uh, yeah. I'm here for the interview."

"You like coffee?" he asked her gruffly.

He said my name.

She was afraid he would ask her that.

"Yes."

She would learn to like it.

"You know how to clean?"

"Of course," she told him, half-lying.

"You start tomorrow."

He *said my name.*

He shook his hands dry, then barged back into the next room.

Reese stood, stunned.

"Welcome to Bean There," the girl said, smiling. "Good luck."

Reese looked to her. "Uh, thanks. Trish, is it?"

"Sure, why not?"

Reese smiled at her in a way that felt completely unnatural, then bowed away from her.

"Well?" Vivian asked, flocking to Reese's side. "What happened?"

"I got the job," Reese asked.

It was the only thing she was sure about.

For now.

2005

Reese had never seen so many balloons in her life.

Small, oval-shaped ones. Big, boxy balloons. Balloons that filled every square inch of the Lakes' ceiling.

"Are the clowns on strike yet?" Reese asked, dropping her backpack to the floor. "Because honestly, if they haven't unionized yet, this is sure to do it."

"Happy birthday, Reese!" Mrs. Amy called, shooting a popper off in her direction.

"What she said!" Wendy echoed.

The two of them looked scarily alike. It was as if Mrs. Amy had single-handedly reproduced her. Even their freckles were placed the same.

"Thanks," Reese said, tugging at a nearby balloon string.

"You want to see your cake?" Mrs. Amy asked. "I'm pretty excited about it, I have to say. It's very you."

"So it's in the shape of a detention slip?"

"Exactly," Wendy said.

The Lake's home was the kind of house that you'd imagine would fit nicely on a postcard. In the winter, there was always a fire burning in the fireplace. In the summer, there was always lemonade in the fridge. And not the cheap, store-bought kind. The real, fresh-squeezed, fifty-cents-a-cup kind of lemonade.

At first, it was really jarring to be in a house like this, the kind of house that made you automatically feel comfortable enough to hog the couch. But after a while, it began to feel less like a house and more like a home.

Reese liked to think of it as the Lake plus Reese home. She even had her own coffee mug in the cabinet and her favorite brand of Pop-Tarts in the pantry.

It only made sense that they'd throw her a birthday party of sorts now, too.

"You like it?" Wendy asked, as Mrs. Amy set the cake on the table.

Claudia, Wendy's younger sister, came toppling in from outside, scooter in hand. "Reese! Happy birthday!"

Reese smiled and thanked her.

The cake was perfect. No, beyond perfect. It was the kind of cake you give someone you know. Someone you love.

It was strawberry—her favorite—with cream cheese icing and topped with real, fresh fruit. In big red letters, it read, "Happy 15th Birthday, Reese! Love, Your Family."

Family.

Reese didn't think about that word a lot. Words like "mom" and "dad" would occasionally enter into her vocabulary, like little fragments of an overall much bigger sentence that had cracked apart.

Family.

Was this what that looked like?

Rita and Reese were not a family. It was like trying to play a board game with only two people. It may work logistically, but it's not nearly as fun.

"Wow," Reese finally said. She'd never felt more like Orphan Annie than in that moment, wondering if Daddy Warbucks would let her stay forever. "It's so great that I don't even want to eat it."

"Of course we're going to eat it!" Mrs. Amy said. "With our hands, if we have to."

When Mrs. Amy pulled Reese in for a hug, it felt like a holiday. Christmas, maybe. Or Thanksgiving. Like Reese was being bundled up in tradition and baked goods.

She was a mother.

She was a mom.

Reese poised her hands over the cake, looking to Wendy for approval.

"Hey, it's your cake," Wendy said, tipping her head toward the unsuspecting icing.

"I'm going for it," Reese said.

Fingers spread wide, Reese pressed her palms down into the icing. Mrs. Amy laughed an unsure laugh. Wendy shook her head, like she didn't think Reese was actually going to follow through with it.

Reese felt victorious.

In that moment, she wanted nothing more than to destroy this too-perfect present. She wanted to lower the bar. To even the playing field. There shouldn't be anything that perfect in the world. It wasn't natural.

She grabbed two handfuls of cake, eyeing Wendy.

"Okay, no," Wendy said.

Mrs. Amy jumped in with a "Reese, don't—"

But it was too late. Reese chucked the cake directly at Wendy. One whizzing past her and slamming against the fridge. The other made clean contact with her cheek.

For a second, nobody said anything, and Reese felt like she may have gone too far. She had let them see the messy, dangerous side of herself. She should leave now. She should thank them for their time and bolt.

But then, in a moment of pure impulsion, Mrs. Amy reached her own hand in the massacred cake, laughing, and threw a handful of cake at Claudia.

"Mom!" Claudia cried, stunned.

And so the great cake fight of '05 began.

Claudia darted behind the kitchen island to hide, while Reese grabbed a cookie sheet to use as a shield.

Icing flew everywhere.

Cake stuck to their skin.

And Reese didn't know if she'd *ever* laughed so much.

By the end of it, there was no cake left intact.

Which somehow, by some turn of events, made the whole thing even more perfect.

Mess and all.

SEVENTEEN

"I know that you're not allowed to cook in here, but does that mean that I'm not allowed to cook in here?" Vivian asked.

She'd brought the works.

Almond flour.

Coconut flour.

Semi-sweet chocolate chips.

All the essentials for making a heart-healthy batch of pick-me-up cookies.

"Yeah, sure, go for it." Besides, she told herself, Liam owed her. "Do cookies and whiskey go together? Because I'm a fan of pumping alcohol into my system as a means of distraction."

"Can I interest you in a green juice?" Vivian countered. "It'll make you feel great, plus it'll give you a nice glow."

"I don't *want* a glow. I want a buzz."

Vivian thought this over. Then, with a sharp slap, she brought the almond flour to its knees. "Screw this. I'm making margaritas."

Well, Reese thought, *look who's loosening up.*

"That's my girl," Reese said.

Two hours and too many drinks later, Vivian and Reese were hugging their knees to their chests in a laughing fit on the floor.

"You were the worst bride ever," Reese laughed. "Seriously, the way you barked orders and meddled in Wendy-and-Simon-land, I swear."

"I didn't meddle!" Vivian insisted. "I simply created an opportunity."

"Word of advice, Landry? You're never going to win this battle. So just stick with, 'I'm sorry.' It's better for everyone."

Vivian stretched onto her side. "I just want her to be happy. That's all. So, I get over-involved. Would it be better if I just *didn't* care?"

"No," Reese said, softening. She could maybe understand that. "For the record, I think she is. Happy."

"You'd know better than me, I guess. You were there for the whole thing. I just caught the finale."

Reese never really thought about that. The years *without* Vivian. She was kind of like Simon in that way, weaving in and out of Wendy's life, taking time and trying to make up for it.

"So, what? You feel guilty?" Reese asked. "Is that what all that was?"

Vivian blinked. "If Simon's a monster, that means I am, too."

"I can't begin to tell you how wrong you are," Reese said.

"Then don't," Vivian suggested.

Reese sighed. "It all worked out though, right? Wendy's happy. You're happy. I'm seeing you off, waving at you both as you set sail for paradise."

"Yeah. Paradise." Vivian turned her face away.

Cecil whimpered from his bed.

"I should let him out," Reese said. "Need anything while I'm up?"

"No, I'm okay, thank you."

The front door swung open.

Reese and Vivian jumped from their makeshift bed palette on the floor.

"Reese," Liam said, his voice strained and breathy. "Are you home? Oh. What are you doing on the floor?"

"Drinking," Vivian answered.

Liam crossed over to them, sitting on the couch and bending over Reese. "I am so sorry. I said I would be there for you and—"

Reese threw her hand up haphazardly. "Hush. Your voice makes me angry."

"*Your* voice makes *me* angry," Vivian said, smashing a pillow over her head.

"She handles hangovers like a champ," Reese said, mooning up at Liam. "Can you, maybe, go away now?"

"Reese, I'm your friend. You have to know that I wanted to be there today."

Friend.

He was really owning that title, all of the sudden.

Why, though?

Her head spun a little, so she couldn't settle on an answer.

"Sure," Reese said. "But you weren't, so."

"Reese—"

"*Go away.*"

Liam picked himself up off the couch, disappeared into his bedroom and slammed the door behind him.

Slammed.

He never did that.

"You should have heard him on the phone," Vivian mumbled. "He was so worried about you."

"He just feels guilty," Reese snapped back at her. "I'm not an eraser. I can't just clear his conscience for him."

"He loves you, Reese. Cut him some slack."

Liam didn't come out for the rest of the night.

Vivian went home after three more movies and a box of tissues, while Reese got ready for her first day at her new job.

She might be in over her head.

She'd find out soon.

He loves you, Reese.

She couldn't think about that right now.

Or, ever, maybe.

Reese wondered what Rita would think of this whole thing. She felt a slow chill run down her back when she remembered the tea leaf debacle.

Rita wouldn't want this.

Reese paced back and forth in her quiet room. She opened her bedroom door, taking on the cloak of night. She was in over her head, but she was about to be several feet below sea level.

The floor was cold under her bare feet.

The paint of night across the living room sparked her awake.

And there was his door.

Like a secret invitation.

Everything that happened at night was so much more forgivable than what happened in the light.

EIGHTEEN

"Liam. *Hey.* Liam."

She poked at his cheek.

His room looked different in the dark. It looked different with him in it, too. Suddenly, there was so much less space in here. His body was sucking up all the attention.

Liam opened his left eye. "What are you doing?"

"I need to talk to you," she whispered.

"No."

"It's either this or I drink more, and I really want to be fresh-looking on my first day."

He buried himself in the blanket. "Fine."

"Are you sure? I'm not putting you out? Okay, great."

Reese took no time to slip into the sheets beside him and make herself comfortable. From an outside perspective, this could be considered a violation of the ground rules.

But right now, he had to just be a person.

A safe place to dump her garbage thoughts.

You are not the person that I once liked enough to run away from.

"Are you wearing pants?" she asked him. "I feel like this will be a lot less awkward if you're wearing pants."

"Of course I'm wearing pants," he said.

Socks too, she guessed.

"But no shirt?" she asked.

"Can we skip to the part where you tell me that you're sorry?"

You are not the Liam that I sort-of-maybe-loved.

She widened her eyes. "You think I'm going to say sorry? Shouldn't *you* be the one to say that?"

"I did. You ignored me."

She pushed him gently in his shoulder. "Whatever. We're past that. Now, we need to talk about my *hey-I'm-your-kid* speech. I'm no good at speeches. In my brain, I picture it happening in front of an audience, like we're on a stage or something. What do you think that means?"

"Wait, why are you making this speech? I thought you wanted to get to know the guy first?" He was starting to look more alert now, even going as far as having both eyes brightly opened.

"Yeah, sure. But I want to have it prepared, just in case. Also, what's Rita going to think of all this? She's not going to take it well, I'll tell you that. So, then what? She ditches me? Then I'm parentless?"

"Can you do me a favor?"

She nodded. "Sure, what?"

"Breathe."

"Why?"

"Will you just do it?"

You are not you anymore.

You are just a body to touch.

You are just ears to listen.

She closed her eyes and sucked the air in deep through her nose. Then, as her lungs filled to the very top, she let it go, out warm and free from her mouth.

"How do you feel?" he asked her.

"Better, I think."

"He's going to love you, Reese. Everybody does."

Vivian's words rang out in her head:

He loves you, Reese.

He had said it to her once.

She'd almost said it back, too.

"Oh, shucks. You flatter me."

"Reese," he said, his voice turning over with seriousness.

She felt a sharp rush of fear.

Was he going to say it?

No, that was crazy. Vivian was making her crazy.

"Yes?" She braced herself.

"You can get out now," he said, and shut his eyes tightly.

The tension melted off her shoulders. "You know what would *really* make me feel better?"

He opened his eyes again. There was curiosity there. And then that was gone, replaced by something more skeptical.

Oh God, she thought, *he thinks I want to sleep with him.*

"No," Reese said, sticking her tongue out. "Gross, not like that."

"You really know how to flatter a guy."

"The trampoline, you dumbass. Come sit outside with me. I need fresh air."

Liam rolled away from her. "No."

"If you don't," Reese said, taking her fingernail and shoving it into the back of his neck, "I will stay here. And I snore. Loudly."

"You are absolutely exhausting."

Reese would be happy in the woods. She would be happy living out in a tent somewhere, or maybe a treehouse even, where everything was green and new and fresh. She'd be naked, of course. And she would never cut her hair. And every morning, she would wake up, place her bare feet on the ground, and curl her toes into the cool, morning dirt.

This is what she thought about on her trampoline, with only one lone tree in the backyard.

"What's *your* dad like?" she asked him. "Tall, probably. I bet he's tall."

Liam's head rested on his sturdy arms. He'd put a shirt on, but she could still see the veins winding down his triceps. "Uh, yeah."

"Is he like you?" she asked, propping herself up on her elbow. "The strong, silent type? Or do you get that from your mom? Maybe he's charismatic. Charismatic *and* tall."

Liam didn't say anything that time. He picked himself up, one arm at a time, and headed for the house.

Reese rolled onto her stomach. "Hey! Where are you going?"

He shut the door behind him.

"Okay," Reese said, turning back to the sky. "Goodnight, then."

Four a.m.

Her witching hour.

She sat up in her dark, empty room.

She felt the air from the circulating fan hit her skin.

And she dipped her toes to the ground—which was carpet, soft and worn, not the earth, not the dirt—and listened.

As the front door opened and shut.

As the car backed out of the driveway and into the night.

NINETEEN

Reese loved the smell of coffee.

It smelled the way an old black-and-white movie looked, like something you were supposed to like, even if you didn't understand it.

Too bad she thought it tasted like burnt leather.

"New Kid, take this."

A stained green apron came hurling at her head.

Miles didn't look at her as he dragged the chairs across the wood floor, slamming them into place. It was clear he wasn't a morning person.

Check number one in the things-Reese-inherited-from-her-father column.

"Joanie will get you set up," he mumbled.

"Joanie?" Reese asked.

"You can call me that," the barista with the buzzed hair said. Trish. "If you want to see stars."

"I like stars," Reese said, wrapping the apron around her waist. Then added, "Joanie."

Trish, or *Joanie*, stopped and said, "This'll be fun."

It was more of a challenge than a sincere statement, but Reese saw this as an opportunity.

She saw a ledge.

She would jump.

"Get moving, New Kid," Miles said, before disappearing into the back.

Hey Miles, Reese thought, *I'm your kid.*

Hey Miles, turns out your fertile and I'm proof.

Hey Miles, what now?

"Where's he going?" Reese asked.

Trish shrugged. "Home, probably."

Leaving work before it already started? How very responsible of him.

Check number two in the things-Reese-inherited-from-her-father column.

Bean There looked different in its set-up stage. It was like seeing a show without the amps plugged in. Yet, there was something special about seeing the place like this.

Reese liked it.

More than she'd expected.

"You're doing it wrong." Trish gestured toward the tables that Reese had already scrubbed.

Reese was folded over the last one, rag in one hand, cleaning spray in the other. "What? You think I don't know how to wipe down a table?"

"Yes, actually. Come over here. Let's try something else out."

This is like sorority hazing, Reese thought, *without all the smiling.*

Reese dropped her cleaning supplies and made her way around the counter. "What's next, *boss?*"

"Are you strong?"

"Hell yeah, I'm strong," Reese said, flexing.

Trish wasn't amused. "See that trash can? Take these coffee grounds and dump them in there."

The coffee grounds were held in a large pitcher under the counter. All Reese had to do was lift it, walk to the trash can, then dump it out. Seemed easy enough.

"Got it, boss," Reese said, squatting down.

The top was taped at both sides with bright pink duct tape. It was heavy, and she had to use every muscle in her body to keep it from toppling out of her arms.

She flashed a pained smile at Trish as she tilted the pitcher over.

And she could almost *hear* the tape pop.

The grounds, dried and loose, spilled out like a waterfall, and all Reese could do was stare, mouth open. Dumbfounded.

"Oh. My. God." Reese gawked at the empty pitcher.

Trish laughed. She laughed with her whole body. Stomping her feet, clapping her hands, the whole shebang.

"Vacuum cleaner, please?" Reese asked.

Trish bent over the scene with pride. "Don't have one."

"You're not serious," Reese said.

"Oh, but I am," Trish said, beaming. "Better get started. That looks like it'll take a while."

Reese settled her hands on her head.

Unbelievable.

"By the way," Trish added, "we open in fifteen minutes."

It took forty five minutes for Reese to get the floor cleaned up. Even then, there were tiny specks of coffee like ash imprinted in the wood. It was impossible.

"Okay," Reese said, wiping her hands together. "What next?"

"You're on runner duty," Trish said, handing a customer a cup of steaming coffee.

"What's that?"

Trish pointed to the empty mugs on the coffee tables. "Pick those up and wash them. Rinse and repeat."

"Perfect," Reese said, sighing.

After a while, Reese made a game of it. How fast could she spot the abandoned cups? How many swipes could it take her to dry the mugs? She buzzed back and forth from table to table, trying to be the best, wanting to be better and better.

"Congratulations," Trish said, what felt like only minutes later. "You just finished your first shift."

The place was empty now.

How had she only just noticed?

This must be their middle-of-the-day lull.

"I could stay a little longer, you know. I'm down to fifteen seconds per cup."

Trish dismantled her apron. "Calm down. There's so much more excitement to come. Tomorrow, it's your turn for coffee making."

"Wow," Reese said, untying her own apron. "Are you sure? Would you really trust me with such a momentous task?"

Trish threw her apron at Reese as Miles walked through the door. "Hang these up for me, would you?"

Reese focused her attention on Miles.

She'd always imagined that there would be some sort of innate *knowing* between them.

Like she'd walk through the door and he would just instinctively, ancestrally recognize her.

Your life hasn't been missing me.

"New Kid, how'd it go today?" Miles asked, stepping into action, fiddling with the espresso machine.

"Well, nobody died."

"Excellent," Miles said. To Trish, who was halfway out the back door, he said, "See you at home, Joanie."

Reese looked to Trish.

Then to Miles.

Then back again.

"Am I missing something here?"

Miles walked over to the sink. "Joanie's my step-daughter."

Your life hasn't been needing me.

Reese wanted to quit.

She wanted to abandon ship.

Even better, she wanted to sink the whole damn thing.

"Right," Reese said, sleepwalking over to the closet to hang the aprons.

Trish left without another word.

Your life and her life.

Miles kept working, unaware.

So, so unaware.

This life.

Not my life.

There in the closet, tucked in the back corner, was a stupid, hopelessly unused vacuum cleaner.

2007

No one ran away to the circus anymore.

It was a shame, really.

No one had imaginations anymore either.

Not like they used to, anyway.

Reese held on tightly to the ticket in her hand. Granted, this train was more modernized than she'd pictured in her head, but it was still just as romantic.

It would only take her eight hours to get to Memphis. From there, she would hail a cab and head to the Chapel Circus.

Reese didn't have a specific role in mind when it came to her life at the circus. She liked the trapeze, but she had trust issues. The tightrope walkers got to wear great outfits, but she wasn't sure if she had the balance for it.

Hell, she'd settle for the title of ticket taker.

Reese checked her phone. No messages. No calls. Clearly, Rita hadn't discovered that she was gone yet.

Inside the train, Reese settled into her seat. The train might not look magical from the outside, but it certainly felt that way on the inside. The attendants smiled as they glided around in their uniforms. The train hummed.

And then, they were off.

"Where you headed, hun?" The woman in front of her—probably around Rita's age—turned around to face Reese. She was perfectly herself in every way, from her sleek black hair to the adorable gap left by a missing tooth.

"Memphis," Reese said confidently. "I'm going to join the circus."

"I tried that once. Didn't work out so well for me. What do your parents think about all this?" She raised one knowing eyebrow in Reese's direction.

Reese was used to this kind of question by now. It used to make her angry when people automatically used the plural when it came to her parental guidance.

Mom and Dad.

Parents.

It was all too assumptive. But now, her answers came as naturally as a reflex.

"Parent. Singular. And, my mom doesn't know yet."

The woman looked judgmentally at her. "If you were my kid, I'd be searching like crazy for you."

The woman turned back in her seat. Reese checked her phone again.

Nothing.

Yet.

"Can I get you anything?" the attendant asked her.

Reese's eyes were open, but her brain was asleep. She checked her phone. Six hours in and no texts or calls from her mother yet.

Reese sighed. "Have you ever been to the circus? In Memphis?"

"Can't say that I have," he said. He looked like he would fit right in there with his big, clown-like smile. "Is that where you're heading?"

116

"Yeah," she said. "I'm running away to the circus."

He choked on a laugh. "People still do that?"

"Apparently so."

"Well, good luck with that."

He walked away, mocking her silently, she suspected.

Reese picked up the phone. In her spur-of-the-moment-ness, she'd forgotten to tell Wendy where she was heading.

"Hey there, birthday girl! What's up?" Wendy's voice was always so welcoming. At first.

"Nothing too much. I'm on a train."

A slight pause. A deep breath. Then, Wendy asked, "And why, pray tell, are you on a *train?*"

"To join the circus."

"As one does..."

"No, for real. I'm on a train to Memphis, heading for the circus."

Wendy's breath caught this time. "Oh my God, take it back."

"Hey, you're supposed to be supportive."

"Reese, I swear, I will come up there and drag you back by your hair," Wendy said, with a fierceness in her throat.

There it is.

"Have you heard from Rita? She's probably called the National Guard by now. I swear she can be so overprotective sometimes."

Even as she said it, she knew how much of a lie it was.

Wendy knew too, but at least she did Reese the favor of pretending.

"No," Wendy snapped. "But if she hasn't called them, you better believe that I will. Reese, what are you—"

Reese hung up the phone.

She checked her text messages again.

Still nothing.

The air was lighter in Memphis.

Still humid, but a little less.

Everything seemed a little less here.

Home.

Where would she live? Did circus performers live in trailers? Or maybe they stayed in tents. She could do that.

What if she had to pay for her own apartment? Would she even make enough money to *afford* an apartment? Would anyone even lease an apartment to a seventeen-year-old girl?

Wendy would have thought about these things.

Wendy was the responsible one.

She checked her phone again. No surprise. No calls. No text messages.

Reese decided to take matters into her own hands.

She called Rita.

"Reese! You'll never guess. I found the most *amazing* little plant nursery just twenty minutes down the road. What do you think: roses or sunflowers?"

It hurt.

She didn't want to admit it.

But it hurt like pure, unadulterated hell.

"Rita... do you... know what day it is?"

"Saturday, why?"

Reese's bottom lip quivered. She grabbed it harshly with her fingers, then let it go. "Roses, Rita. You should buy roses."

"K, hun, talk later."

And that was it.

End of conversation.

Reese could disappear into the circus, and Rita would never know it. She probably wouldn't even be able to give a physical description of Reese for the missing persons report.

She crouched down on the sidewalk. Her heart felt heavier than her body felt around it.

She picked up the phone again.

"Wendy?" she said as soon as the ringing stopped. "I made a mistake. I'm... umm... I'm so screwed up."

Wendy didn't skip a beat. "You screwed up, Reese, but that does *not* mean that *you* are screwed up."

Reese's lips started trembling again.

This time, she let it happen. This time, it was joined by a new friend, a steady stream of tears down her face.

"I'm going to buy you a ticket home right now," Wendy said. "If you don't want to be alone, then I'll hop on a plane and book a train back with you."

Family.

Was this what it looked like?

Family.

"That's okay. I'm okay," Reese said, assuring her. "I'll see you when I get home."

TWENTY

"I'm bored," Reese said.

Another four a.m.

Another night on a damp trampoline.

The past week had been incredibly weird. Every day, Reese went to work, pretending like she didn't have a father there, pretending like she didn't have a *step-sister* there.

It was too much.

It was so much that she thought she might quit soon.

They didn't act like family. At least, not by any standard model. Miles floated in and out of the shop, barely saying any words at all. And Trish was constantly testing her, using her pranks and her wit to... well, Reese didn't really know why that was happening, exactly.

"Need food?" Liam asked, glasses slipping from his sleep-filled eyes.

At night, there was Liam. Another routine she had down. They'd meet in the kitchen for warm milk—or cat food as he so lovingly called it—and then she'd irritate him into meeting her on the trampoline, where they'd look at the stars and Reese would talk about death.

She stopped wondering if he loved her.

She kicked Vivian out of her head with two feet.

"No, Liam, I do not need food. I need a night out. I need to do something."

"It's 4 a.m. What exactly are you planning on doing?"

"We could go to Bourbon Street. We could get beignets. We could break into the pool. Whatever."

"Tempting, but..."

"What if a hot girl was asking you? I mean, yes, *of course*, I'm hot. But I'm talking about a hot someone who isn't me. You wouldn't tell her no, would you?"

He probably would, she realized.

He hadn't even mentioned another girl, unless in the hypothetical sense.

Thank God.

Wait, what?

"I would, actually," Liam said.

"Regardless," Reese said, "I'm going to go out on a limb here and say you've never done one impulsive, downright ridiculous thing in your whole life."

"If you say so," he said. But it wasn't honest. It was a *just-to-get-you-to-shut-up* statement.

"In fact," Reese pressed, sensing something more, "I'd bet you've never done anything in your entire twenty-seven years of life, knowing you'd get caught, knowing you'd get in trouble, but doing it anyway, because the *fun* of doing something spontaneous and different was worth it."

"Sure, Reese," he said, still cryptic. "Can I go to sleep now?"

Reese sat up, cross-legged. "What are you not telling me?"

"I'm not telling you that you're a crazy insomniac who's driving me out of my mind... oh, wait."

Reese balled her fist and gave him a fairly decent jab to the side. Liam winced. "Spill."

"If I show you, will you leave it alone?"

"*Show* me?"

She made no promises.

"If I show you," he said, again with the illusive *show*, "do you promise that we can stay here? No trespassing, no drug purchasing, no illegal activity whatsoever?"

"For tonight, yes."

Liam exhaled. He knew better than to fight her. One more exhale. And then he stood.

His shadowy figure loomed tall above her, like a lone stalk of wheat under the moon. He was thin, yes, but somehow demanded more room in the world than he actually required.

And he lifted his arms above him.

And removed his t-shirt.

"Woah," Reese said, before she could help it. Maybe it was because of Liam stripping for her. That simple fact alone warranted some kind of reply.

But it was more than that.

It was because of the visible indents of the abs that had mysteriously emerged.

Don't you dare stare, Reese.

It was because of the strong, perfectly placed pecs that appeared from out of nowhere.

Seriously, Reese, you can look away now.

Then, he turned his back to her.

And it was because of the tattoo—yes, tattoo—on the back of his right shoulder.

You're screwed, Reese.

"You happy now?" he asked her.

The tattoo was simple but outspoken. A deep, inky black number "15" carved into his back in block lettering. Strong. God-like. New.

Nearly-nerdy, straight-laced Liam had a tattoo.

You always fall for guys with tattoos. That's your type.

Vivian had been right.

The proof was there on Liam's surprisingly muscly back.

"Well," he muttered, turning back around and reaching for his shirt.

Falling for Liam had been a turning point for Reese.

He was the good one.

He was different from the string of low-life boys.

He was proof that she could change.

Realizing she hadn't spoken in a solid minute, she said, "What's the 15 for?"

You can't change, Reese.

"I don't really feel like talking about that," he said, settling back beside her. "You've maxed your quota of questions for one night. My turn."

"But—"

"No," he said. "I showed you mine, now you show me yours."

Her stomach went up in flames.

Was that suggestive?

Possibly.

He mooned up at her from beneath marry-me eyebrows. He was practically begging her to mash her face into his.

You're exactly the same, Reese.

"Fine," she said, willing to play along. "What do you want to know?"

"Crazy thing you've done. Go."

"Crazy thing I've done? Man, that's hard to narrow down."

"I've got time," he said. Bent back over his elbows. Hidden, magic muscles tucked back away in Clark Kent fashion.

Reese could think of a million dangerous, destructive things she could tell him. The sort of stories she'd break out at parties for bragging rights. But she didn't want to tell him any of those things. She wanted to tell him something good.

"I'm Catholic," she said. "Mostly. I mean, I don't practice, but yeah."

You tried to be different, Reese.

She didn't like that he made her want to prove she was good or different or better.

But she liked that he made her want to try.

Liam reared his head back dramatically. "No."

"Yes."

"Well, I'll be damned."

"It's possible."

Later into the night, when sleep finally hit, Reese fell hard. For abs. For rimmed glasses. For the number 15.

You failed, Reese.

TWENTY-ONE

"He has a tattoo."

"Who has a tattoo?"

"Liam. Liam has a tattoo, and now he's not cute, black-rimmed glasses Liam, he's tribal-ink, tatted-up, dangerous Liam and what the hell?"

"I've never heard you use that many adjectives before. Are you having an aneurysm?"

Reese was driving home. Not Liam-and-Reese home, but Wally-and-Rita home.

Maybe she was distracting herself.

Maybe she was making this into a bigger deal than it actually was.

Still, everything was more than a little confusing.

"Psh, no," Reese said, taking a solid, controlled breath. "I'm just kidding. Liam has a tattoo. I mean, it's just weird, okay?"

On the other end of the line, Wendy was probably smiling. She was probably shaking her head just a tad, being irritatingly right about her non-expressed words.

Is everyone right except me?

"Sure," Wendy said. "Totally unexpected."

"What's that supposed to mean? That long pause you just did?"

Wendy laughed. "You're acting crazy. Crazier than usual."

Reese relaxed. Wendy was right, but only a little.

Wendy didn't know the whole story.

She'd buried that with her Liam feelings.

"So, Nashville. Cool city, huh?" Reese said, changing the subject.

"It's alright," Wendy said.

"Isn't this supposed to be the dreams-do-come-true part of your life? I think you can do a little better than just alright."

Wendy sighed. "You're right. I'm being ungrateful. Allow me to readjust my attitude."

"I'd appreciate that, thank you."

"So, any father/step-sister updates? So weird, by the way. Do you need any advice? Claudia and I would be *happy* to give you pointers on not killing each other. Nineteen years, and going strong."

"Trust me, Trish and I aren't even the same dimension as you and Claudia. It's like I opened Pandora's box and a brand new life exploded from it. I've suddenly got two sets of families and I was barely managing the one."

Reese pulled into her parents' driveway. Everything looked the same. And, she realized, it felt the same too. In reality, it wasn't the same at all though.

"It's all going to work out," Wendy said, reading her mind, as always.

Of course it would.

It always did.

Rita was acting weird.

Weirder than normal.

For starters, she was wearing pink. Not pale pink. Not unintentional hints of pink. It was a deliberate, ridiculous pink that swallowed her upper body whole.

As if this weren't enough, she was *singing* to herself as she poured the tea into the china. Not chanting, om-like singing. This was La Vie En Rose, and she sang it with power and fervor, as if Reese weren't even in the room.

Reese glanced over at Wally, who looked equally confused. He wrapped the end of his beard in his left hand.

"Um, Rita," Reese ventured. "Is everything... alright?"

She sang another line, then said, "All is well, my little bumblebee."

Reese glanced outside at the actual bumblebees that still inhabited her parents' backyard. Maybe Rita was talking to them.

"So, how are the new digs, Greaser?" Wally asked.

Reese clicked her heels together under the table, Dorothy-style. "Great. I have a dog. Well, I mean, he's not technically mine, but I feed him sometimes, so I share custody."

Rita glided over to them, setting the teacups gently in front of her family members.

Wally talked around her, "Anything good on the job front?"

"Yes, actually," Reese said, taking a sip from her steaming cup. "I, uh, got a job as a barista... at a local coffee shop."

Rita danced back into the kitchen, literally, not figuratively. It looked like a variation of a two-step and lyrical ballet. There was nothing composed about it.

Turning back to Wally, Reese saw the awareness in his eyes.

He knew.

She wasn't sure how, but he did.

"Groovy," Wally said through a clenched jaw. "Where's that at?"

Reese kept her eyes hooked on his. "It's on Magazine Street. Bean There. That's the name."

"Haven't heard of it," he said, for Rita's sake, she assumed.

"Meditation break," Rita said, giving a flick of her wrist before flitting upstairs.

Reese and Wally kept their eyes locked and their mouths shut until they heard the click of Rita's door.

Reese fired off the questions. "I know you know, but *how* do you know? And, by the way, who crushed happy pills into her Earl Grey this morning?"

Wally leaned in, keeping his voice low. "We'll get to all that, but first, you need to quit your job, and you need to do it now."

She'd never heard his voice sound like *that* before. So rigid. It made the hair on the back of her neck stand up.

"What? But you said—"

He looked over her shoulder, then back. "I know, I know, but your mother. If she finds out you're spending every day with—"

The door clicked open again.

"Shh," he whispered. "Don't say anything."

They listened as Rita walked back down the stairs and into the kitchen again.

"All is well," she said again, then followed with, "but I won't be meditating any longer. More tea, anyone?"

TWENTY-TWO

She was not getting the hang of this.

When it came to creating latte art, there were three factors you really had to master: the pull of the espresso, the frothing of the milk, and then the combining of the two.

She went wrong in nearly every *single* area.

Her espresso pulled too slowly.

She overheated her milk.

And, because she was focusing so much on trying to create the perfect milky flower, she usually lost track of how much milk she was actually pouring and wound up overflowing the cup.

Then Trish would make a face and Reese would have to start all over again.

And, of course, the customers were thrilled with this whole scenario on Monday mornings, as they anxiously stamped their feet and checked their emails.

"Move over," Trish would eventually say, taking the lead.

Trish was amazing in the driver's seat. She could take three orders at a time, and have the rush hour crowd out the door in twenty minutes. Reese wasn't sure why they hired her at all. Not when Trish could so clearly handle it all on her own.

"I'm no good at this," Reese said, around ten o'clock. "It's like you're speaking a foreign language to me."

"Maybe we should go over this again," Trish said. "I can't keep picking up all the slack around here."

See? She totally cares.

"Show me again, I guess," Reese said.

And Trish tried. Twice.

"You overheated the milk again," Trish said patiently.

"No," Reese said, staring down at the frothing pitcher. "No, that's not possible."

"Just, take a walk, Reese. Clear your head or something," Trish said, pouring the ruined milk down the drain.

Reese needed a cigarette.

It had been months since she'd smoked one—partially because Liam had made it *very* clear that it was against house rules—and today, she was pretty sure that she couldn't go another minute without one.

She texted Wendy: "Bad family day. My sister thinks I'm an idiot. Advice?"

Again, Wendy answered nearly immediately: "Welcome to my world. Show her your math skills. Or color her hair. She needs to see something you're good at."

Reese responded: "Thank you, buddy."

As she took her first drag, Miles pulled up in his old, vintage two-door. The thing was so ancient that it could probably have great-great-grandchildren by now.

"Sweet car," Reese told him, rolling her cigarette back and forth in her fingers.

He looked permanently tired. Reese wondered if his face always looked this way or if it had something to do with life at home.

The topic of Trish's mother had yet to breach the surface. She was the big question mark in Reese's new family, although Reese tended to picture her as a fabulous, nocturnal musician who spent her days in a bathrobe with a glass of gin in her hand and her nights jamming out on a guitar.

Or something like that.

"I could use one of those right now," Miles said, nodding toward her cigarette.

She thought about it a moment, then handed him one. He held it up to the lighter, then breathed in the nicotine.

"That's the life," he said, claiming a spot next to her on the wall, kicking one leg up.

The family that smokes together...

"I didn't know you smoked," she said.

He smiled. "You don't think I fit the profile?"

"Guess you're right," she said.

There were so many things she knew that she should want to ask him. It turned out that she didn't actually want to ask him the questions that she'd stored away all this time.

She just wanted to know what he liked to do for fun.

Where he went to school.

Who he was as a person, out in the world, at every and any age.

"So, how do you like it so far?" he asked her.

"It's okay," she said. "I'm less than spectacular. And my boss is kind of a tyrant."

He laughed. "You joke, but it's been said before."

"No way," she said, unable to imagine that.

"Oh, yes," Miles said, crossing his arms. "This kid, barely out of college, moved here from somewhere up north. I asked him to work the early morning shifts, and well, there you go."

"He sounds like a model employee," Reese said.

Miles nodded. "If these walls could talk, I'm telling you."

"You know, Trish is really great," Reese offered, hoping he'd give her more information on her new sister.

"Sure is," he said, leaving her hanging.

"How long has she been here?" she asked.

He thought about it. "Let's see, she's twenty-three and I met her when she was nineteen. So, she's been working here on and off, for what, four years?"

"She's *twenty-three*? But she acts so—"

"I know. Mature for her age. She gets that from her mom."

Does she get anything from you?

In a lot of ways, Reese had inherited so many things from Wally. He gave her permission to be childish. He taught her how to play blackjack. He was the one who saved her from being alone. She didn't know much about biology, so she had no idea the power of nature versus nurture.

Who wins?

Wally or Miles?

Miles or whoever Trish's dad was?

"Well, this was fun," Miles said, crushing the cigarette under his foot. "Shall we?"

She copied him, pushing the cigarette into the gravel with the ball of her foot. "We shall."

2000

"So," Reese said, staring at him coldly from across the picnic table, "what are your intentions with my mother?"

The *him* in question was Wally Snead, a dairy farmer from Bush, Louisiana with a crazy beard that fell all the way down to the table, coiling there like a snake. He happened to be dating her mother, who was wildly in love with him.

"Well, sweetheart, I intend to love her for the rest of my life, 'till death do us part."

Reese squinted at him. "You know, Wally, a lot of people say that. But every year, the divorce rate is growing higher and higher, so what do you have to say for yourself?"

"Well, let's be fair here. I don't think I'm responsible for all the divorces in the world. Just the one."

She folded her arms. "So, the truth comes out. How do you explain your track record, mister?"

"I won't lie to you, Grease Bucket. Is it okay if I call you Grease Bucket?"

She wanted to say no, but she'd never had a nickname before, so she told him that it was fine.

"What do you know about marriage, Grease Bucket?" he asked her.

She brought her finger to her lip, thinking. "Nothing."

"Well, lucky for you, I have the secret, all ready and waiting for you. Think you're ready to hear it?"

Reese didn't know if she was ready for this secret quite yet. She was only ten, after all. But she could take this secret and tuck it into her back pocket, should she ever find anyone she loved enough to keep.

She closed her eyes. "Okay, I'm ready."

"The secret to marriage is that it only works if you're both on board. The second somebody jumps ship, it's Titanic city."

Reese tried to make sense of his statement. She didn't really know what marriage had to do with ships.

"So, did she hurt you?" Reese asked.

He smiled very softly. In that moment, he looked more like a grandpa than a step-dad. His hair was fading to gray, and he had wisdom tucked up into his eyes.

"Yes, ma'am. She hurt me real good."

Reese extended her hand out to him. "Okay, Wally. You seem like a pretty good guy. And since you've been hurt real good, then I trust you not to hurt my mother real good. Deal?"

He shook his head. "I would like to accept this, except there's one minor flaw to your statement."

"So you *don't* want to date Rita?"

"Hurt people hurt people, Reese. And don't you ever forget that," Wally said.

That made sense to her. She hurt people all the time. Rita hurt people, too. But looking at Wally, he didn't look like he'd hurt anybody. Not even an ant.

"I won't forget," she promised him.

Later that night, when Wally had gone back to Bush, Rita and Reese relaxed together on the couch.

"Did you have a great birthday?" Rita asked.

Reese tucked her toes between the couch cushions. "I had the best birthday. Wally's... he's really nice, Rita."

Rita smiled. "I'm glad you liked him. Seems like he liked you a whole lot, too."

"So, when you get married, would it be okay if I called him Dad?"

Rita pushed the glasses down to the tip of her nose. She'd brushed out her hair for the night, so it fell in big, frizzy sheets around her face. "You know how I feel about parental terms."

Reese actually *didn't* know how Rita felt.

"Could you... tell me again?"

Rita wrapped her hair over to her right shoulder. "Terms of endearment such as Dad or Mom or Grandpa imply a sense of ownership, which is duplicitous. People don't belong to people. So, there you go."

There you go.

Rita did not belong to Reese and Reese did not belong to Rita.

Wally did not belong to Rita and Rita did not belong to Wally.

That's why people left, then.

Because they could.

That night in her bed, Reese watched the clock until the time reached for midnight like a hand to hold. She'd been ten for a whole day. People had told her for weeks upon weeks how turning double digits would change her life. That ten was the age when you grew up.

She flipped through the day in her mind, turning it over and over, searching for something to learn.

In fact, she'd learned a whole lot.

Hurt people hurt people.

People don't belong to people.

She tossed those phrases back and forth in her mind like a tennis match as she fell asleep, knowing, somewhere way down deep, that she may never stop repeating them.

TWENTY-THREE

It was cold.

Cold for Louisiana, anyway.

Her feet were the coldest part of her body, but the cold traveled up the back of her calves and shot through the rest of her body like a pinched nerve.

She couldn't pinpoint what got her here.

She just knew how she wanted to feel.

Where do you go when you want to feel free?

A bar.

A church, maybe.

In the end, though? It was a pool.

In the dark of night, you couldn't see it from the street. There was no reason for her to get caught, no realistic chance at someone finding her, alone, with her bare body about to jump in the freezing cold water.

"Just do it," she told herself. "Just jump in."

Her toes grazed the top of the water. Her whole body tensed.

Behind her, her phone vibrated on the lounge chair. She paused to check it.

Liam texted: "Where are you? Working late?"

She only sort of hated that he wanted to check up on her.

People don't belong to people.

She texted back: "Swimming. Be back soon."

She dropped the phone.

And without giving it another thought, she dove. At first, the shock was so immediate and chilling, that it felt like her whole body had caught on fire. After that passed, the sheer overwhelming feeling of cold filled her system.

She screamed.

"You okay?" someone yelled from beyond the fence.

And now, panic.

"All good here. Thanks, though!"

She didn't have a towel, she realized now. She could make a mad dash for the bushes and hide there until the stranger passed, but by that point the frostbite will have settled in. Could you even get frostbite in south Louisiana?

The gate clicked open.

"I was driving passed and thought you might want dinner—oh, Christ."

Liam.

Reese couldn't move. Not her body. Not her mouth.

"What the hell, Reese?" He turned his back to her, but he didn't look like he was going anywhere either.

"It looked like fun," she found herself saying. "I'm slowly losing all feeling in my extremities. Tell me, how quickly do people die from this kind of thing?"

"Get out before we find out."

"Okay, I'll meet you at home."

He didn't move. "You don't want me to... help or something?"

"Help me? How exactly? I mean, unless you want to join..."

"Quit it. Come on, we should go."

Reese splashed the water around her. "What are you, scared?"

"About your health? Yes."

"You're scared we're going to get caught." She took a few steps toward him, quietly, so he couldn't hear her.

"I am not."

"That doesn't sound very convincing to me." She was almost to the edge now, her hand inching toward his ankle.

"Will you just hurry up?"

"If you insist," she said.

Reese grabbed his leg in one, swift motion, pulling him backward into the water with her. He cried out, and tossed his phone to the chair, mid-fall.

When he surfaced, his mouth begged for air. "Holy crap, it's freezing."

"That'll pass. Soon, you won't be able to feel anything at all."

He opened his eyes.

And she remembered. She was naked.

"You're an idiot, you know that?" he asked her.

She didn't cover herself up.

And he didn't look away.

"You know you love it."

She watched him. He watched her, too. Right there in her eyes, holding his gaze steady and strong. Never looking down, never looking for anything more.

Somehow, this felt like more of a violation than if he'd just stared at her body. She could deal with that. She could expect that.

But the way he was looking now? It was like he was searching for her soul.

"We should go home," he said, probably catching onto her fear.

She nodded. "Yes. We should."

He let her leave the pool first, turning away as she slipped her shirt over her head, her pants over her bare, damp legs.

"Okay, I'm decent," she told him.

"You sure about that?" he teased.

She turned to look at him. "Don't make me throw you back in there."

He walked right up to her. His face leaned down to hers, leading with his mouth. "Then you're coming, too."

"Admit it. You had fun."

He didn't say anything, but his body said everything. He raised his hand and tucked it under her jaw. His hands were cool on her neck. His thumb, ridged and rough, ran over her cheek, before he pulled back and stumbled away from her.

"See you at home."

"Yeah," she said, the wind officially knocked out of her. "See you at home."

TWENTY-FOUR

Reese stumbled down the street.

He loves you, Reese.

She tried to ignore that heartbeat of a line, but every time she tried to silence it, there it was, beating away in her chest.

What would happen when she went home?

Maybe he would kiss her. She could live with that.

Maybe he would have sex with her. No, he wouldn't.

But what if he wanted more? What if he thought he could vault the past back into the present? Maybe he'd never learned that lesson the way she had, the one that pounded itself into her brain with every stitch in Simon and Wendy time.

"Why are you thinking so much?" she said out loud to herself. "Who *are* you?"

Great question.

Who are you?

She picked up the phone as the house was nearly in sight.

It rang and rang, again and again.

"Come on, Wendy," Reese said, stopping just two houses away.

The ringing stopped. The voicemail started.

"Hi, you've reached Wendy Lake..."

Except she hadn't.

Wendy was not there.

Wendy was not here.

People don't belong to people.

"I'm losing it," Reese told herself, pacing in circles in front of the neighbors' house.

She couldn't call Vivian.

She couldn't call Rita.

So who could she call? Who could she reach for?

"Hi," Reese said, when she heard the click of a phone being picked up. "How, uh, how are you?"

There was a moment of pause on the other end of the line. "Why are you calling me, Weller?"

Reese smiled at Trish's voice. "You know you don't look twenty-three."

"And you don't look twenty-six. What game are we playing?" Trish asked. She sounded intrigued, which made this more fun for Reese.

"What was your major?" Reese asked.

She was outside of her own house now.

Liam was inside.

Waiting, maybe.

"Political Science. Now let me guess yours. General Studies? Couldn't pick one major so you had to pick them all?"

Reese laughed. "Much more thrilling than that. Accounting."

"So you're a numbers person."

"And you're a word person."

Reese realized she was searching for a string of likeness between them, which, of course, didn't make sense because they weren't related by blood.

She guessed she couldn't wait him out any longer.

Eventually, she would need to go inside.

"Well, this was fun," Reese said. "Good talk."

She could imagine the face that Trish was making on the other end. "Good talk, Weller. See you bright and early."

"Bright and early," Reese mimed, then hung up the phone.

She marched into the house, prepared to kill all things good.

Liam couldn't be more beautiful if he tried.

The way his stupid hair fell just above his eyebrows.

The way his stupid eyebrows married together at the bridge of his nose.

The way his stupid eyes settled on her like he knew her or something.

"Hi," Reese said nervously.

She hated feeling nervous, so she usually made a point to skip that state of being altogether.

But not tonight.

"Hey," he said not-nervously. He was never nervous. "Do you want some wine?"

She felt like she was coming out of her skin.

"Like lungs want air," she said.

As he filled her glass, she looked around their house. Well, it wasn't really their house, actually. They were renting this life. They were renting each other. Until one day, they'd move out and move on.

People don't belong to people.

"Here you go," he said, walking up close to her and slipping the glass into her hand. "Want to lie on the trampoline with me?"

She laughed nervously. She wasn't in her own body anymore. She was renting it. "I knew that trampoline would win you over eventually."

"Yes," he said, holding the back door open for her. "It won me over."

There were rules.

She wasn't allowed to break them.

And yet, he was breaking them left and right.

Was that fair? Was any of this fair?

"Is it just me or are the stars like *super* bright tonight?" Reese asked.

He laughed, but not at her. "I guess it's time for me to come clean. You were right about this purchase. It's beautiful out here."

She was choosing this, she knew.

She had every right to sit up and walk back into her house, back into her room, and back under her blankets.

And yet, she didn't.

"Reese." He said her name with respect that a lot of people often forgot to give her. "I know we said there were rules..."

She dove in, then, as if he were that cold, biting pool. She'd held it in as long as she possibly could, but she couldn't do it anymore.

Reese kissed Liam.

And he kissed her back.

There weren't wine glasses anymore, as Liam had tossed them somewhere in the yard. His body rolled on top of hers, his hands cradling the back of her neck.

She'd forgotten how long it had been since she'd been held like this. Over five months, actually. Not since before she'd moved in with...

Liam.

Had she been *waiting* for him?

Had she been *holding out* for him?

No.

Maybe.

He kissed her neck and she felt like she might die.

He loves you, Reese.

But she didn't love him.

I don't love him. I don't love him... right?

That's why she stopped this in the first place, wasn't it?

She couldn't love anyone that way.

She'd tried. She'd thought she did, anyway.

"Reese," he said her name again. "I—"

She turned her face away from his. "Liam, I'm sorry, I can't."

It spilled out of her mouth like one lonely word.

Liam pulled his face away from her. He rolled onto his back and fixed his eyes on the sky. "Okay."

"I don't want to lose you again," Reese said. It came out more desperately than she intended. "You're my best... you're my best friend."

That was true, it turned out.

She was never alone with Liam in her life.

He made her feel like she was good.

She existed.

"You won't," he said.

And he leaned over and kissed her cheek sadly, before he picked up the broken glasses, and tossed them in the trash.

TWENTY-FIVE

She was distracted.

She hadn't told anyone about what happened the night of the skinny dipping incident.

Though it was only a few weeks ago, it felt like a lifetime. Liam had kept his promise; she hadn't lost him. He stayed awake with her in the middle of the night to talk, but it wasn't quite the same. It was like they'd both jumped and landed just a few inches away from where they had started.

It looked close enough, but it wasn't exact.

The customers were complaining, Trish was irritated, and Miles eventually had to pull her aside.

"New Kid." He still called her that, even though it had been months now, and there were *plenty* of other newer kids around. "What's the deal?"

I don't know how to let anyone love me.

Got any fatherly advice for that?

Now would be the perfect time.

She used to imagine what that might look like, when she used to have her heart broken, over guys who didn't matter.

The last time she found herself crying over this very idea was when she broke up with Ben. Marriage-material Ben, or so she let herself pretend. She wished that she could have a father who would hold her tightly and tell her it would all be okay.

She wished for a father who would threaten to break Ben's limbs.

"Personal problems," Reese told him.

Miles nodded. "Let's take a break. I'm due for a beer. You in?"

It was 11:30 in the morning.

"You bet," she said.

Check number whatever in the things-Reese-inherited-from-her-father column.

"So what made you decide to open a coffee shop?"

The bar was a hole-in-the-wall neighborhood place, with regulars already assuming their designated chairs. Reese loved these kind of bars. They had a certain kind of charm about them that was so uniquely homey, that you felt compelled to stay for hours.

There was history here.

Miles lounged over the counter. He never stood completely upright. It reminded her of the way her teachers used to nag her about sitting up straight in her desk.

Maybe posture is hereditary, she thought.

"I've always been a solo worker," Miles said. "I wanted to work for myself so I made it happen."

"Cool."

"And you?"

"Well, gee." Reese wrapped her hands around her glass. "I've wanted to be a barista my whole life. As a coffee-hater, I can't think of a better career choice."

He laughed, which was more like a grunt, but she guessed that was the best he could give.

"You're a millennial. Shouldn't you be pursuing some kind of made-up career like life coach or fashion blogger?"

She nearly choked on her own spit. "I can't believe you just said fashion blogger."

"Whatever."

"I don't have a dream. Never really did," she said bluntly. "I'm not an artist. I'm not a visionary. The only things I've ever been good at are binge-drinking and taxes. Not exactly a career path."

He seemed to be processing the idea in his brain. He glanced around the bar for a beat or two, until his eyes landed on a nondescript wood panel in the floor.

"What?" she asked.

"Nothing," he said. He straightened his back as much as his spine would allow. "Just sounds like the makings of a bar owner to me."

Reese Weller, owner of a fine, nighttime establishment.

She'd never really owned anything important before, but somehow, it wasn't actually the craziest idea she'd ever heard.

"I think you need capital for that kind of thing," she said, shooting down the idea. "As you can see, I'm hardly investable either."

"Save now. Plan now. Once you get something figured out, we can talk about a loan."

She wasn't sure if she'd heard him right, since he mumbled and started to walk away.

"I didn't mean—"

"We'll talk, New Kid," he said. "Look, I may not be rolling in dough or anything, but I could help. You remind me a little of me."

Her body flared up in goosebumps.

I am a little of you.

She felt that phrase pass through her cells and bury itself into her heart. It meant more than she thought it would. Another phrase she could keep with her forever.

"Thanks," she told him. "That really means a lot."

"No problem. There's your first business lesson. A boss is nothing without his people. You got me?"

Reese felt like she should write that down. "How do you find the right people? People you can trust, I mean."

"It's not easy, at the start," he said, taking a sip of his beer. "You read their resumes, you bring them in for interviews, that sort of thing. Eventually, you'll get so good at it, you'll be able to tell with only a look."

"Is that how you hired me so quickly?" she asked him.

He blew out a puff of air. "It all comes down to instinct. I could tell you had it. Whatever *it* is. Plus, you reminded me of someone."

"You, right?" she said, laughing, liking the idea of it more and more.

He nodded. "No, somebody else." He shook his head. "Anyway, just start somewhere. We'll talk later."

They would talk later.

She and her father were talking.

It still didn't feel real yet.

2009

Reese didn't know alcohol could taste like this. The one time they tried drinking beer senior year, she and Wendy nearly vomited, shouting, "It tastes like pee!"

But there was something about holding a glass of tequila in her hand that made her feel cool. More powerful somehow.

And because it was her birthday, she didn't have to pay for a cent of it.

"To being nineteen!" Wendy shouted.

A group of frat boys stopped and gazed in their direction, looking like vultures salivating over road kill.

They looked to each other and raised their eyes, as if to say, *"Who's up?"*

The guy with the gargoyle grin stepped forward and said, "Did someone say birthday?"

"No," Reese said, "but it's good to know you can read."

She pointed at her crown that read, "Birthday Girl," in plain English.

"I was going to be nice and offer you a shot, but since you're being so—"

"So what?" Vivian said, stepping up. Her dainty fists perched against her hips in what was a laughable expression of intimidation.

"Forget it," the guy said, returning to his pack with a disappointing, struck-out look.

Wendy draped her hands around Reese and Vivian's shoulders. "Who needs boys? We are sassy lady warriors who can buy our own damned drinks."

"Shots on me!" Vivian exclaimed, darting away through the crowd like her feet were ice skates.

"See?" Wendy said. "I knew you'd like her."

It was actually true. She'd fought it for months, worried that Wendy's first best friend would come storming back into her life, set on replacing Reese. But that never happened.

Wendy and Reese were family.

And now, Vivian fit that too.

"All I'm saying is that if that shot isn't tequila-based, then she's out."

"Fair enough," Wendy said. She had on her drunk, reflective eyes. Like she was about to spit out poetry or something.

"Spit it out," Reese said. "Come on, what were you going to say?"

Wendy smiled. "I love you two more than I love any boy. And I just want us to eat cake and tell our sob stories while we watch sappy movies."

Reese laughed so hard that tequila burned in her nostrils. "Okay, Wendy. Let's go get you a drink."

That night, the three of them took the bus back to Reese and Wendy's apartment. They all stumbled inside like chicks breaking out of their eggs, kicking off their heels immediately and slipping into pajamas.

"I'm starving," Vivian whined, throwing herself onto the couch.

"Pizza!" Wendy suggested. "Let's order *all* the pizza!"

Reese picked up the phone first and ordered three different medium pizzas, which would probably last them all of one day.

And then Wendy got her wish, almost.

They turned on Casablanca and stretched their comforters across the living room floor to make a pallet. The pizza boxes spilled open on the floor and they ate their slices while lying on their backs, as the drunkenness slowly left them.

"I don't know if I want to get married," Vivian said. "Is that weird? I mean, maybe it's because I've never felt like that about anybody before. But I just don't really see *till death do us part* in my future."

Reese chomped down on pizza crust. "It's not weird. You don't have to get married if you don't want to. You can just marry us."

"There's an idea," Wendy said, in the middle of the pretend mattress, stretching her legs in the air. "I don't want to think about marriage anymore. That picture's all blurred and fuzzy now."

"Just because it's not Simon, doesn't mean it's not in your future," Vivian said. "It's the same view from a different lens."

"That's a good point," Wendy said, her eyes closed.

"I don't think I know very much about love," Vivian admitted.

"I don't think I know *anything* about love," Reese followed up.

They all laughed.

"Well, I love you both," Wendy said. "So, I happen to know a lot about love."

Reese sighed. "Love is interesting. It's up, it's down, it's a million miles a minute. It's the forever part that seems stale. If I had my way, I'd fall in love a hundred times, each one hotter than the last."

Wendy shoved her. "You don't mean that."

"I do too!" Reese stared up at the ceiling. "Think about it. You get to relive that first love feeling over and over again."

"But what about stability?" Vivian asked. "What about somebody to grow old with? What about knowing that at the end of the day, he's there, knowing the good and bad parts of you, and loving you anyway?"

Nobody said anything for a moment.

Then Wendy did, saying, "Spoken like a true marriage naysayer."

"I'm not a marriage naysayer," Vivian said. "I just don't think it's for me personally."

Reese stretched her arms out and over her head. "You're welcome to my many boyfriends. There are plenty to go around."

Wendy tucked her arm through Reese's. "Oh, Reese. Always so generous."

That night, while Vivian and Wendy slept, Reese was wide awake, imagining the next few years.

She could see Wendy married first, with maybe a baby or two.

And Vivian would be next, despite what she said.

Reese would be in love again.

And again and again and again.

TWENTY-SIX

She couldn't believe she'd gotten him to agree to this.

With Vivian's help, they went all out with the decorations. Fake eyeballs floating in the punch bowl. Fake cobwebs covering nearly every nook and cranny of their house. And of course, the costumes.

Reese prided herself on being the perfect Poison Ivy. Green jumpsuit. A trail of leaves climbing up her body. And, of course, she was back to her trademark red locks. Newly dyed and dangerous.

"You have to go as Batman," she had told Liam. "The hosts need to complement each other."

"We compliment each other all the time," he'd fired back. "Just the other day, I said how nice it was that you brushed your hair for a change."

"Clark Kent, then?"

Liam hadn't said no.

So she'd continued with, "You've already got the glasses. All you need is a Superman t-shirt and you're set."

That had won him over.

Seeing him now, Reese couldn't deny that he was the perfect Clark Kent. His serious jawline. The smile that broke through like a freaking rainbow, the one that he never hid anymore. And the glasses that fit him just so perfectly.

She used all of her muscles to hold herself back from removing his glasses, throwing them across the room, and kissing him hard.

"Don't get too close," he told her, pulling her out of her slightly inappropriate thoughts.

More than slightly.

"Huh?" she asked.

He pointed at her then to himself. "Poison Ivy. Superman. She manipulates him with her mind control. So, as you can gather, I don't want to get too close."

That makes one of us.

She wanted to get close. She wanted to get so close that their bodies suffocated the air molecules between them to death.

She may not know how to love him, but that sure as hell didn't stop her from wanting him.

"Mind control, you say? That seems like a handy trick."

He backed up from her, jokingly. "Not so handy at all, actually."

Reese smiled.

And her body ached all over.

"Happy birthday, Clark," she said.

"Thank you, Pamela."

The swarm of costumes that descended on their typically quiet house rivaled most birthdays Reese had ever had, which was saying something. Reese didn't realize how many people *loved* Liam. When they talked about him, it sounded like they were venerating a saint.

And the worst part was that it was all warranted.

How am I supposed to get over you like this?

She couldn't.

So, she got under a glass of wine instead.

"Reese!" the crystal decibel of Vivian's voice pierced the crowd.

She weaved through the bodies toward Reese, revealing a perfectly put-together flapper costume complete with jeweled headband and frilled dress.

"Where's Gatsby?" Reese asked.

"Hanging with Clark. Great crowd tonight."

Reese nodded. "And even better decorations. Want something to drink?"

"No, I can't stay long."

There was a flash of something in Vivian's eyes. For a split second, they went dark, like she'd just lost something. Like something had gone away. Reese thought about asking, but she had given up on that topic of conversation.

You can only ask the question so many times before the answer, or lack thereof, gets old.

"Okay," Reese said. "Whatever you want."

Vivian huffed, like Reese had poked a nerve.

"Let's go find the guys," Reese suggested.

She couldn't believe she'd gotten him drunk.

Liam, the mild-mannered, responsible one, could barely hold his cup up at this point. And he was *dancing*. Right there in the living room, to an old school, big band song of his choosing, he was dancing as if the whirling of his arms and the stomping of his feet were the only things keeping his blood pumping through his body.

Oh, and alcohol.

Lots of alcohol.

"Careful," Reese yelled over to him. "If you spill on the rug, it'll be the end of life as we know it."

He kept dancing. "Who cares about a rug? I've got the music in me."

Stop being charming.

Owen coughed into the crook of his arm to keep himself from spitting his drink everywhere. "Check my pulse. That last comment nearly just killed me."

"Nearly? Darn," Reese said, grinning at him with a big cheesy smile.

"Who is this person?" Owen asked, pointing over at Liam, who kept spinning one of his friends in and out, toward him, away from him, and back again.

Stop being attractive.

"Because I don't think I've *ever* seen him like this," Owen added.

"That's my roommate," Reese said proudly.

"Y'all are good for each other. I gotta admit, I thought it might be a disaster. But, here we are."

Reese shrugged. "He's a good guy."

"He's the *best* guy."

Stop being so god-awfully good.

"Easy there, tiger. You're taken."

And then.

Well, and then, it happened.

When Sophie walked in with her blue John Lennon glasses and her barely-there crochet top, everything shifted.

TWENTY-SEVEN

Movies told the story of time slowing down in big moments.

The main character watched the person she liked or loved or liked to love meet the girl who's going to take him from her.

The music faded out.

Everything else was background.

That's a lie.

Liam danced in double time.

Sophie speed-walked through the crowd.

And when they turned and bumped into each other, the spark that ignited between them turned to a wildfire in a single blink of Reese's eyes.

It started that quickly.

And Reese saw it all, so swiftly that she wondered if her mind was tricking her. That maybe it wasn't reality, but a distant parallel universe, playing out in her brain.

"That's your old roommate, isn't it?" Owen asked.

Reese nodded.

It felt like a knife to her gut.

Sophie caught her eye, probably said something like *nice to meet you* to Liam, then walked over to Reese.

"Hi," Sophie said, her voice strained. The tension sent Owen running.

"What are you doing here?" Reese asked. She hadn't invited her. At least, she didn't think she did.

Sophie tucked her hands into the pockets of her jean shorts. "My friend Molly works with Liam, and when I heard you were the one giving the party, I thought, well, I thought I'd come make peace."

Reese could see Liam looking at Sophie from the kitchen. She knew he wouldn't try anything with Sophie, as long as she was in the house, too. He wouldn't want to make anything awkward.

Reese, on the other hand, had no problem with that.

"I'm really happy to see you," Reese said, wrapping Sophie up in a hug.

She wasn't happy.

She wasn't anything, really.

She felt frozen over, like someone else was moving and making the decisions for her.

Sophie let go first. "Can we meet for lunch soon? I know this isn't really the right environment for talking, but I'd love to get together."

"Sure, yeah," Reese said, distracted by what she was about to do.

"Good," Sophie said, smiling. "Well, I'm going to go grab a drink."

"Actually," Reese interrupted her, "what do you think about Liam?"

Stop.

Sophie turned to look at him, then back at Reese. "Honestly?"

"Honestly," Reese said. "Safe space."

"I think he's super hot," Sophie admitted.

Don't.

"Well, he's not dating anyone. I think... I think he'd really like you."

"Really?"

Reese grabbed Sophie's hand. "Come on, let's go find out."

This was not what she wanted to happen, and yet, she was the one *making* it happen.

Sophie and Liam laughed at each other's half-jokes.

Sophie and Liam talked like two, heartsick teenagers.

Sophie and Liam couldn't keep their eyes off each other.

Wait.

"Well," Reese said eventually, "I'll let you two talk. I'm going to get a beer."

Vivian intercepted her path immediately. "What's the story?"

"The story? What story?" Reese changed her mind. She went for tequila instead.

"Sophie? What's she doing here after everything that happened? And why is she so *close* with Liam right now?" she asked.

People don't.

People don't belong.

People don't belong to people.

Reese walked away from Vivian.

She let the music wash over her.

It washed away the party.

It washed away Sophie.

It even washed away Liam.

Reese found herself on the floor of the laundry room. She knelt in front of Cecil's kennel. He didn't whine at her, but he did lift his left paw up to meet her hand through the bars.

"For the record," Reese told him, "I may actually be in love with him."

Cecil cocked his head to the side, like he was listening.

"Blink once if you think I'm a crazy, stupid idiot."

He looked at her with intense, unwavering eyes.

She felt a slight tear escape out of her eye. "Good boy."

Slowly, she rested her head on the tile, tucking her knees into her chest.

Cecil laid his body down beside her.

And she closed her eyes, wondering what in the hell she'd just done.

TWENTY-EIGHT

In the bright light of morning, the house was a wreck.

There were beer cans in the sink and in the bathtubs. All of the furniture was rearranged to create a dance floor. And, best of all, Cecil had panicked from the noise and peed in his crate, which had spilled out to the tile and soaked up into her hair.

Reese had a faint memory of that. She'd tried to let him out in time, but he just couldn't make it.

And clearly, drunk Reese couldn't be bothered to clean up after him.

So now, she had piss in her hair.

Liam was going to flip.

Except, he didn't get up.

It was already 9:30, way past his customary rise-and-shine time. Plus, it was Sunday. Cleaning day. Reese chalked this up to the fact that he'd been so *drunk* the night before, and decided to get to work.

She scrubbed the kitchen.

She washed the dishes.

She threw away the beer cans.

She even straightened out the furniture.

And still, Liam slept well into the afternoon.

Finally, Reese decided it was time to check for a pulse. Carefully, she knocked on his door and whispered, "Liam?"

No signs of life on the other side.

"Liam?" she said again, turning the knob and carefully pushing the door open.

She couldn't take it back.

Not when she saw Liam's bare chest rising up and down.

Not when she saw his arm curled around a sleeping, bare-backed Sophie.

Not when Liam opened his eyes and looked straight at her, finger to his mouth, silencing her.

"God," Reese whispered, closing the door. "Sorry."

There were pangs of regret somewhere roiling inside of her. Last night came crashing back down on her. Reality. That's what this was. A choice she'd made, a direction she'd chosen. And yet.

She glanced toward the kitchen.

There it was, in plain sight.

The dish towel hanging on the fridge door.

A gentleman's agreement.

She was pacing through the living room when Liam shut his bedroom door, now covered by a gray t-shirt.

"Wow, it looks so clean in here," he said. "Guess things weren't as out of hand as I thought."

"Yeah," Reese said. "Look, I'm so sorry... I didn't know..."

Liam shook his head, turning to look behind him. "We gotta talk."

He took her hand and whirled her outside before her head could make sense of it.

"Okay," he said, breathing deeply now that he was outside. "That was *not* planned."

Reese kept her cool, swinging her hair behind her back. "It's called alcohol, Liam."

"I know, I know. But there's just a lot to think about here. I mean, Sophie. And you know I haven't dated in a while." She could practically see his brain flipping through the laundry list of excuses in his mind. "And I mean, there's you."

"Me?" she asked. "What about me?"

He balled his hands and shoved them into his pockets. "We haven't talked about this yet. Dating other people."

Dating.

He was dating her?

Liam and Reese had never signed a contract of celibacy. Although, looking back on it, there should've been a clause about sleeping with each other's friends.

I wanted this. I wanted this... right?

So, really, there was only one thing she *could* say. "Come on, Liam. It's okay."

"I remember you saying something like that last night." He sighed. Was he expecting a different answer? "I just need you to be sure. I need this to be okay."

Reese imagined a Liam switch in her brain. Emotions aside, she had the power to flip it on and off. She had the agency to make a choice right now.

Liam needed somebody.

But right now, that somebody was not her.

So, she flipped the switch off.

"Liam," she said, grabbing ahold of his hands, trying to memorize all the lines in them. "Did you have fun with Sophie?"

"Yes," he answered skeptically.

"And do you want to see her again?"

"Um, yeah. I do."

Reese smiled. "Then that's all that matters. Start there. See what happens."

Liam smiled back. A little sad, maybe. "Right. Okay then."

"See? You're so dramatic sometimes." She shook out her hands like she was washing them clean of him. "Now go back to her before she thinks you ditched."

Almost giddily, he leaned in and planted a quick kiss on Reese's forehead before darting back to bed with his tow-headed princess.

Hurt people.

Hurt people.

2015

"Where's... uh... Wendy?"

Her legs felt like jello underneath her. And Vivian, who was in just as good of shape as she was, draped her arm around Reese, letting her whole body weight settle on Reese's shoulders.

Reese was so drunk that she hadn't seen Wendy leave. She was so drunk that she couldn't be sure if Wendy had ever been there in the first place.

"Who?" Vivian yelled back. She lifted her body off of Reese, and slowly readjusted the pink wig on Reese's head. "There. Don't. Lose. Birthday. Hair."

Reese nodded, briefly losing control of her head.

Slowwww.

The room was so slow.

Or maybe, it was fast.

She grabbed onto the person next to her.

"You okay?" His hand was on her back.

She shook her head.

Wendy.

Right.

Find Wendy.

"I gotta go home," she said.

The stranger, dark-haired and blurry-faced, squared off to her. "Do you need me to call you a cab?"

She tried to focus on him. He had glasses. He had a mouth. He had a boy-beautiful face. "No."

"Wait, are you Reese?"

She backed away. Did she know him? No. Did he know her?

"It's okay," the maybe-stranger said. "I'm Liam. Owen's friend?"

Liam.

Real Liam.

Not-her-type Liam.

"Oh," she said, throwing her arms around him, "I know you."

He laughed and it sounded warm in the way that tea felt in your throat. "Yes, you know me."

Looking over his shoulder, she saw Simon alone at the bar. She remembered now. Simon with Wendy. Simon leading Wendy out the front door.

"Liam," she said, pulling back sharply, "I have to go, but just wait right here, okay? Right. Here."

"Okay," he said. "I'll be right here."

Reese toppled over to the bar. Her legs were stilts, breaking and straightening and surging her forward. And Simon found the bottom of his cup. It was straight in the air. And all the liquid ran *down down down*.

"Hey." Reese hit him. "Where's Wendy?"

He focused hard on the bar. He asked for another drink. He might as well have asked for a dark cloud to hide under.

"Hey!" Reese hit him harder. "Where's *Wendy*?"

"Your house," he mumbled. Sulked.

She sat down in relief. "Good."

"Reese?"

"What?"

"If I ask you a question, will you be completely honest with me?"

Reese hated Simon most of the time. It wasn't a secret. "Fine."

"Totally honest, Reese."

"Just shut up and ask already."

The bartender handed him another drink and he swallowed it down hard. "Am I the worst thing that's ever happened to Wendy?"

Reese stood up. Tried to say this soberly. "The fact that you're asking me that proves so much."

"Like?"

"Like maybe you are? Like maybe you leave people? You're a people-leaver. That's who you are." That was definitely not delivered soberly.

"You're right." He didn't look up. "I don't know how to not be in love with her."

"Well," Reese sighed. "You don't know how to *be* in love with her either."

There were two types of love.

The feeling kind.

The action kind.

You can feel it and not show it.

You can show it and not feel it.

Wendy deserves both.

"Stay away from her, Simon," Reese said. "For once, just stay away."

Simon took another sip. "For once, you and I are on the same page."

Reese felt like she was forgetting something.

She was on the move again, stumbling around the bar, looking for whatever she lost.

"Reese?"

She turned her head.

The boy with the glasses was behind her.

"You!" Reese exclaimed. "I think I've been looking for you."

He cupped her elbows in his hands, steadying her. "Well, you told me to wait right there, so here I am."

"Liam," she said. "That's your name."

"And you're Reese." He said it like a secret. "Are you looking forward to the wedding?"

"What wedding?"

He looked confused. "Um, Owen and Vivian's wedding?"

"Oh, yes, but I don't believe in all that stuff."

Now he *really* looked confused. "Love? Marriage?"

"Well, I mean, I have a boyfriend, so I guess I'm supposed to, but honestly? I don't." She leaned in close so that her cheek was pressed against his, her lips at his ear. "Plus, my boyfriend is cheating on me, so."

His hands climbed up to the back of her arms. "I'm so sorry. That's... that's horrible."

"Yeah well." She waved the rest of her sentence away.

"I mean, this isn't my place to say, but," he said anyway, rounding his shoulders back, "why don't you end it with him?"

"I don't know," she said honestly. "Maybe I should."

He smiled, at least she thought he did. It was a layered smile, like the real one was hidden underneath there somewhere.

"If you do," he said, "you should call me."

She rested her hands on his chest. She felt his heart beat. "And why is that?"

"Because I'd like to take you out."

His eyes looked like stars behind his glasses. Maybe it was the alcohol. Maybe it was the glare. Either way, he was celestial.

"Okay," she said. "Okay."

TWENTY-NINE

Wendy was waiting for her at the gate, like she was a kid back from a summer abroad.

"You're here, you're here, you're here!" Wendy chanted.

Reese knocked Wendy over. She ran right into her, pushing Wendy smack down onto her ass. Wendy winced, but she laughed through it.

"I'm so happy to see you," Reese said, holding her tightly.

"You're my favorite surprise," Wendy said, hugging her back. "Now, what's wrong?"

"What's wrong is that I'm starving and I need to eat cake while we tell our sob stories and watch sappy movies."

Wendy smiled. "Your wish is my command."

Chocolate made everything better.

They sat in Wendy's apartment, beside Plant the plant, and told their sob stories over cake, as Casablanca once again played in the background.

"Well," Wendy said, "what are you going to do now?"

Reese, through her mouth full of cake, said, "Well, now I'm going to start dating again."

"And how did you reach that brilliant conclusion?" Wendy asked.

"Because I got what I asked for," Reese said, folding her arms. "I didn't want to love him, so I didn't. And now, I've got to get out there. If I don't get out there, I'll go crazy."

Wendy licked the icing off her fork. "If you say so."

"I do say so," Reese said.

"Then might I say, I think you may be more romantically stable than any of us."

Wendy looked at Reese. They had shared heartbreak in their eyes. Wendy was trying, but she was a relationship girl, not a dating girl. And Reese, well, she was the complete opposite.

"Hey," Reese said, reaching out and grabbing Wendy's hand. "You must be losing it, if you just called me stable."

"You're right." Wendy stood up, tugging at Reese's hand. "Want to have a Disney sing-along with me?"

"You know I'd rather birth quints, but sure, why not?"

They splattered over the carpet.

Their vocal cords were fried.

Still, Wendy managed to speak. "I miss you so much that it hurts."

"I think that's just all the singing," Reese joked. "It'll pass."

"I'm serious," Wendy said. "What if I said that I wanted to come home?"

Reese sighed. "Do you want the tough love speech or the sensitive love speech?"

Wendy rolled onto her stomach. "Tough love speech."

"Okay," Reese said. "Here goes."

Wendy braced herself.

"You came here for a reason," Reese said. "You want this amazing, beautiful life as an artist, and you're making it happen. So, yes, you miss us. And we miss you. But don't come home until you've lived your dream all the way through."

Wendy wiped away a small fragment of a tear.

"You know where to find us if you need us," Reese said, reaching up and patting Wendy's cheek.

"You're right," Wendy said. "You really are on a roll today. When did you get all sage and insightful?"

It was a joke, of course.

But when Reese really thought about it, Wendy was right.

She wasn't the same. She didn't go out anymore. She didn't make out in bars. She *never* drank during the weekdays.

Who are you, Reese?

She needed to reverse it.

She needed to go back to who she was.

All fun, all the time.

Except.

"I think I want to open my own bar," Reese said, rolling onto her stomach now, too.

"Shut up. Are you serious?"

"Somewhat," Reese admitted.

And she might actually let herself believe that she could. The idea was incredibly overwhelming. It made her want to drink right then and there, but still. She wanted to make something of herself.

Especially if she was going to tear everything else down.

"What does Rita say?" Wendy asked.

Reese shrugged. "Rita... has been off lately. She quit meditating. She's walking around like she's the human embodiment of an antidepressant."

"Well, I, for one, am extremely on board for this. I think you should call it *Wendy's Place.*"

Reese pinched Wendy's cheek. "You got it, buddy."

The next day, as Reese said goodbye to Wendy, she felt like she was saying goodbye to herself, too.

Partially because she was leaving Wendy.

Partially because she was leaving the part of herself who might love Liam.

Partially because she was leaving the sage-and-insightful Reese behind, too.

I know who I am. I know who I am... right?

THIRTY

He had settled down.

He had earned himself a family.

Miles and Frances had a relationship that didn't look like it quite fit from the outside. He was the dirty, devil-may-care, detached coffee guy. And she, well, was nothing like Reese expected.

Reese had been failing at the latte art, yet again, when Trish laughed over her shoulder. Ever the prankster, she'd purposefully stuck her finger right in the center of Reese's failing heart art.

"First Lady's book signing tomorrow night. Cancel your wild plans," she'd said.

"Michelle?"

Trish had shaken her head, amused. "Frances, birdbrain. My mother. First Lady of Bean There? Get it?"

"Yes I get it. I'm not stupid."

Trish had proceeded to explain that Frances aka the First Lady of Coffee was a brilliant chef. She'd worked in the best kitchens of New Orleans, apprenticing under the greats at Antoine's and every Brennan restaurant she could name.

"She's the master," Trish had said simply. "And her new cookbook's out, so this'll be a big draw for Bean."

The next few days were a frenzy of pre-planning madness. Every day brought a new delivery, a new set of tablecloths, a new chafing dish. It seemed like Frances was slowly morphing the place from casual coffee lounge to upscale dining prestige.

It was impressive.

Like Viv's wedding, without all the sand.

All the while, Miles stayed clear. It had almost been a full week since he'd shown up, to the point where Reese actually missed him.

In the mildest form of the emotion, of course.

When he did show up, he had a no-sleep look.

"Looking good, boss," Reese said, serving him up a mocking thumbs-up.

"Can it," he said.

"Careful. You'll grow gray from all that angst."

Miles sat down at the counter with all the energy of a sloth, before sinking his forehead to the surface.

"Coffee, New Kid. Just. Coffee."

Reese had never made him coffee before, as strange as that sounded. What kind of person hired someone without a performance review? Stranger still was her reaction to his question. A nervous twitching in her fingers. She didn't get nervous. She got to work.

And yet.

"Me?" she asked. "Sure you don't want Trish?"

He growled, deep in his throat. "Just do it."

She knew how he took it. Espresso. As dark and oaky as she could make it. Luckily for her, the beans did most of the work.

"So," Reese started, "we all set for tomorrow?"

"New subject," Miles said, sitting up. "I can't talk about catering or flower arrangements or freakin' farm fresh eggs anymore."

"Okay, well, tell me about Frances. What's she like? How'd you meet?"

Miles studied her, probably wondering what it mattered to her. He squinted, puffed out his chest, then finally released a tense breath.

"Frances is..." he struggled for a word. Maybe all the words. "A force."

"Like a tornado?" Reese asked.

"Nothing like that," he said. "Tornadoes are short-lived. All over the place. Frances is... a tsunami. She builds slowly, then demolishes everything that gets in her way."

Reese didn't know what to make of that statement. She didn't know what it said about Miles that he used *that* analogy.

"You'll see," he said as she handed him his espresso.

He took a sip, held the heat of it in his mouth, then swallowed. "Nice."

When Frances walked through the door, Reese understood the First Lady reference. She wore all white as if daring stains to cross her incredibly precise path. She walked confidently with her phone between her hands, texting and gliding like she had an extra set of eyes on her forehead.

This woman picked Miles?

"The tables are all wrong." Frances said to no one and everyone.

Then, in all her white dress glory, she began to shove the table closest to her forward. The flowers almost toppled from their vases as she leaned into the table.

A few cater waiters flocked to her assistance, in awe, as the rest of the room was, by this woman's presence.

Her energy was like a hot air balloon shoved into a closet.

Reese had decidedly found her new hero.

She strode up to Frances confidently and said, "Frances? I'm Reese. It's nice to finally meet you."

Frances, to Reese's surprise, shook her hand firmly with a smile. "Great, can you give me a hand with these books?"

Frances turned on her heel and headed outside, with Reese struggling to keep pace behind her. She didn't say much to Reese as they opened up the trunk filled with boxes of books, thick and hardback, but explained to place them in her husband's office.

"Where is Miles?" Reese chimed in, as she felt the weight of the books weigh her flimsy body down.

This job was heavy in sneakers.

She couldn't imagine it in Frances' sizable heels.

"He's at home," Frances said casually. "Miles doesn't deal well with conflict. Or chaos. Two inevitable before-party aspects that I personally thrive under."

That much was undeniable.

Reese was about to ask about the cookbook itself, when they dropped the first batch of books at the room.

"Thanks for your help," Frances said quickly. "I'll get the cater waiters to handle the rest."

And like a blur, she was off again.

Miles showed up around 9:15.

If you could call him Miles.

This Miles-like man came through the front door in a navy suit with a *tie*. And not the mocking kind of tie that you wear to holiday parties or football games. This was an ironed, perfectly knotted red tie that some-how transformed him from grungy to grown-up.

She could see it now, for the first time.

Their resemblance.

It wasn't any specific facial attribute or a recognizable mannerism that they both shared.

It was much more nuanced than that.

Like Miles, Reese could master the appearance of change, too. She could be a trainwreck one day, then glitz and glam the next. And it didn't matter what she looked like, or what she wanted you to think she looked like, because it was always Reese.

He waved at her from across the room, his head kept low, aimed at the ground.

She watched him walk over to Frances, who was signing books from behind a lily-lined table.

From a few feet away, he gave her the same wave that he'd given Reese.

From Frances' ivory throne, she nodded simply.

Then he turned and walked away.

I am a little of you.

THIRTY-ONE

Sophie asked Reese to her favorite lunch spot. Vegan, sprouts, quinoa heaven.

Rita would love this.

Sophie wore her velvet crop top and the bracelet she'd bought that was woven from sex slavery survivors.

Reese didn't, couldn't and wouldn't hate Sophie. In fact, she really liked her. She was actually the perfect fit for Liam, which Reese could admit in the moments she decided to shovel away her pride.

"I'm so glad you could make it," Sophie said, hugging Reese tightly.

"Well, how could I resist your invitation to eat grass for lunch?"

Sophie laughed. "I miss that. Always so witty. Wheat grass shots are completely optional."

It was meant to be endearing.

It felt more like an insult.

Of course, Reese knew it was all in her head. She held up her menu. She might be mostly okay with this, but she would not talk first.

"I'd really like to get the awkwardness out of the way," Sophie said. "I owe you an apology."

Reese wasn't expecting that one.

She owes me an apology?

"I shouldn't have kicked you out like that," Sophie stumbled over her words, like she was summoning up all of her emotions. "It was an awful thing to do and I regret it. Really, I do."

Still, Reese said nothing.

She sipped her water.

Trying to wrap her head around this.

"So, I'll cut to the chase then," Sophie said. "I would like us to be friends again. I mean, things are going really well with Liam, and I know you mean a lot to him. And to me too, of course."

There it is, Reese thought.

It was brilliant, really. Pretending to be sorry. Smiling in all the right places. Extending the olive branch of friendship.

Some people might buy this reformed act of apology.

Reese knew better.

She dragged her hand over her heart, dramatic and pointed. "So, things are going well with Liam then?"

"They are," Sophie said, her face lifting with hope. "I've never dated anyone like him before. He's so... sure of himself. It's really attractive."

Reese agreed in her head.

I'm Liam, would you like to dance?

She tried not to replay that scene in her head again, the one she always went home to, the wedding that changed everything.

"Well that's great," Reese said, with only a hint of sarcasm. "I'm really happy for you."

"Thank you," Sophie said. "I didn't think I'd be happy again after... well, you know."

It was Reese's turn to apologize. Sophie had served it up perfectly, whether she'd intended to or not.

"Look, Sophie," Reese leaned forward, ready for the guilt trip.

"No, don't apologize, please," Sophie said, stopping her. "Yes, the details were not so great to live, but, you did me a favor. I was drowning in that relationship."

See, Reese told herself, *I knew I wasn't all wrong.*

Still, it didn't feel all that great.

They swapped stories over quinoa and kale salad.

Sophie talked about her latest poetry slam.

Reese talked about her new job, leaving out all the familial pieces.

"So give me the scoop," Sophie said, trying to bond again. "What do I need to know about Liam?"

Oh God, here we go.

"I don't know," Reese said, feeling strange about this line of questioning. "What do you want to know?"

That he's incredibly neat, kind and forgiving?

That he shows up for people he loves?

That he is the only person I've ever—

"Has he dated anyone recently? Any serious ex-girlfriends?"

Reese should've known that question would come up.

Oh God, here we go.

"Well, um, I don't know if I'm supposed to be the one to bring this up to you, or maybe you already know? God, I hope you do. Since you asked... Liam and I, well, we sort of dated."

Sophie's face fell. "You... and now you..."

"No, it's not weird, I swear," Reese insisted. "There's no reason to worry or anything like that."

Sophie didn't look comforted by that. "Well, thank you for telling me."

"You're welcome," Reese said.

Oh God, here we go.

2003

Reese knew how to die.

Water.

Fire.

Pills.

It was *living* she wasn't so sure how to do.

She tried not too think to much about this as she bent over her Aunt Mitzi's casket, trying not to feel the twinge of jealousy in her stomach. Reese didn't want to die. She just wanted to be remembered.

"Doesn't she look peaceful?" Rita asked over her shoulder.

Reese shook her head. "Why does she look so fake?"

"Because her soul isn't here anymore." Rita said this like it was a fact. But did she really know? Maybe Aunt Mitzi's soul was hovering right over them. Or maybe not.

Wally peaked closer. "I think it's all the damn makeup."

Reese laughed into her sweater.

"Sorry," Wally whispered.

They stood there for a while, watching. Reese wondered what they were waiting for. It wasn't like Aunt Mitzi was going to change anytime soon. She wouldn't change again. She'd be exactly this way forever and ever.

Forever.

"Wally," Reese asked, flanking to his right, "do you believe in Heaven?"

Wally glanced over his shoulder, waving at Rita, who had gone to greet more relatives. "Grease," he started, his voice low and secretive, "I believe in good. And Heaven is good, so sure. I sure do believe in Heaven."

"What about Hell?" Reese asked.

She didn't know if she believed in Hell, exactly. Fire. Damnation. But, she was pretty sure she was starting to believe in God. And because she believed in God, she maybe believed in a place without him.

It wasn't a big conversion or anything. She'd simply seen a statue of a cross days before and decided that she wanted to believe in something.

God seemed good enough.

Wally sighed, tugging at his ear. "Isn't it bad juju to talk about Hell at a funeral?"

"You sound like Rita."

He paused, thinking on it. "I guess if I believe in Heaven, I'd have to believe in Hell too, now wouldn't I?"

"I don't know," Reese admitted. "I don't know how it works."

Aunt Mitzi had died from a hole in her heart. Reese didn't know the medical term for it, but in reality, she didn't need to know. She understood now that she lived in a world where people could get actual holes in their actual hearts.

It wasn't fair.

It wasn't right.

So, she had to believe in good.

She had to believe, because there had to be a reason.

The service was as most funeral services go. The pastor said nice words and bible verses. People cried. People said goodbye. People made it about themselves. Everything was very ordinary at best.

It wasn't until the burial that Reese actually found something beautiful. Something good.

When they lowered Aunt Mitzi into the ground, everyone was quiet. Outside, the world was green and warm and free. And when everyone sang over the grave, Reese could feel what felt like God.

This is it, she thought.

People didn't belong to people.

People belonged alone.

Doesn't she look peaceful?

Aunt Mitzi would be remembered. Maybe not be everyone, but by people who mattered. She had lived a wild and warm life. She had lived.

This is it.

Reese would live big and bold and beautiful.

So that when she did die, when she got holes in her heart, there would be stories.

There would be tears.

There would be love.

Happy birthday, Reese, she told herself. *This is it.*

THIRTY-TWO

"This place reeks of baby powder and estrogen."

For Reese, there was nothing worse than shopping with a friend. And this wasn't just any shopping. This was *baby shower* shopping, which was the equivalent of a shopping atomic bomb.

"I'll be quick, I promise," Vivian said, pushing her cart around the store with vigorous intent.

Reese trailed behind. "Do you register for this shit?"

"Yes," Vivian said. "But Lord knows that I am not going to buy a hundred dollar baby rattle. No ma'am. This way."

Vivian made a sharp right turn, almost taking out a thumb-sucking toddler.

"Clothing? That's risky, right?" Reese asked. "Side note: is this our new reality? Baby showers and nipple cream? I was barely getting used to the marriage plot."

Vivian compared onesie to onesie. "Babies come in sizes? What happened to one size fits all? And, what the heck is nipple cream?"

"Maybe you should get a bigger size. That way, the kid can just grow into it. Or, maybe it will be a super big baby, and voila, a onesie."

"That's a terrible thing to say," Vivian said.

"It was funny and you know it."

"Okay," Reese said, weaving in and out of the stands. "Maybe we should look for something else. Like a nice bonnet. Do babies still wear bonnets?"

"No," Vivian said, "I can buy baby clothes. This is not a freaking Rubix cube."

"Alright, alright."

Reese wished Wendy were here. Without her, Reese and Vivian were like two impossible siblings. They were always just a few words away from a brawl.

Family.

Was this what that looked like?

"So," Vivian said, glancing over a yellow-striped onesie, "How's Liam? Are he and Sophie still hot and heavy?"

Reese knocked a onesie off its hanger.

There seemed to be no end to Sophie and Liam in sight. It wasn't like she was standing around waiting for them to get bored of each other, but she wasn't *not* either.

She was happy and she wasn't.

"Oh, it's cool," Reese said. "I mean, living with Liam's like living with a girl. So, there's no real tension there. Plus, he's so *boring*. So, you know, that's good."

Vivian stopped to stare down Reese. "What?"

"Never mind," Reese said, realizing she didn't fully answer Vivian's question, realizing that she wasn't making any sense at all.

"Owen and I were hoping to have the two of you over for dinner soon," Vivian said. "Do you think we should invite Sophie, too?"

Liam would want her to say yes.

"Well, I don't know. That sounds like something you should probably ask him." She caught Vivian's expectant stare. "Okay, fine, you should ask her."

"What does Liam like? Chicken or fish?" Vivian asked. "And how about *Sophie?*"

Vivian never bothered to hide her judgment. She wore it like a badge of honor on her chest.

So, of course, Reese kind of liked that Vivian judged Sophie.

It meant that she didn't have to.

Reese threw a onesie in the cart. "Why are you asking me these questions?"

"Well, you know him better than I do."

Reese felt unstable in her footing. "So, what? You think because we dated once that I have some kind of, what? Inner access to his soul or something?"

Vivian stopped shopping. "No, I think because you *live* with the guy, that you might know him just a tad bit better than I do. What's going on, Reese?"

Reese wouldn't look her in the eye. Partially because Vivian had an unmistakable way of getting the truth out of people, and partially because the baby clothes seemed to be judging her now, too.

The only safe place to look was the floor.

"Reese?"

She shook her head. "It's nothing, alright? I mean, it's not *not* nothing, but can you please not ask me about it? It would be *so* wonderful if you just didn't ask me about it."

Vivian considered it. It looked like it pained her to stop pressing the issue, but eventually she said, "Alright, I won't ask. If..."

"If what?"

"If you don't ask me why I don't want to have babies yet."

Well, this took a turn.

It came out of nowhere, and seemed sacrilegious to say in front of all the baby clothes, but, in the sake of fairness, she would not press the issue either. "Alright, I won't ask either."

So they kept on shopping, going back to never saying anything important at all.

THIRTY-THREE

The house was tucked into a halo of oak trees, behind a perfect picket fence, beneath perfect oak trees, beyond perfect porch lights. Reese couldn't imagine what it was like to live this way, right now. She couldn't wrap her head around the idea that one of her best friends lived just beyond there. Married. Settled.

"Don't make me go in," Reese said, her back pressed up against Liam's car. "I'll get matrimony all over me. I'm not sure how many showers can wipe off the stench."

"Four a day. Five, if you're feeling particularly putrid."

"Putrid? How do you even know that word?"

He brushed a hand against his shoulder. "I've got skills."

Oh.

Good.

God.

"I'm dying. Hospital. *Pronto.*" She collapsed onto the sidewalk, gripping her stomach, the skin of her knees scraped.

Liam went to respond, but the door opening cut him off.

"Am I interrupting?" Owen asked suggestively.

Reese threw a tuft of grass at him. "You wish."

A blonde head popped up from over Owen's shoulder. Reese stayed on her knees.

"Reese, are you okay?" Vivian asked, genuinely concerned.

"Oh yeah, just you know, practicing... for volleyball." Reese slowly climbed back onto her heels, brushing the dirt off her knees.

"Volleyball?" Liam whispered.

"Yeah," she whispered back, "you know, like sliding? That happens, right?"

"Get in here, you crazy kids," Owen said, waving them in.

"Way to make an entrance," Liam said, as they walked side by side.

She blew the hair out of her eyes. "I do what I can."

Inside, Vivian offered to take Reese's purse, which wasn't really a purse at all. It was a tote bag that read, "THIS GIRL WANTS A DONUT," and held crumpled-up receipts and a rubber band that doubled as a wallet.

"Careful, it's heavy."

Vivian took it in her hand, and the weight of it sunk her forward. "Geez, Reese, what's in here? A dead body?"

"I'm not quite sure, actually. I don't clean it out regularly. I think there's a book in there. Maybe a few bags of coffee."

"I'm not even going to ask." Vivian tucked the tote bag onto the stairs. "Is that okay? I don't want to hang it. May break the peg right off the wall."

Reese felt awkward. She hated this conversation already.

Hi, I'm Vivian, I'm a good-natured housewife, Reese mimicked in her head.

But please don't ask me why I don't want babies.

"Sure, yeah, it's fine," she said.

"So where's Sophie tonight?" Owen asked Liam.

"She had to work, actually," Liam said. "She asked me to give you this."

He handed Vivian the apology bottle of wine: a red blend of whatever from somewhere in France.

Reese studied Vivian's face.

Just as she suspected, it was overtaken by *why-didn't-you-tell-me-sooner, I-already-set-three-places* face.

"That's so thoughtful," Vivian said blithely. "Owen, how about you take Liam for a tour and maybe a beer?"

"I'd like in on that action," Reese said, raising her hand.

Reese couldn't pass up a chance to make fun of Owen. If he said the word *sconce*, she was prepared to record it and set it as her outgoing voicemail message. If he mentioned the word *escrow*, she would be there to trip him, because, well, that never got old.

"Owen, hun, where are the bell peppers?" Vivian met them in the hallway that led to her own bedroom.

"Viv, where'd you get this vase?" Reese asked, lifting it from the table, daisies and all. "I have one that looks just like it, except instead of polka dots, it's got little cat faces."

"Bell peppers?" Owen asked, swinging his beer bottle at his side.

Vivian swallowed a breath. "I asked you to get bell peppers on the way home, remember? I called you... we talked... then I texted you after as a reminder."

Everyone looked at Owen, who seemed to be weighing this around in his head. It finally registered, but it was only a flash of recollection, before he lifted his hands and shrugged.

"Babe, I don't know. My phone's been acting up lately."

Reese went to say something about the vase again, but Liam stepped on her toes. Literally. "Ouch."

"You said you were almost to the store. And you texted me back, remember? Here, I'll read it." She lifted the phone to her face. She didn't sound *mad*, like Reese expected. She sounded empty. "'Absolutely. I'll buy six and we can send them with leftovers.'"

Reese wasn't sure if she wanted to stick up for Owen or slap him for making Vivian's lip quiver like that.

"I know that I'm supposed to apologize now, so I'm sorry." Then Owen made his biggest mistake yet. He turned his eyes downward, and gave Reese a slight, obvious smirk.

Reese hands shot up. It needed to be clear that she was innocent in this. She was not a participant here.

Vivian sucked in her cheeks and shook her head, right before stretching her face into an eerily energetic smile. "That's alright. There's broccoli. At least there's broccoli."

She turned and retreated back to the kitchen.

"So," Owen said, oblivious, "where were we?"

THIRTY-FOUR

Somewhere between the sound system in the living room and the hand-painted corn hole boards, Liam pulled Reese aside.

"I know what you're thinking and don't," he said. He let his tongue run over his bottom lip for a brief second, and Reese tried to look away.

"What have you been smoking tonight? And why are you keeping it all to yourself?"

He checked down the hall to make sure no one was listening. "Stay out of it, okay? You're only going to make this dinner worse by saying something to Vivian."

"Okay, but—"

"They're *married*, Reese. This isn't a casual fling that you get to offer your opinion on. It's different now."

She glared up at him from heavy eyelids. "I love how you're trying to tell me what to do. It's a valiant effort."

"I'm just saying. Up to you." He backed away from her in one, intentional movement.

"Thanks for your *permission*, master." She gave him a sarcastic salute. He was right, she knew. But he didn't need to know that.

Alone now, she slipped her phone out of her pocket.

Reese texted Wendy: "SOS. This party sucks. Where's the vodka? P.S. Has Vivian mentioned anything about her and Owen? They're acting the way I like my tequila. On the rocks!"

Almost immediately, Wendy answered: "WTF? Back up. Start over. What's happening?"

Reese slipped into the bathroom to call Wendy.

"I can't talk long," she whispered, "but there were bell peppers and weird telepathic exchanges and then Vivian walked away all robotic-like and it's freaking me out!"

"One more time in English?" Wendy said, muffling her own voice, too. "Are they passive aggressively fighting?"

"I mean, I think so. Liam told me not to butt in, but this whole situation feels too Stepford to me. What do I do? Just pretend like this is totally normal?"

Wendy paused. "You drink. Moderately, Reese. None of your over-the-edge, reckless abandon intake, okay? I'm talking a refined, happy hour-like buzz, you hear me?"

"Why didn't I think of this before?" She felt better already. "Maybe I can sneak a cigarette while I'm at it."

"No mixing." Reese could practically hear the smile on Wendy's face. "And you're welcome."

"Move home. I'm not responsible enough to take care of Vivian all by myself."

The door swung open. Vivian, her face pink and dewy, looked like she'd just finished baking her own head in the oven.

"What are you doing?" Vivian asked. Seeing the phone, she added, "Is that Wendy?"

"No, I was just brushing my... hair." Reese rushed her words before hanging up the phone.

Vivian smiled her forfeit. "Dinner's ready."

Reese nodded. "More alcohol, please."

The table was set with folded cloth napkins that you might find at a grandmother's house. The plates were possibly more than Reese's monthly rent, and she didn't trust herself around them.

"Do you like the wine glasses?" Vivian asked, sitting down and folding her dress underneath her.

"I like that they're full," Reese said.

Vivian folded her napkin in her lap. "You don't recognize them?"

Reese held hers up close. "Should I?"

"You bought them. For our wedding."

Liam gave her a cautionary look.

Owen laughed, almost knocking his glass completely over. "Good going, Weller. A truly thoughtful gift."

"Liam," Vivian said, "tell us more about Sophie. I feel like I don't even know her."

Reese squinted at her. "Um. Hello. She was my roommate. You've picked her up from the airport before."

Vivian hadn't forgotten, of course. This was a game that Reese wasn't sure how to play yet.

Vivian kept her attention on Liam.

Liam, for his part, chewed, and said, "Um, it's still new, but she's great." He glanced at Reese, for just a fracture of a second. "It was... unexpected."

How diplomatic of you, Reese thought.

"Unexpected," Owen chimed in, binding his hands under his chin. "That's one way of putting it."

Vivian grinned. "I think it's romantic."

"Really?" Reese said, folding herself over the table. "Romantic? You think it's *romantic?*"

Again, Vivian didn't look at her.

Didn't address her.

Didn't even acknowledge that she'd said anything at all.

"So, Liam," Vivian pressed on, "how's work going?"

Liam, catching onto the game now, served the question away. "Boring, really. Reese is the one with the exciting job. Hey," he said to Reese, "tell them the story about the chai guy. The one where he carried in the live rabbit."

"A rabbit?" Owen said, intrigued.

"Yeah," Reese said, jumping in before Vivian could stop her. "There's this man who comes to Bean There every day, and last week, he brought this ginormous, magician-white rabbit—"

"So, Liam," Vivian said, taking her entrance as Reese took a breath, "how's Cecil doing?"

No one said anything.

Owen set his fork down carefully.

Liam offered eyefuls of apology to Reese.

"Okay, Vivian," Reese said finally. "Cut the crap. What did I do now?"

Vivian's eyes grew wide. "I'm sorry?"

"Ah," Reese said, shoving her pointed finger across the table toward Vivian, "you lose. You talked. What's up next? A staring contest?"

"Do y'all have plans for Mardi Gras?" Liam interrupted, practically shaking a white flag between them. "Reese and I thought we'd invite everyone over to stay with us. We're only a few blocks from the Endymion parade route, and we could just bunk out at our place for the week."

"Dude, that sounds *awesome*," Owen said.

"We might be busy," Vivian said, her focus aimed at Reese. "My family goes on a ski trip every year." Locking eyes with Reese, she added, "I was going to ask you to join us, Reese, but it's mostly couples."

Her tone wasn't cruel.

Her words weren't, either.

But the spirit of them? That was smeared in spite.

That's it.

Reese slammed her hand on the table, causing her plate of food to jump and land with a *clank*. "I'm sorry you hate your husband, Vivian, but if you keep this up, I swear to Jesus I will punch you in the throat."

"*Excuse me?*" Vivian's voice hit its highest decibel. She looked genuinely shocked.

Maybe she was.

"Wait, she hates who now?" Owen asked.

"Reese," Liam said, wrapping his hand over her shoulder to guide her back into her chair. She hadn't even realized she'd been standing.

"Your strategies are tired, Viv." Reese's voice was rising without her permission. A bubble. A wave. *A tsunami.* "Everyone knows that you take *everything* out on people who don't deserve it."

Vivian's jaw came unlocked, before she set it firmly back into place. "I'm... I'm..."

"Sorry? Are you sorry?" Reese had lost it now. She was a train derailed. "Screw this. Liam, I'll be in the car."

Outside, in the dark, the house looked anything but perfect. She could see the cracks in the pavement, where wayward weeds broke through. She could see the broken gutters, the brown patches of grass under the half-dead porch lights.

"Reese." Owen stood awkwardly behind her now, his hands uncomfortably fallen to his sides. "I thought I knew what I would say at this point, but clearly I have no words."

"I'm done, Owen," Reese said. "Don't try to make me feel bad about what happened back there."

"I won't," he said. "But, I will ask you to go easy on her."

"I'm tired of going easy on people. I'm tired of people altogether."

He looked hurt, like he'd been hoping for a different answer. "I wish that I could tell you it will get better. That she'll get better."

Hurt people hurt people.

"You have my number," she told him, before walking to the car, slipping in and slamming it shut.

2012

One shot.

Two shots.

Three shots.

Four.

Reese paced around their apartment, making circles with her steps, her stride matching the speed of her thoughts.

What if it never gets any better than this?

The countdown was officially on.

With only a month left of college, Reese and her friends were staring down the barrel of the gun called adulthood. Life was charging onward, whether they liked it or not.

"You're making a bigger deal out of this than it really is." Vivian swung her legs over the kitchen counter, pouring shot after shot for Reese.

Wendy sat up from the couch. "Reese, it's your last college birthday. We should be out. Not *stressed* out."

"You don't get it," Reese said, circling still. "This is it. The end. The big finale."

What if it never gets any better than this?

She liked life right now.

The boyfriend.

The classes.

The friends. Finally. The friends.

Life was all starting to look the way she wanted.

"You know what you need?" Vivian offered. "A *big finale* birthday."

Reese grabbed another shot. "I'm interested, seeing as a month from now, life as we know it is coming to a deadly end."

"Okay, that attitude is not welcome in our party plans," Wendy said, standing. "Viv, what's on the agenda?"

Vivian smiled. It was the mischievous one that made an appearance every so often. The one that signaled something big on the horizon. "A party fit for a Reese."

No bars.

No boys.

No booze.

Well, no more, at least.

Vivian drove with a mission, taking Wendy as her accomplice.

"Okay," Reese said from the backseat, hanging her hands on their chair backs, "what are we doing?"

Wendy lowered her window, letting the breeze flood inside. "Will you just let us surprise you for a change?"

"No," Reese said, bending in between them. "I'm the spontaneous one. You two are the straight-laced, rule-following do-gooders. Stop trying to steal my job."

"Does she sound bitter?" Wendy asked.

"Bitter as beer," Vivian concluded.

Reese tensed her shoulders.

Wendy noticed. "Sit back and relax. Let us spoil you, damnit!"

What if it never gets any better than this?

First stop: The Dollar Place.

"Well," Reese said, closing the door behind her, "it's original, I'll give you that."

"You have ten minutes to pick out ten of the most random things you can find," Vivian said. When Reese didn't move, Vivian added, "Now!"

Reese sprung into action, deciding to play along.

She tore through the store, picking out items that made her laugh, items that made her roll her eyes and items that made her wince.

A stick-on mustache.

Generic brand tampons.

A kaleidoscope.

She rushed out the store, post-checkout. "How did I do?"

Vivian checked her phone. "A minute to spare."

"Let's go!" Wendy said, running toward the car.

What if it never gets any better than this?

"Okay, don't show us what you have yet," Vivian instructed.

"We're saving it for *the big finale*," Wendy added.

Reese nodded. "Okay, I'm sold."

Second stop: Grocery store.

Vivian pushed a cart at Reese, who caught it before it knocked her in the stomach.

"Your second mission?" Vivian crossed her arms, taking herself quite seriously. "You have six minutes to buy your six favorite snack foods."

Reese squinted at her. "Six minutes? That's—"

"Now!" Wendy called, jumping up and down.

Reese's legs wheeled her around the store. She didn't have much time, so she decided to outsmart the system. She placed herself in line, throwing in items from the aisle beside the register.

The man who checked her out tried to start up a conversation, but she interjected, "Sir, I'm on a scavenger hunt. There's no time!"

When she made it back to her friends, Vivian announced, "Four minutes flat!"

"Let's go," Wendy said, sliding into her seat.

She could feel her heartbeat.

It pounded inside of her, signaling that she was alive.

Life.

Life is in here.

"Okay," Vivian said, putting the car in park, "we're here."

Wendy grinned back at Reese. "You ready?"

What if it never gets any better than this?

All the world had fallen to holy darkness around them. Holy, because it was the three of them. Holy, because they were with the dead.

"A cemetery?" Reese questioned, trailing behind the other two. Vivian fearlessly opened the gate with Wendy close behind. "You brought me to a cemetery?"

They didn't answer her.

They just kept walking.

Past the headstones. Past the gloomy oak trees. Past the mounds of unmarked soil.

Vivian stopped in a small glen away from the actual graves.

"Here," she said, sitting down with her legs tucked under her.

"Here," Wendy agreed.

Reese dipped her knees to the ground, letting the rest of her body fall along with her. "So... what now?"

"Reese Weller," Vivian said, emptying the contents of Reese's purchases on the ground, along with an old shoebox, "tonight, we say goodbye to life as we know it."

Reese wanted to cry.

She could feel the moisture springing up in her eyes.

"You guys," she started to say.

"Shh," Wendy said, "you'll ruin the ceremony."

Vivian seized the control back. "In this shoebox, we, your dearest friends, have collected your memories. Tonight, we honor your legacy. We pay homage to the twenty-two years that we now lay to rest."

Reese reached for the box, and no one stopped her. Reverently, she lifted the lid. Inside, she found photos they'd collected. Reprints of a life fully lived.

What if it never gets any better than this?

Finally, she found her people.

Finally, she found acceptance.

Finally.

Family.

This was what that looked like.

THIRTY-FIVE

Sophie wasn't a beauty queen. She was an environmental activist, a meticulous recycler and a devoted vegan. She had shoulder-length champagne hair that she never brushed, but looked flawless anyway.

She partied, but otherwise? She was smart, passionate and downright impressive.

Of course Liam was into her.

Of course.

He'd been coming home later and later in the evenings, sleeping through their 4 a.m. meet-ups, needing Reese slowly and obviously less and less.

So, Reese wasn't the slightest bit surprised when one Saturday night, he didn't show up at all.

Reese passed out on the couch. Thin blanket draped over her. Half a bowl of soup on the table in front of her.

She could hear Cecil whining.

"Goddamnit, Liam," she mumbled, eyelids like bricks, shuffling her feet into Liam's empty room.

It was light outside when she unlocked Cecil from his crate. He bolted to the back door, whining more.

Just as the key turned in the lock.

Liam strolled into the living room with greasy, spiked-up hair and half-opened eyes masked behind his glasses.

"Oh good, you let him out," he said, reaching for the orange juice, going at it mouth-first.

"Yeah, you're welcome," Reese countered. "Poor dog was sitting with a bladder full of piss, thanks to you."

Liam was unfazed. "Reese, it's 6 a.m. He's held it for longer than this before."

"And that makes it right? Jesus, be responsible, why don't you?"

Liam huffed and set the orange juice down on the counter.

"What?" Reese said. Demanded, maybe.

He shook his head. "Nothing. I'm gonna go shower now, unless you have something else to add?"

She could keep going.

She decided against it.

"I'm good for now," she said.

"Perfect."

Reese slid onto the couch, and kept sliding until she reached the floor, thinking she could stay down here forever, trying her best to forget that Liam was in the other room, washing the sex off his skin.

He walked out repentant. "Can we start over? Turns out I'm not at my best when tired."

"Sure," Reese said reluctantly. "I mean, I don't have much of an option, I assume."

"Hey, what's going on with you?" he asked, sitting down on the couch, just above her. "I mean, first you're fighting with Vivian, and now me. Is something going on with your dad?"

Reese folded herself into a ball. "If I told you it was my period, would you leave me alone?"

"No, probably not."

"Didn't think so," she said. "I guess, I'm just... jealous."

She had to tread carefully with this one.

She had to control the narrative.

"Jealous?" His eyes sparked with emotion. Fear, satisfaction, confusion. It was all in there.

"Of course," she said, "Why wouldn't I be? I never get to hang out with you anymore. I mean, I'm happy for you. Really, I am. It's just, you're my friend, and I miss you."

He didn't look like he bought it.

Probably because underneath she was crying out, *I may have made a mistake and I don't know what to do about it.*

He ruffled her hair. He was going to follow her lead. "Reese, I'm sorry. I miss you too. How about a trampoline night tonight? Just you and me?"

She nodded. He was making room for her. Just like he always did. "That sounds like a plan. Right after I go out."

"You're going out? That's great," he said, only partly excited.

"Yes, so you better wait up," she said, smiling.

"Okay, I'll be right here."

She gritted her teeth.

It's what he'd told her the night they met.

The night that he waited there, as she walked around the bar, searching for something she'd forgotten that she'd lost.

THIRTY-SIX

"I just think it's convenient, that's all."

Reese curled her newly restored orange locks in the bathroom mirror. She was going out. She didn't care who came with her. She didn't even care where she was going, as long as she was going there.

"What's convenient?"

Wendy's voice boomed over speakerphone. "Sophie. She knew you and Liam had a whatever, right?"

"Wendy, Wendy, Wendy. Life is not a romantic drama, okay? She didn't know about Liam, because I never brought him around. Not when she was there, at least. Plus, Sophie and I never talked about real stuff. That was the beauty of our friendship."

"That's depressing."

"My point is," Reese continued, "that Liam is a free man, okay? Sophie may be an opportunist, but oh well. To each his bloody own, you know?"

"So what's the plan?"

Reese blinked her eyelashes trapped in the eyelash curler. "The plan is simple. I go out, get boys to buy me drinks, and have a damn good time."

"You're not self-destructing, right? Because I will fly in and intervene if I must."

"If you do," Reese said, "can you make sure it's a fun, party-style intervention? They are typically too depressing for my taste. I recommend a bouncy house to lighten the mood."

"I'll see what I can do."

Someone knocked at the door. "Hey, I'm heading out."

"Wait, one sec," she said to Liam. To Wendy, she added, "Be right back."

On the other side of her bathroom door, Liam was wrapped into a stupidly attractive, brick red sweater.

Stupidly attractive glasses.

Stupidly attractive stubble.

"What's up?" he asked.

"Just making sure that you *definitely* don't need me on Cecil duty. You know, I'm not really sure when or if I'll be coming back tonight or not, so I figured you should know."

Liam looked at her from over his glasses. "You're not coming home tonight?"

"I don't know," she said. "I'm flexible."

"I thought it was a you-and-me night?" he asked.

He looked hurt.

Maybe.

"Liam, I'm a grown woman with a healthy sex drive who doesn't need to be questioned by her male roommate. I'm going out. That's as far as my planning has gone."

"Okay," he said, outwardly confused. "Have fun. Let me know if you need a ride."

"Okay," Reese said, drawn-out and annoyed. Then before she could stop herself, she said, "Hey, Liam?"

"Yeah," he said.

"I'll see you tonight."

She watched his face, which was confused as it had ever been. "I'll be right here."

Back in the bathroom, Reese steadied herself over the sink, looked herself dead-on in the mirror.

"Wendy," she said. "I need to start seeing someone. Like yesterday."

"Shouldn't be hard for you," Wendy said. "You are a grown woman with a healthy sex drive, after all."

"This is why we're friends," Reese said, stripping off her t-shirt and her uncertainty, then choosing to be decided instead.

At the bar, she sat alone, pounding back drinks.

She tried not to think about Liam, which was proving to be harder than she realized. Maybe she just needed to make out with someone. If she stuck her tongue in someone else's throat, then maybe it would break the spell.

"Can I buy you a drink?"

Perfect timing.

The man beside her might not be the smartest, as he'd asked to buy her a drink when she had a perfectly full one in front of her, but she didn't need smart. She needed a face. A prop. And he was perfectly adequate.

"No," she said, "but I'd like to try something."

She leaned over and pressed her mouth to his. He responded forcefully. She recoiled. It just... didn't feel right.

"Sorry," she said. "It's not working for me."

He glared at her. "Whatever."

Then he walked away angrily.

This isn't going to work like this, she realized.

210

She was going to have to get much, *much* drunker.

"Can I get two more of these?" she asked the bartender, and she readied her bladder for what was to come.

THIRTY-SEVEN

Reese had a conscience.

It was buried under deep layers of stone and soundproof walls, but it was there underneath somewhere.

And right now, it was screaming at her to stop.

Don't take that next drink.

The fourth one. The one that would tip her right over the edge, sending her straight toward—

"Another round?" the bartender asked.

She forfeited her cup over to him, nodding for more.

Don't go home. Not yet.

"Liam?" she heard herself saying. "Pick me up, please?"

He didn't hesitate. "I'll be right there."

He would be right here.

He always said so.

He always showed up.

Don't say anything stupid.

"Is everything okay?" Liam had the moon behind his face. He glowed. "I mean, apart from being totally plastered."

She could tell him now.

That she made a mistake.

That she wanted to be with him.

Don't touch him.

Reese draped her arm over his shoulder.

"Easy there," he said.

He helped her inside. He helped her all the way to her room.

"Thank you," she said, gazing up at his face.

"Why don't you change?" he offered. "I'll go heat up the milk."

Don't wear that.

Reese felt good.

Her nightgown was black and lace.

It held her up. It held her tight.

She flipped her head over and tried not to puke. Then she slipped her hair over her back.

Don't leave this room.

She walked out into the kitchen. "What time is it?"

He looked at her, looked away, looked back again.

"Um, late," he whispered.

Liam looked at anything that wasn't her.

Don't look at him.

Reese draped herself over the counter. She pushed her chest out.

The microwave beeped and he took out the milk.

She smiled.

He set the cup in front of her.

"Thank you," she said.

"Welcome," he answered.

Don't move.

She reached out and touched his hand. "Can I ask you a question?"

"I'm pretty tired," he said, looking toward his room. "Can it wait?"

She nodded.

He didn't leave. "On second thought, go ahead."

"Have you ever been in love?"

Don't ask.

Liam sat down beside her. "Yeah. I'd like to think so, yes."

Reese felt hot.

"High school girlfriend? College?"

He shook his head. "Never a girlfriend. I've fallen in love with best friends before. I've always been the best friend."

She leaned forward. "Unrequited love. What's that like?"

"Of course you'd be unfamiliar with it." He took a sip of milk. "I'll give you the synopsis: it's not fun."

"I'm unfamiliar with love in general."

He clutched his hair in his hands.

Don't you dare.

"No, wait," she said. "I lied."

She had a conscience.

She could feel it in her bones somewhere.

The thoughts trailed across his face.

"You... um, you lied?"

She nodded.

She felt the fear in her eyes.

Don't kiss him.

Reese took his head in her hands.

And it looked like he let her.

Then she pressed her lips against his, soft and steady.

He stood up sharply. "What are you doing?"

She stood up with him. "What?"

"I'm with Sophie."

"It's not serious."

The alcohol persisted.

She was going to be sick.

Don't throw up.

"I have to—"

Reese ran out of the room.

Her tears mixed with vomit.

He was at her door. "Here," he said. His hand was on her back.

"No," she begged. "Go away."

He didn't.

He never did.

Don't love him.

2016

Reese knew how she would die.

Alone.

That's how everyone died, after all. The *how's* and the *why's* of the story didn't matter, because in the end, you're dead all by yourself.

She snapped herself back to reality.

This was her party and she should not be thinking about death right now.

"Are you having fun?" Sophie flocked to her side with a cup full of water, and maybe more.

Reese nodded. "Well, it's not the worst party I've ever had."

"The power of positive thinking!"

Across the room, Wendy and Vivian looked like fish out of water. They hovered around by the bookshelves with their eyes scanning the crowd of strangers, like a tight little closed-off unit.

Reese paused.

She didn't know anyone either. The entire room was filled with people she barely knew. After twenty-six years of life, Reese couldn't stop herself from wondering...

Is this all there is?

Wendy caught her eye and waved.

Reese held up her hand and mouthed, "One second."

Reese looked at the stars.

Alone.

Her bare feet sunk into the cool grass and she just let the sky look down at her face. There was so much more to life. There had to be.

She picked up her phone and started scrolling through her text messages.

So many happy birthday wishes.

So little that actually mattered.

And then—

Liam texted: "I wasn't going to send this, but here you go. Happy birthday, Reese. Hope you got everything you wished for."

The message wasn't remarkable.

But the boy on the other end of it?

He was.

Reese didn't think about it until the phone was ringing.

"Hello?" He sounded like he'd been asleep.

She wrestled with the almost words in her throat. "It's my birthday again."

He sighed. "Yes, I know."

"I'm twenty-six. Am I still mid-twenties or did I just get promoted?"

She could hear him breathing, but he didn't say anything for a while.

"Reese," he breathed, "why did you call me? Shouldn't you be at your party?"

Is this all there is?

"Yeah, of course. You're right. I should go."

"It's okay," he said.

She hung up quickly.

She wasn't the girl who called her ex on her birthday.
She was the party girl.

Reese went back to the party.
Alone.
Reese took tequila shots.
Alone.
Reese got wasted in a room filled with people.
Alone.

THIRTY-EIGHT

The 7 a.m. rush packed into the small space. Trish was like a hockey player, cutting left and right across the floor, shouting names and orders all while biting down on an imaginary mouthguard.

Reese lived for this crowd now.

After *months* of practice, she'd finally gotten the hang of it all.

The latte art.

The perfect espresso.

The ridiculously specific orders from the so-called regulars.

She found it hilarious when the customers got angry. When they asked for the wrong coffee size, then complained. When they accidentally picked up someone else's order. When they bitched about service when their coffee had been waiting there ready for ten minutes.

There was a buzz about the morning.

And it was *exactly* what she needed to distract her from her quiet house.

Liam hadn't spoken anything real to her in weeks.

She didn't expect him to, either.

"Mocha latte. "

"Medium non-fat vanilla latte."

"Large almond milk latte."

The rush made the hours fly past her, like she was gripping to the tail of a kite on a blustery day.

But once 10 a.m. hit, the world slowed to a crawl.

Reese bent over the cash register while Trish restocked.

"Are you bored?" Trish asked, as she lugged a bag of beans from the stockroom. "Because I'm so bored that I can practically feel the wrinkles forming on my face."

Reese stretched her arms over her head, feeling her lower back pop. "Oh, yeah. I can see 'em, too."

Trish threw a towel at Reese's head.

"Okay," Reese said. "Let's liven this place up."

"You're reading my mind," Trish said, taking a mental inventory of the place. "I'll make you a deal. We clean this place up in the next five minutes, and you can help me play the greatest prank *in history* on Miles."

Reese smiled.

Now this is what she needed.

"You're on."

Before she covered her hands in suds and dried coffee grounds, Reese checked her phone.

Rita had texted: "Heading to see you. I'm looking forward to seeing you at work."

Reese felt her ab muscles tighten.

Well, Trish was right.

This would be the greatest prank in history.

Had Miles mentioned he'd be coming in today?

She couldn't remember.

"Hey Trish?" Reese called.

"What?" Trish yelled back.

"Is Miles coming in today?"

"Not that I know of. Why?"

"No reason."

Panicked, Reese shot Miles a quick text: "Super busy here. Better steer clear."

She figured that one should work. She had to be strategic about this. If she'd told him it was quiet, he was sure to show up. If she asked him flat out, he'd get suspicious.

So, fingers crossed, she'd made the right move.

Reese texted Rita back: "What time? How about we go out for lunch?"

She was proud of herself. She was really thinking through this one.

Reese turned on the faucet and plugged the drain. Generously, she poured the detergent in the sink. She sunk her hands in and scrubbed.

"Two minutes left on the clock!" Trish said, shimmying the mop around the floor.

The back door clicked open.

Both Reese and Trish stopped what they were doing.

"Morning," Miles said, nodding and ducking into his office.

Trish dropped the mop. "Well, there goes that plan."

Reese had a moment of panic.

Rita texted: "Just got off the bridge. Be there in five."

She didn't think twice about it.

"Okay," Reese said, flying over to Trish, her voice low and hurried. "I need you to do me a huge favor and I need you to not ask me why."

"Excuse me?" Trish asked.

Reese stood next to her, searching the room. "Never mind."

She'd have to find another way.

"No, hang on," Trish said, leaning against the mop. "I'm intrigued."

Reese turned back around. "I need you to get Miles out of here. Now."

"One condition," Trish said.

"I told you not to ask why."

"You're going to have to tell me why," Trish said in tandem.

Reese didn't even listen.

Five minutes.

"Whatever, deal."

Rita was off the happy pills.

The pink was long gone, replaced by a shade of dark green, that made her look like she'd wrapped herself in the plants from her living room.

"It's lovely," she said of the place, but her face said differently. It was stoic, almost. Rita was never stoic.

"Thank you," Reese said.

"Shall we go?"

Reese thought she'd feel weirder about this. Seeing her mother here after all these months of lying. Because that's what it was, wasn't it?

One lie after another.

"Sure, yes, let's go."

After a tense lunch, Reese carried herself back into the shop, war-worn.

She wasn't handling things well.

Liam wasn't speaking to her.

Vivian wasn't speaking to her.

Wendy was too busy to answer her calls.

And then, there was her family, which was probably the most crumbled of all.

Trish sat at the counter waiting. "Finally. I've been dying to hear this big, earth-shattering secret."

You hit the nail on the head.

Reese didn't sit down.

"Miles had sex with my mother and they made me."

Trish shook her head. "That's... a weird way of saying that..."

"Well, it's true."

"You're not saying—" Trish looked like Reese felt. Confused. Aching.

"That Miles is my father? That he has no clue? Yes, that's exactly what I'm saying."

She didn't feel any differently.

Reese had expected this big crescendo of a moment.

In the end, though, it was just a secret. The same as anybody else's.

Trish curled her fingers around the back of her neck. "Oh my God."

"I know." Reese faded onto the floor.

"*Oh my God.*"

Reese nodded. "Take all the time you need. You're gonna need it."

THIRTY-NINE

"So, what does this make us?" Trish asked. "Belated step-sisters?"

"I don't really know how to be a sister. I'm not even capable of being a fully-functioning human being."

"Well, the good news is that you can blame that on daddy issues now. Or, at least you have a daddy to pin it on."

Reese hadn't thought about it like that. "Man, that's good. If nothing else, I'll always have that."

Trish inspected Reese's face. "You know, you look like him."

"You think so? I don't really see it."

"Trust me. You both have that screw-the-world way about you. It's compelling, I guess."

Did Reese want to screw the world?

Not really.

She just wanted it to lie still while she threw a party on top of it.

"Is there anything you want to know?" Trish asked. She was spread out on the floor beside Reese now. They flipped the sign to CLOSED, but it didn't matter. No one was showing up, anyway. "I mean, I've lived with the guy. I know things."

"I'll take the abbreviated version of... well, his life."

Trish hooked her knees in the air. "Well, he's not very interesting, I'll give you that. He's just a guy. He fell in love with Frances. They got married. And... yeah. Sorry I couldn't interest you more."

"It's okay. I was never one of those girls who imagined her dad as a superhero. Although, it would've been useful."

Trish nodded. "Me either. Mine left me at five, so I still have a good mental image of him. It's a decent souvenir."

"Are we supposed to want them? I mean, I've worked with Miles for months now, and we still haven't had that parental moment yet. I don't remember why I showed up here in the first place, to tell you the truth."

Trish sighed. "I don't know. I haven't thought about mine in years. And it's never when you *think* you're supposed to think about them. Not at graduation or birthdays or anything like that. I always think about him on random Tuesdays when I can't fall asleep. You know what I mean?"

Reese did.

The triggers didn't seem to be consistent to her.

She couldn't set her clock to them.

"Maybe I should quit," Reese said.

"No, you can't do that. You should at least tell him, since you're here."

Reese laughed. "So I should tell him out of proximity?"

"Look, I'm no good at this either. But, if it were me, if my dad were standing here, I'd say something. I don't know what, but I would. You've got to get brave."

"I can do that," Reese said, believing it. "Maybe you're right. Maybe it's supposed to mean something."

"I'm always right."

"See? I'm learning so much about you already."

They stayed outstretched on the floor for hours.

Reese wanted to know everything about Trish, and, to her surprise, the reverse was also true.

They shared embarrassing stories about their childhoods and stupid haircuts.

They talked about their friends.

They left no subject unturned.

Trish sat up. "Oh my God, it's dark outside."

Reese lifted off the ground, too. "I don't think I've ever talked that much in my entire life."

"I find that hard to believe."

Reese reached for her tote bag and found she had missed calls from Liam and Wendy. It was already 8:30.

"I should probably get going," Reese said. "We should go out sometime. I bet you know all the best bars."

"I don't know if you could keep up with me," Trish said, taking off her apron.

Reese slipped on the strap of her tote bag. "Oh, I will take that bet."

Trish knocked herself on the forehead, like she just remembered something.

"What?" Reese asked.

"I forgot. I do have an interesting fact about Miles. Probably shouldn't tell you, but what the hell."

Reese wavered slightly in her stance. "What's the story?"

"He's in pretty significant financial trouble," Trish said, leaning in closer. "I mean, may-have-to-sell-the-place kind of trouble."

Reese fell onto the chair. "Way to bury the lead."

"I know, I know, but it's recent. Today, when I told him someone slit my tires—ahem, when I slit my tires—he drove me over to the repair man, and we waited for my car—"

"*That's* how you got him out of here?" She had to admit that she was impressed. "Little extreme, wouldn't you say?"

"I'm a professional," Trish said, grazing over that topic. "Anyway, he was on the phone with the bank or a lawyer or something. He said something to the effect of January."

"January? We're a week away from Christmas. How did this happen?"

"Reese," Trish reasoned, "we spent all afternoon on the floor of this place. Not a single person so much as knocked on the front door. What do you expect?"

Trish was right.

Things had been overwhelming slow lately.

Life around her had just been too chaotic for her to sit back and notice it.

She looked around nostalgically at Bean There. Her favorite chair tucked into her favorite corner, that smelled like old newspapers and a faint cigar smoke. The mismatched art on the wall. Miles' quiet office.

"Well, we can't just let this happen. I'm an accountant, maybe he'll let me—"

"What? Play the savior? Miles built this place from nothing. You really think he's going to be so forthcoming about this with you?"

No, Reese didn't.

But she'd figure something out.

FORTY

The house was quiet again.

Cecil trotted over to her, his tongue tucked to the left side of his mouth, smiling.

"Need a cocktail?" she asked him.

He panted.

"Yeah, me too," she said, walking toward the kitchen.

The door opened just behind her.

She froze with the bottle of wine in one hand and the glass in the other. "Hey."

Sophie rolled her coat off her shoulders. "I'd join you, but I'm on a cleanse."

"Again? Remember what happened that last time?" Reese asked, pouring her drink.

Sophie laughed, walking up to the counter. "Oh my God, when you had to pick me up from the library because I got too dizzy to drive my car home?"

"And I bought super greasy french fries that I shoved in your mouth?"

"And you yelled at me like a drill sergeant?"

They couldn't stop laughing.

And then, they did.

The room tensed as Liam entered it, greeted by all the friendship that once lived there.

Reese and Sophie's.

Reese and Liam's.

Just like that, Sophie gave a sympathetic smile, and wordlessly headed toward Liam's room.

Cecil didn't leave Reese's side.

"You're still friends with me, right?"

Cecil yawned, then trotted over to his bed, falling asleep instantly.

"Figures," Reese said.

An hour later, Reese was naked in her bed, watching reruns of *Law and Order*.

"The boyfriend did it," she said to herself. "It's always the boyfriend."

Her phone rang as the detective crossed into the interrogation room.

"Hello," Reese said, without checking.

"I need you to come and get me."

It wasn't an outrageous request, except for the fact that it was Vivian who was making it.

"Um, where are you?"

"I don't know. Can I send you my location? I can do that on my phone, right?"

Reese sat up. "What do you mean you don't know where you are?"

"Okay, I sent it. Please leave as fast as you can. Don't speed."

Reese clicked over to the map.

"Holy shit."

"I know."

"Well," Reese said, stepping into her underwear, "see you in four hours."

She was sitting on the curb in front of an empty Starbucks when Reese pulled up. Vivian's head was in her hands, a spout of blonde hair spilling over her shoulders, her normally perfect posture crumpled down like a used napkin. When she lifted her head, her face was pale and stoic. Reese didn't know what she expected.

Tears, maybe? Doubtful.

Fear, possibly? No, not Vivian.

But not this. Not in a million years.

Reese parked her car right there in the street, hopping out of the car.

"I've never wondered what Beaumont, Texas looked like," Reese said, sitting next to Vivian. "And yet, here we are."

Vivian didn't say anything. She stared ahead at nothing, a blankness in her eyes that made Reese wonder if anyone was behind them.

"Okay," Reese said. "I want to ask you questions, but I also want to get back home before dawn, which at this rate is not happening."

Vivian stood, opened the door, and slid into the seat like a ghost.

Reese followed. "Okay, so you're not talking. I get it. But what are we going to do about your car...?"

"Leave it," Vivian said. She had this empty look in her eyes, like she'd tucked her soul away.

"Okay, I'm going to repeat this for you. You want me to leave your car in Texas."

Vivian nodded. "Just drive."

Reese still wasn't convinced.

"I called a tow truck. My uncle is driving from Houston to get it in the morning. He and my aunt are coming to visit and will bring it then. Happy?"

Reese backed out of the parking spot, still thrown. "Happy."

They hadn't spoken in two hours.

Vivian dosed in and out of sleep, occasionally jolting awake, staring out of the window, then lulling herself back to sleep.

In the middle of nowhere, Vivian stayed awake.

There were words she should say, Reese knew. She could recognize a cry for help, but was it really a cry if she'd never wanted it to be heard? It was one of those *if a tree falls in a forest* kind of moments. What do you do when the person in pain never wanted that pain to be noticed?

Wendy would know.

But she couldn't call her now.

"Vivian," Reese said, in the gentlest voice she could manage. "Will you talk to me?"

"It was a mistake," Vivian said. She sat perfectly still. Like a Madame Alexander doll.

"Viv, I just picked you up off a street curb in the middle of the night, in a completely different state. If I were a therapist, I think I could really dive into the meaning of this, but as it happens, I'm a barista, and I don't know what this means until you tell me what this means."

Vivian took a deep breath, and let it out so slowly that she could have blown out the candles on five different birthday cakes. "I don't *know* what it means. Something broke. And I just needed to go away."

Reese didn't understand.

It was like Vivian was speaking a different language.

"Vivian," Reese said again calmly. "Does Owen know where you are right now?"

Vivian's face remained unchanged. She simply said, "No."

The world always seemed more right with a hamburger and a basket of fries. Sure, there were problems. But they seemed far away when you were shoving greasy food down your throat.

"Can I pose a theory?" Reese asked, as they drove down the miles and miles of road ahead of them.

"Mhmm," Vivian said through a cramped mouth.

"You and me and Wendy. There have been big changes and big lessons lately, and none of us have been... handling them as well as we should, if we handle them at all. We're all just trying to figure this out."

Vivian sniffled. Reese looked over and saw her sobbing into her hamburger.

It was the most absolutely hilarious image she'd seen in a long time.

And so, she laughed.

A little at first, then, an outright overtaking of laughter.

Still chewing, Vivian said, "You're laughing? Why are you laughing at me?"

That only made the laughing happen more.

It was so loud and obnoxious that Vivian, through her tears, laughed right along with her.

"My side hurts," Vivian said through her fit.

"My eyes are watering," Reese said in agreement.

They kept driving and didn't say much else.

And Reese thought that maybe it was okay that they didn't have it all figured out yet. Maybe no one really expected them to.

2008

April Fool's Day.

The day of her birth was literally one big joke.

Reese had seen it all. From fake pregnancy scares to the healthy-food-in-the-donut-box trick, Reese spent her birthday as the butt of every joke at school and work.

The only place that ever seemed safe was home.

Home was where she could be alone.

But this year? Her last high school birthday? This year, she was the prankster.

So far, she'd spent the morning switching the coffee in the Lakes' house to decaf, setting Wendy's cell phone language to Japanese, filling Claudia's hairdryer with baby powder, and unplugging the internet cords in the library, just barely, so the librarians wouldn't notice.

And now, it was time for class.

She brainstormed her other prank ideas in her planner, as her teacher talked about slopes and tangents:

1. Cover Rita's car in Post-It notes

2. Throw all of Wally's clothes in the pool

3. Stuff unwrapped pads down Wendy's locker

When class ended, her teacher handed out last week's test papers, the last one before their final.

"Weller, Reese," he called.

She walked up to the front of the room, distracted by all of her prank ideas. When she grabbed the paper, she almost couldn't believe it.

A+.

She double checked her name.

The teacher leaned forward and said, "Don't go broadcasting it, but that's the highest grade. Congratulations."

Numbers made sense to her.

If she could fit her life into infinite sets, she might be able to understand it more clearly. She would take debits and credits over words and language any day.

Reese sat outside in the breezeway, staring at her test. She'd always been a good student, but she'd never been a great one. Never the top of the top.

It felt... *amazing.*

She picked up her phone, hiding it in the sleeve of her sweatshirt, so her teachers wouldn't notice.

"Hello, are you alright?" Rita answered.

Reese smiled. "Guess what? Actually, you'll never guess, so I'll just tell you. I made the highest grade on my Calculus test."

Reese leaned back and waited for her moment of glory.

There was nothing but silence on the other end.

"Rita? You still there?"

Rita took a breath. "It's a shame the way they rank children by a letter on a piece of paper. It trains you to seek outside approval to define yourself. It's such a shame."

Reese's heart sunk. "But Rita, grades will help me get a better job."

"Where you will seek approval from your bosses and your coworkers. Where you will spend your life trying to attain impossible standards, all for monetary gain."

"Rita, that's *life*," she said loudly. She never raised her voice to her mother like that. "What would you rather me do? Drop out? Live in a field?"

Rita sighed again. "I can't tell you how to live."

Yes, you can, Reese thought, *because you're my mother.*

That night, Reese thought about her future.

She would go to college.

She would get a good job.

She would live life.

Reese held her test in her hands. Maybe it was just a piece of paper. Maybe she couldn't find worth in an arbitrary letter grade.

She picked up her phone and called Wendy.

"Hey," she whispered. "Wendy?"

"Hmm." Wendy mumbled into the phone, clearly stirring out of sleep.

"It's still my birthday," Reese said. "You still have to listen to me."

Wendy sighed begrudgingly. "Okay, you win."

"I got the highest grade in Calculus today."

The sound that charged out of Wendy's voice was partly shock and partly excitement. "You didn't? You did? You didn't."

"I did," Reese said proudly.

"Wow," Wendy said, thinking it over. "You beat Elizabeth Trapper. I didn't think it could be done."

"Think I'll beat her out for valedictorian now?"

"Without a doubt." Wendy said, smiling, no doubt. "I'm so proud of you. After all of the hours you spent studying, you earned it. We should celebrate. Tomorrow."

"Okay," Reese said, closing her eyes. "Tomorrow."

She fell asleep without hanging up the phone, knowing there'd be someone there for her in the morning. Even if her phone was dead, even if Wendy was in a different house, on a different block, under a very different roof.

Wendy would still be there.

That's all she needed, really.

Someone there.

FORTY-ONE

This wasn't your typical company Christmas party.

It was more like a cross between a frat party and a high school re-union. Without the formality of an office, the Bean There workers were free to relax and hang out. They were friends, in a way. More pals, less coworkers.

Reese was pretty proud of her gifts. They'd thought about playing White Elephant or Secret Santa, but in the end, no one wanted to take charge of that endeavor. So, Miles ruled that if you wanted to buy gifts, do it. If not, then don't.

Their artificial tree stood tall at the front window, and the bundles of presents underneath were overflowing onto the carpet.

Reese grabbed her present for Trish first, and handed it over to her with a grin. "I know, I know. Presents are lame. But still, I got you something. So, open it."

Trish rolled her eyes, but ripped open the packaging regardless.

Inside the box was a new name tag that read, "Joanie/Trish."

And Trish didn't hesitate to pin it to her chest and say, "I'll wear it with pride."

"You like, Trish?" she asked.

"Joanie."

Reese cupped a hand around her ear. "What's that you say?"

"In light of recent events, I think it's about time you start calling me by my actual name." Seeing Reese's face, she added, "Don't make this into a thing."

"Hold still," Reese instructed. "I'm going in for a hug."

Joanie cringed. "No don't—"

But it was too late. The hug was in full force. Reese squeezed Joanie tightly, then released her quickly. And it was nice to have a friend like Joanie. Or a sister like her. It was nice to know her now.

"Okay," Reese said, pulling away. "Back to Santa time."

She'd spent weeks thinking about what to get Miles. In fact, she spent more time bouncing gift ideas around in her brain for him than she'd spent studying for finals all through college.

Her ideas ranged from the idiotic to downright ridiculous.

A toaster.

A coaster.

A giant pink balloon with the words, "IT'S A GIRL!"

Nothing fit quite right.

Vivian suggested, "How about a cigar humidor? That would be a really nice gesture."

Too expensive.

Wendy suggested, "Get him a nice card. Preferably one from the con-gratulations-you're-the-father section."

Too stupid.

So, ultimately, Reese decided not to decide. She went to three stores to find something, anything, that might work. Every time the salesperson would ask, "Can I help you find anything?" She'd reply, "Yes, I'm looking for a gift for my boss who is also my father but has no idea."

This tended to confuse said salesperson, but he or she would try her best to help anyway.

In the end, Reese bought a noncommittal, nonthreatening bottle opener. It wasn't much. Although, it did double as a keychain, so that was something.

Holding the wrapped gift in her hand now as she walked up to Frances and Miles, she felt pretty stupid. She felt so stupid that she was about to turn back around and give up on the whole idea, when—

"Reese!" Frances said, waving her down. "We got something for you."

Reese dragged herself over to them, just as Frances presented her with a gift wrapped in the largest bow she'd ever seen. It was red and green, of course, and she swore it smelled of gingerbread. She hated opening gifts in front of other people. The expectation. The way people inevitably knew that she hated their gift, as much as she tried to hide it.

"Faster, faster, you're not going to save the wrapping!" Frances urged.

As she peeled away the last piece of tape, she gently opened the box that was tucked inside. Under a layer of bubble wrap, there was the most elegant piece of crystal she'd ever seen. It was crafted in the shape of a coffee cup, even bending and swirling into the fine lines of steam off the imaginary liquid.

And Reese had no freaking clue what she was going to do with it.

"Wow, thanks, this is amazing," Reese said anyway. "Thank you."

Miles shrugged. "I had nothing to do with it."

"Just a little something for you," she said. "Since I know he doesn't thank you guys enough."

"I pay them. Isn't that enough?" Miles asked, tucking his hands into his pockets.

Then Frances was gone, off to deliver more gifts.

Reese stood awkwardly with the gift in her hands. "Uh, so I got you something. Don't get excited about it."

"I won't." He ripped the wrapping off in one fell swoop. Then, he nodded in approval. "Just what I needed. Thanks, New Kid."

"Am I graduating from that nickname anytime soon? I'd settle for Sophomore Kid."

My Kid, maybe.

"We'll see," he said plainly.

She rocked back and forth on her feet, waiting for him to say something else. "Okay, well, back to present-giving for me."

"Just a sec," he said, reaching in his pocket. He pulled out an envelope, bent in half. "Don't get excited about it."

"I never do," she said, running her thumb over the seal.

Reese could tell he wanted to say more. Maybe something heartfelt. But, in lieu of this, he placed a strong, telling hand on her shoulder. It was better than words. It was wholly Miles.

Frances waved him over from the drink station. He sighed and said, "Merry Christmas."

"Merry Christmas."

Hey, she thought, *our first holiday season.*

When he'd walked away, she split open the envelope that was burning a hole in her hands.

Inside was a twenty dollar bill.

But more importantly?

The scribbled note that read, "For your bar."

He remembered.

He cared.

FORTY-TWO

She heard the door to Liam's room open and close. Cecil's paws clicked against the tile.

Reese couldn't resist. She made her way out into the kitchen.

"Am I on Cecil duty?"

At the front door, Liam slipped his arm into a sleek black jacket. His keys jingled in his hands, and when he turned to look at her, he looked like he'd been caught robbing a bank or something.

He swiftly tucked his keys away. "I'm just going out for a bit. Won't be long. I'll be back before your witching hour."

She eyed him closely.

He looked guilty... but of what?

"Okay," she said, turning to go back to her room.

"Will you come with me?" he asked hurriedly.

She wasn't sure if she'd heard him right, but she wasn't about to ask him to repeat himself.

How long had it been since they'd had any sort of meaningful interaction?

Long enough for her to forget what it felt like.

She nodded. "I'll get changed."

Sliding into his car not five minutes later, Reese sat uncomfortably in her jeans, the leather of his seats wrapping around her thrown-together ensemble.

"You're being mysterious," Reese said quietly.

Liam grinned. "Just trust me."

Somewhere uptown, on a side street off St. Charles that Reese didn't recognize, Liam pulled his car into an empty spot behind an obnoxiously large truck.

"Are we here?" Reese asked.

Liam gave her a warm smile before stepping out of the car. "Yep." He shut the door.

"Well, wait for me." Reese tried to run on her toes to catch up with him.

Liam walked ahead of her, not bothering to look back, heading for a hole-in-the-wall building. Over the front door a sign read in electric pink lettering, "Delia's." Reese trotted across the street and tucked inside the door.

The place, though you'd never guess from the outside of it, was packed wall-to-wall with people. Reese looked around, but Liam had been swallowed up by the crowd.

Everything in the place was covered with a hazy layer of smoke, the neon lights were the only clearly visible elements in sight. Signs reading, "Drink and Be Drunk" and "Down in the Nola, Baby."

And then, there was the music.

Jazz.

Crashing over their heads, the mixture of the trumpet, the piano and the bass made their conversations dull under the weight of it. And something else.

The saxophone.

She could hear the fullness of it, could feel it pulsing in her own heart, like the music had somehow found its way into her skin. Now *this* was the way to make an impression.

"Reese." Liam flagged her down as he walked in her direction. "Over here."

She followed him to a table marked RESERVED, a small two-top snuggled in the sea of people, directly in front of the band. Liam took a seat.

"Since when are you VIP?" she asked.

"I know a guy."

Reese rolled her eyes. "You know a guy? Please be more vague, I dare you."

He laughed, loosening up a little. "I know the band."

"Really?"

"Sure," he said. "The guy on the trumpet? That's Schmitty. He owns a brewery in Abita, but every Wednesday night, you can find him here. That woman over in the corner with the perm? That's his wife, Karen."

Reese followed the invisible trail his fingers made between them and the amazing instrumentals. "Okay, I buy it. Who's on the bass?"

"That's Dale. He's a waiter at Mr. B's. He's hoping to make enough money in the next year to put himself through culinary school."

There was no hesitation on Liam's face. He really did know these people. Just as she prepared to ask him how, a waitress approached their table.

"Liam Blake, I know you did not bring a girl into my bar, when you so clearly pledged your love to me."

Not a waitress, but the owner.

The woman, her skin dark and beautiful, was probably in her early thirties. She had a stained apron around her waist—a look Reese knew well—and on her left hand was a stunning diamond ring.

"Louise," Liam said, standing up to hug her, "I could never replace you."

Reese nearly fell over from the stranger in front of her. Liam, being flirty. Liam, being comfortable. Liam, in his element.

"Louise, this is my roommate, Reese."

Reese stood to shake Louise's hand, but found herself caught up in a tight hug instead.

"Roommate? Like I don't know what *that* means," Louise said, winking.

"Oh, no," Reese corrected, waving her hands like she was trying to stop an accident on the highway. "We really are just roommates."

"It's strictly platonic," Liam interjected before Reese's words could get away with her.

"Mhmm," Louise said, unconvinced. She pointed at Liam, then to Reese, then back again. "You sure look like a couple. And it's a shame to waste all that"—she circled her finger around them—"on friendship."

Liam gave her a pleading look. She added, "Okay, I'll drop it. Drinks? What are you having, sweets?"

"Anything with tequila."

Louise looked at Liam. "I like this one." She grabbed their menus and said, "Be right back."

"You didn't order anything?" Reese asked.

"I didn't have to."

"Are you saying you have a usual?" Reese couldn't hide the shock in her voice.

Is this where Liam had been sneaking out to when she first moved in? To a seedy bar with the best live jazz she'd ever heard? All alone?

Reese had been wrong.

She didn't know him at all.

"So how do you know everyone?" Reese asked.

Liam pretended not to hear her, his eyes fixated on the band.

"*I said*—"

"I heard you." Liam's answer was decisive and clear. He wasn't going to answer her questions. Not on her time table, anyway.

There was something about jazz that reminded Reese of the inside of her own mind.

Maybe it was how the notes didn't quite fit together in the way she expected them to fit.

Maybe it was the way the music rose and fell then rose back again.

Maybe she just liked the way it made her feel.

"I'm sorry things changed," Liam said, just loud enough for her to hear it.

She shrugged. "They always do."

"How have you been?" he asked, treading carefully.

She smiled. "I've been pretty great."

"How's your dad?"

"He invested in my future bar." She took a sip of her drink. He nearly spat his out.

"And—I'm afraid to ask—how's Vivian?"

Reese shrugged. "Haven't seen her since I picked her up on the side of the road in Texas."

"Man, I really have missed a lot, haven't I?"

After that, the floodgates opened. They dove in and out of every topic like it was an Olympic sport, and every time Reese thought they were done, they found something new to share.

"I missed this," Liam said, swirling the last splash of beer around in his cup.

"Yeah, me too," Reese admitted.

He looked up at the band like he was watching a memory. "My dad started this band."

They rarely talked about his family.

He'd mentioned his brother every now and then, but he lived up north. And his mom worked long hours in Baton Rouge, so she never came to visit.

But his dad? Never mentioned. Not once.

"Oh, yeah? What instrument does he play?"

Liam gave her a sad, bluesy smile. "Played. He *played* the saxophone."

She recognized that face.

It was the one she wore when she realized the man on the phone was the mailman, not her father.

It was the one Vivian wore sitting on the Starbucks curb in the dead of night.

Wendy had worn it, too. Over and over again.

This was loss.

"When did he pass away?" she asked, as gently as she could.

He gave her a heavy smile. "A month before Owen's wedding. 2015."

Liam pointed to the tattoo blanketed by his shirt.

His tattoo.

In memoriam.

It all made sense.

Reese counted backward. A month before their wedding? "Wait, but that was—"

"He died the week before I met you."

She disengaged. It made sense, him coming around all of the sudden, but then again, it didn't make sense at all.

"Why didn't you tell me?" she asked. Her soul felt raw. The alcohol helped.

He leaned back in his chair, opening himself up. "I wasn't ready."

She understood that.

"Well," she said, trying to find the words, "I'm sorry."

"It's ok—"

"And here I am," she said in realization, "waltzing into your life and making everything about me and my dad quest."

He laughed. "You were my favorite distraction."

She winced, slightly.

You're mine too, she thought.

FORTY-THREE

Bourbon Street was never a good idea. Bourbon Street on *New Year's Eve?* That was the mother of all terrible decisions.

Yet here they were in a sea full of tourists, surrounded by hurricanes and beads and bouncing, naked breasts. Every day was Mardi Gras here, and every night was an explosion of sex and lights and bar fights.

"Where do y'all want to go?" Sophie asked, rubbing a hand through her thick hair.

Reese shrugged. "Wherever I can get a drink."

Sophie smiled. "That's literally everywhere."

"Works for me," Reese said.

Liam couldn't look more uncomfortable if he tried. He kept his eyes on everyone at once like a sheepdog herding his flock, and he avoided the gazes of the half-naked women.

"Relax," Reese teased him. "They won't bite. Unless you ask."

He faked a laugh. "Sure."

She couldn't stand the smell of the stale Bourbon Street air. You could practically taste the burning alcohol on your tongue, and the crowds of people pushed past in droves.

Reese wished they were tucked away again at Liam's small, secret jazz club. Hiding away in the real New Orleans, just she and Liam, alone.

Vivian treaded lightly beside her. "Whose brilliant idea was this?"

"Don't look at me," Reese said. "For once, I'm not the instigator here."

"Still don't believe that. Why did Sophie plan this again?"

Ahead, Sophie slipped her arm through Liam's, looking up at him like he was the pillar of perfection. Reese shrugged. "I don't know. She's trying to break Liam out of his shell or something."

"Well, did she have to take us down with him?"

Reese realized that she wouldn't change anything about Liam. His old man slippers. His scheduled Sunday cleaning days. He was so perfectly himself that she wouldn't dream of altering that in any way at all.

She hoped Sophie felt the same.

Sophie turned back to them. "I've got it! How about we go to Cat's Meow and karaoke? Doesn't that sound like a blast?"

Reese could hear Vivian scoff under her breath. Owen, however, got fired up. "Are you kidding? Karaoke? I'm so in that I'm already there, mic in hand, belting out my Aretha Franklin power ballad."

"I have never been more embarrassed for you," Reese said, hitting him on the shoulder. "I didn't even know that was possible."

Liam shifted closer to Reese and whispered, "Karaoke?"

"It could be worse," she said, thinking of something clever to say. She couldn't. "Actually, no it really can't be any worse than that."

"I'd kill for some earbuds," he said.

"I'll do you one better," she told him, curling her lips into a smile. "I challenge you to a battle of shots."

"Why do I feel like this won't end well?"

She smiled. "Because it won't."

They encountered three bachelorette parties before they even reached the bar. The whole place smelled like cigarette smoke and fog machines, and the lights pulsed around them. The girls on stage belted out to a song from Grease, in their pink lady jackets and colorful wigs.

Reese decided she could get on board with it, even if she wasn't much of a singer.

"Okay," Liam said, facing her. "What are we going for?"

"Tequila," Reese said. "Always tequila."

He raised an eyebrow to her. "Jumping right in, are we?"

"Hell yes," she said. She grabbed both of his shoulders, giving him the most serious face she could muster. "Liam Blake, we never do anything halfway."

"If you say so."

She smiled. "Of course I do! I'll get Vivian up on that stage even if I have to shove the microphone down her throat."

"Sounds violent."

Sophie pushed her way through the crowd. On her left hand, she now sported a light-up ring that flashed pink, green and blue in alternating patterns.

"Guys," she said. "I put our names down!"

Liam grinned as she came close. Reese fired off petty insults in her head.

Get a room, losers.

"You did?" he asked her, his voice shifting into soft respect. "Well, what are we singing?"

"I thought we could sing YMCA. Get the crowd going, you know?" She bounced on the balls of her heels as she talked.

"I'll be the cop," Reese volunteered.

Sophie leaned into Liam, her hands pressed against his chest. "I want you to be the cowboy."

He blushed. "Oh yeah?"

Reese practically threw herself over the bar. She made eye contact with the bartender and demanded, "A round of tequila shots, please."

Vivian winced at her shot. "I can't do this."

"Yes, you can, Vivian. Hold your damn nose if you have to," Reese insisted, two shots propped in her hands.

"Does that help?" Vivian asked.

Liam bent toward them. "Not at all."

Sophie counted them off. On three, they all threw their heads back, letting the sharp taste of tequila fill their mouths. One after the other, Reese emptied the two glasses. When she looked up, Vivian's face puckered.

"I can't finish it," she said. Her glass was still half-full.

"Oh, give it to me, you big baby." Reese grabbed it out of Vivian's hand and threw that one back too. "Okay. Now, we can officially start our night."

Sophie mooned up at Liam. "I love you."

Something inside Reese died. She didn't know if it was an important part or if it was something she could resuscitate back to life, but whatever it was that Sophie had just killed now left a gaping hole in her body.

Liam's face softened. He lovingly swiped a stray piece of hair away from Sophie's face. "I love you too."

A bullet wound.

"Reese?" Vivian was calling her name. She hadn't noticed. "Are you okay?"

Reese swallowed a tear. She reached over and swiped a boa off a passing bachelorette partier. "Never been better."

There were more shots. More bad covers to 80's hair bands. More exchanged looks between Reese and every other passing guy.

"We're on," Sophie said emphatically.

Reese slapped the fake police badge onto her chest, thinking that this whole night was incredibly stupid. She flexed her arm muscles. She cracked her neck. Then, she put on her party face, grabbed a microphone and blew love-me-damnit kisses to the crowd.

They cheered, every eye following her as the music pumped through the speakers.

Reese worked the stage, bending low over the crowd to sing at the boys below, throwing her hands into the air and letting them sensually slide down behind her head.

And Liam never looked at her.

Not once.

Sophie, on the other hand, tried to participate. Strategically placing herself in Reese's strut line, Sophie tried to sing in her direction, but Reese wasn't having it.

She was a solo act.

Always had been, always would be.

Reese went to belt the final Y-M-C-A, when her eyes met his in the crowd.

Ben.

Her heart went crazy, speeding up so fast that she could feel it in every part of her.

Then, it got worse. Right beside him, with a face like deer in the headlights, was Simon Guidry, the devil himself.

She had a few options. She could either run off this stage and into the next bar, stand here and take it or ignore them completely. She went with option D.

On the last note of the song, she looked at Ben and she looked at Simon.

She raised both middle fingers in the air.

One for each of them.

Vivian caught up with Reese at the bar. "Well, what an unexpected turn of events."

"They hang out now? Is there a club or something? The Band of Boys with Bad Dating Histories?" Reese ordered jello shots now, hoping that this would work better with Vivian's particular palette.

"If I were a bolder person, I would go over there and tell them where they can shove their drinks." Vivian's mad face was mild and well-mannered, but it was a welcomed change.

Reese handed her a drink. "I like this. Pissed-off Vivian. Go on."

"It just sucks," Vivian said, swirling her finger on the side of the cup to loosen the jello. "Ben cheats. Simon chokes. Why are guys such assholes? Why do we let them get away with it?"

"What are we gonna do about it?" Reese said, baiting Vivian.

"We're going to have a conversation with them."

"With our fists?"

Vivian crinkled her nose. "No. With our words."

"Okay, you lost me."

A flash of recognition crossed over Vivian's face. Reese followed her eyes and saw Simon talking to a girl near the stage. She was leggy in leather, her hair pulled back into an unkempt, teased ponytail.

"Asshole," Reese mumbled.

Vivian gripped Reese's wrist. "I have the best idea."

Reese didn't know that Vivian was capable of being so diabolical.

It was immature.

It was stupid.

It was undeniably spiteful.

And she loved every minute of it.

Confidently, Vivian marched right up to Simon, her arms swinging to the beat of the music. The girl in the leather politely excused herself and headed for the bathroom. Reese made her move.

In line behind the girl, Reese fanned herself with her hand. "Could it get any hotter in here?"

"Seriously," the girl said, taking the bait. "Wearing this outfit was a bad decision."

"You look familiar," Reese said. "Have I met you before?"

The girl shook her head. "I don't think so. Maybe you've seen me here?"

"Maybe," Reese said, pretending to think deeply on the subject. "Oh I know! I think you were talking to my friend. Simon Guidry?"

"Yes?" There was a question in her voice, like she was trying to connect Reese and Simon.

"Oh, don't worry. He really is just a friend," Reese assured her.

The girl relaxed. "You scared me for a second there. Wouldn't be the first bathroom brawl I've been a part of."

This girl is my hero, Reese thought.

"Woman to woman, I feel I should warn you—"

The leather girl perked up. "Tell me."

"I feel bad saying this, since he's my friend. But you seem really nice, and it would be rude of me not to tell you." Reese brought her voice down to a whisper. "Simon has herpes. *Down there*."

The girl's eyes went wide. "Oh my God."

"Yeah, I know. And he's not afraid to spread it around, if you know what I mean."

"That's disgusting," the girl said, looking over Reese's shoulder to look at Simon.

"If it were me, I'd want to know. God knows they don't warn you about those things, you know?"

The girl looked like she might vomit. "I think I'm gonna—" She pointed to the door.

"Of course," Reese said, smiling. "Have a great night."

Reese walked back to her friends, victorious.

"That was amazing!" Vivian's voice was so loud it could bounce off the ceiling.

"Shh," Reese said, checking around. "Don't ruin it now. Remember, no telling Wendy about this. She doesn't need to hear the S-word right now."

"Shit?" Vivian asked. The alcohol shone through her light blue eyes.

Reese laughed. "No, Simon."

"Right," Vivian said, nodding. "Can we get more jello shots?"

"I'm on it," Reese said. "You go find Owen."

Reese walked through the crowd. Halfway to the bar, she bumped into Liam, who was heading back from the bathroom.

"Hey," he said. "Haven't seen you in a while."

He always looked annoyingly excited to see her. Irritatingly happy to be around her. She wished he'd quit it already.

"I've been around."

He studied her face. "Are you alright?"

"Sure, why not?" she asked.

She walked away, feeling that hole from her phantom bullet wound again.

At the bar, she saw Ben standing just a few people away.

And she didn't stop walking.

"Ben," she said to him, turning him toward her.

He was exactly the same, aside from a few pounds around his stomach. His shaggy brown hair stuck with sweat onto his forehead. His burly arms could still wrap around her.

All she had to do was ask.

"Reese," he said, caught off guard. "You look good."

"Take me home," she told him.

"What?"

She knotted her hands around the back of his neck as she pulled his lips down to hers, pulling her life down with her.

2011

He texted her late in the afternoon: "Happy birthday, babe."

She answered: "Took you long enough."

Ben texted: "Birthday dinner tonight. Wherever you want."

Reese texted back: "Macaroons in Paris should be fine."

Ben texted: "Hibachi it is."

There was nothing less romantic than sharing a birthday dinner with your boyfriend and a family of six. They were celebrating, too. The middle child, all snot-nosed and grubby-handed, had just turned eight.

They screamed bloody murder when the chef set the grill up into a mountain of flames, and this was the most rewarding part of the evening for Reese.

"I thought you might have planned something," Reese said, stabbing her fork at her fried rice.

"Planned something?"

"Yeah. Like a party or something. I mean, God, I'm twenty-one today and I'm sharing my birthday with a third grader."

Ben barely looked at her. "We could go out. Want to text Wendy?"

"You must be kidding. You want me to plan my own birthday celebration now? What are you even good for?"

He elbowed her playfully in her side. "I'll show you later... you know, after a drink or so."

"Not a chance," Reese said, dropping her napkin on the table. "I'm sorry. I'm being a brat."

"No, I just didn't realize you wanted—"

"I'll be right back," she said, excusing herself.

In the bathroom, she splashed cold water on her face. She knew she should feel guilty for talking to Ben like that.

What did she expect from the guy? A carpet of rose petals and a champagne bath? He could barely pass chemistry.

When she was mean to Ben, she never felt bad about it, and he never resented her for it.

Maybe that's why he was comfortable.

He couldn't hurt her.

Ben dropped her off at the bar, where Wendy, Simon, Vivian and Owen were waiting.

Their faces lit up as the bouncer slapped a wristband on her arm. It could've been the alcohol making them all dewy.

But when she walked up to them, they embraced her in a giant group hug, screaming *happy birthday* in her ear.

"Really feeling the love here, guys," she said, wriggling out of their embrace. "Now, who wants to dance?"

"Where's Ben?" Vivian asked, looking around.

Reese propped her hands up on her hips. "I told him to go home."

"Why?" Wendy asked. "Did y'all have a fight?"

Reese shook her head. "No, it's my present. I get to be single for my birthday."

Simon looked at Owen, and vice versa.

"I'm gonna go—" Owen started.

"Beers, yes," Simon finished.

They left and the girls drew nearer.

"So what does that mean, exactly?" Wendy asked.

"What are you planning to do about this? Or is this another one of your jokes?" Vivian asked.

Reese threw her hands up in the air. "Enough questions!"—she grabbed them each by the hand—"Let's dance!"

Ben hadn't specifically *said* she could be single for the evening.

They'd had a fight in the car, and she'd told him he couldn't come. That was it. Nothing earth-shattering.

But Reese would be damned if she let this night go down without making the best of it. Her birthday was her favorite day of the year, and she wanted to make it last.

"Are you having a good time?" Wendy asked, ever the people pleaser.

Reese twirled. Mid-spin, she spotted a tall, tan guy posted up against the wall like a model. She spun back.

"I'd be having a *much* better time if I had *that guy* over here," Reese said, nodding in his direction.

"Don't," Vivian warned.

Reese smiled. "I'm going for it."

She lost track of time.

Somewhere between dancing on the stage and dancing in mystery guy's arms, her phone had died.

Reese hadn't crossed any lines, but her mind was coloring right over them. Finally, her night was turning around.

"Reese," Wendy said, marching up to her, "Ben's outside. He said he's here to take you home."

Reese made a face. "I didn't ask him to do that."

"Should I tell him I'll take you?"

Ben would be a baby about this. He'd probably show up at her house anyway.

"No, that's okay," Reese said. "I'll go."

She said goodbye to mystery guy.

She said goodbye to singledom.

But somewhere, tucked into her back pocket, she remembered a card she could always play:

People don't belong to people.

FORTY-FOUR

She knew this bed.

The smell of old socks.

The bong in the corner of the room.

She didn't have time to process it fully when Ben rolled over toward her and draped a heavy arm across her chest. He wasn't trying to hold her. He was trying to claim her.

X marked the spot.

Finders keepers.

Reese stared up at the ceiling. Maybe this wasn't so bad, after all. Part of her still loved Ben, probably. There was enough attraction there that could serve as the perfect distraction from the disaster that was her current romantic life.

If she tricked herself into loving Ben, she could trick herself out of her feelings for Liam.

It wasn't subconscious.

It was survival.

She reached over, under the weight of Ben's arm, and grabbed her phone. The screen lit up with texts.

Three from Wendy.

Five texts from Vivian. Three calls.

Ten texts from Liam. Four calls. Two voicemails.

Obviously, she'd ditched.

Without checking her voicemails, she called Liam, wrapping a blanket around her bare body and walking out into the living room.

"Where the hell have you been?" Liam's voice sounded grated from alcohol and smoke. He answered before the phone could even ring.

"I know, I'm sor—"

"I have been scouring the city for you, Reese. I called your dad, your mom. Jesus, I almost called the morgue. Where the hell are you?"

She blinked. The sun flooded in from the untucked blinds, and she struggled to adjust. "Liam, I get it. You're pissed."

"I can't do this, Reese. I can't be wandering the streets of New Orleans, hoping that you're not lying drunk and dead in the street somewhere."

She didn't know what to say.

She could feel a fiery anger rising up inside her, even though she had no right to it.

He wasn't wrong. She'd messed up. But when her heart felt like shards of glass in her chest, she had no other choice but the deep end.

"Fine," she told him. "I never asked you to take care of me. I never asked that you come rushing to my side like some kind of white fucking knight."

"No, but you sure as hell expected it."

Had she?

Had she been leaping off the cliff just so he'd be at the bottom, ready to catch her?

She hoped not.

"Well, you're off the hook." She padded her voice with a layer of confidence. "Ben and I got back together last night."

Liam took an exasperated breath. "Ben? Ex-boyfriend, cheater Ben?"

"Well, those aren't his favorite modifiers, but yes."

There was a long pause.

She could still hear him breathing long, pacifying breaths.

And when he did speak, his voice was resigned.

"If you want to wreck your life, by all means, don't let me stop you."

He hung up.

In the pale light of morning, everything felt wrong. This apartment. That guy. The old Reese with her drinking and falling and failing.

She shook her head, and with it, her reservations.

Reese crawled back into bed beside Ben.

"Ben," she said, tucking the comforter underneath her chin. "We should do this again sometime."

His lips were at her neck. "I never got over you."

"I know."

Later that afternoon, Reese drove home with the plans of seeing Ben again later that night. If it hadn't been clear earlier, it was clear now. They were back together, whatever that meant.

Fidelity? No.

Commitment? Never.

Distraction? Sure.

Bag in hand, Reese stared at the door to her house, willing herself to go in, but dreading the thought of seeing Liam up close. She hated disappointing him, but she hated that she *cared* about disappointing him even more.

It was her own fault. She'd had every opportunity to be with him. She turned him away.

What if there is something fundamentally wrong with me?

It was like there was a core piece of her soul that hadn't fully kicked into place yet.

She wondered if it ever would.

Turning the knob, she pushed her way into the house.

Liam hunched forward on the couch, his cupped hands pressed against his mouth.

"Hey," she said.

He didn't look at her. Instead, he stood up and walked back to his room, slamming the door shut behind him. He didn't want to talk, of course. Despite everything he'd said, he still wanted to make sure she'd gotten home safe. That was the only explanation she could think of.

Cecil sighed from his bed.

"Hey boy," Reese said, stooping down over him. "It's okay."

He whined, so she went to the back door and let him out into the backyard. But he wouldn't go. Instead, he sat there, crying softly to himself, for no other reason than because he could.

"You and me both," she told him.

Then she walked over to her room, closed the door and climbed into bed. If she could sleep it all away, then maybe she could convince herself that none of it had really happened at all.

FORTY-FIVE

Trish, now Joanie, said for the hundredth time, "Tell him, Reese. Today. What do you have to lose?"

And, like always, Reese replied, "I'll tell him. I'm going to tell him."

What do you have to lose?

Everything.

The possibility of everything.

One night, just as it was starting to get dark, the wind kicked up outside. The clouds crawled with full bellies closer to them from the horizon.

Miles and Reese were the only ones left.

What do you have to lose?

"You should get going," Miles said, scraping the bristles of a brush against the floor. "Beat the storm."

"I can help out," she said.

Her stomach flipped in on itself.

She knew.

If she was going to tell him, if she was ever going to tell him, she had to do it now.

She couldn't explain it.

She just knew.

"No, really. Don't want you to drive in this kind of storm. In fact, why don't you go ahead and text me when you get home? That way I know you made it safe."

She laughed, picking up a lonely cup from a two-top table. "Wow, is this what it sounds like when you're concerned? How unnatural for you."

"I can be concerned," he mumbled.

"You know, for a second there, you almost sounded parental."

He laughed. "I've had practice."

What do you have to lose?

"I don't know how to say this." He wasn't looking at her. It was better that way. "I really don't know how to say this, so. I'm Rita Weller's daughter. I'm *your* daughter."

His broom stood still, just before it fell to the floor, the handle landing with a reverberating crack. Miles didn't look at her initially. He stared outside, just as a plastic bag took flight, hitching itself onto the antenna of a nearby truck.

Then he looked in her direction.

It seemed like the whole coffee shop could collapse around them, the storm could morph into a hurricane, the world could stop entirely, but there they'd be.

Standing still.

Frozen in time.

"How did you—"

"I internet-stalked you," Reese said.

Miles tugged at his hair, his eyes filled with distress. "Look, Reese—"

"It's okay, Miles," she said, steadying herself on the top of a chair. "We don't have to do this part of the finding-out-who-your-daddy-is ordeal. I just want you to know I exist and that I know you exist."

"Reese—" He bit his lip, then started over. "I didn't know. I don't... I don't know what to say."

It was clear.

She could read it all over his face.

He really *didn't* know about her.

And now, they didn't need each other.

Miles had a family, and she did too. Reese was grown up and he was settled.

What could they want from each other now, so far down the line?

What do you have to lose?

Nothing.

And that was okay.

It would have to be okay.

"You're right about that rain," Reese said, pointing outside just as a crack of lightning bolted across the sky. "I better get on the road."

He didn't say anything as she lifted her tote bag off of the chair. He didn't tell her to stop. He didn't tell her he was sorry, that he was wrong. He didn't say anything at all as she opened the door and sprinted out into the rain.

FORTY-SIX

She was thankful for the rain.

It kept her calm as she drove home. Not Liam-and-Reese home. Wally-and-Rita home.

There wasn't much thought behind this decision, just pure emotion, only slightly numbed by the rain.

It was never about Miles.

All this time, she'd thought she'd been waiting for her father to show up, she'd thought she'd wanted him to just *notice* her.

It was never about Miles.

Reese knocked on the front door, then let herself in.

"Rita," Reese called. "Rita, where are you?"

Wally turned the corner. "Grease, what a surprise."

"You knew. You knew he didn't know." Reese had never talked to him like that before, but she wasn't Reese right now. She wasn't... whole.

"Reese—" he started.

She didn't stop. She marched outside. "Rita."

In full beekeeper's gear, Rita carefully lifted a frame from the box.

"MOM."

Reese couldn't see her mother's face through the mask, but she could imagine it.

It was the same face that she'd seen at ten.

That was the year that everything shifted.

That was the year that her life fell away from her.

"People don't belong to people, right, MOM?" Reese said. She could hear herself sounding like a lunatic. "Or did you forget? Did you forget you were supposed to want me?"

Rita didn't move.

All of the words were unbuckling from Reese's chest, like she'd been holding them there as armor.

"It hurts," Reese said. Her face was leaking. "It hurts me, Mom."

Rita moved tentatively toward Reese now.

Reese was shaking.

"I never pushed you," Reese said. "I never asked for more than you could give. But I'm asking now."

Rita said nothing.

And then she turned her back to Reese, returning to her bees.

The tears rolled out of Reese's eyes in buckets, but there was nothing more she could do.

"Rita," Wally said, crestfallen.

Reese walked back toward the house. "It's okay. Really. I'm used to it."

"She doesn't mean it." Wally said, following Reese to the door. "You know how much she—"

"Do I? Because I can count on one hand how many times I've heard her say it."

Reese slammed the door behind her.

It wasn't good enough.

It was never going to be good enough.

2001

"I want a funeral-themed party," she told Rita.

Reese was strangely obsessed with death at eleven. She loved stories about young, deceased celebrities who died before their time.

Marilyn Monroe.

JFK.

Kurt Cobain.

She'd spent hours researching on her mom's rusty desktop and when it came time to pick her birthday theme, she couldn't think of anything better.

Rita should have been more surprised by this, but she barely even bat an eyelash.

"How do you throw a funeral-themed birthday party?"

"I have a few ideas," Reese said, twirling the last of her cereal particles in the tinted milk. "We could rent a hearse."

"Mhmm."

"Maybe we could camp out at a graveyard. You know, turn it into a sleepover."

"Sure, good thinking."

"And then, there could be eulogies."

"Eulogies?"

"Yeah. For me."

This was what gave Rita pause. Just a brief one, though.

"Why do you want people to eulogize you, Reese?"

"I like the idea. People saying nice things about you. Memories. Things like that."

What she didn't tell Rita was that in her mind, she imagined herself in a casket, playing dead. While each of her very few friends would stand up, one by one, saying how they would miss her and how much they loved her.

In her dream, she pictured the last of the line fading back to their seats, leaving one stranger behind.

This man would be crying more than the rest of them.

He would kneel beside her, resting a warm hand over her pretend-cold forehead.

"Reese," he would say. "I'm so sorry. I'm so sorry I never knew you."

He'd choke back a sob.

He'd be the only sound that mattered.

Until finally, he'd choke out the last words, "I love you now, then, and always."

She didn't know what happened from there, but she believed it would be the start of something good.

"How about fake tombstones in the backyard, a new death gown, and a cake that looks like fake dirt?" Rita offered, probably thinking of a way to explain this to the other kids' parents.

Reese was ready to counter, but Rita said, "That's the best I got for you."

"Deal," Reese said, disappointed.

Reese waited on the bottom porch step.

She always liked this step. Maybe because it was so close to the ground. Maybe because she could reach her legs out and touch the grass with her feet. In any case, she was on this step when she realized that no one was coming.

She let the minutes go by her.

One.

Two.

Three.

If she stayed on this step, watching the road, then there was always the chance that someone could still show.

No, not just someone.

Him.

Rita sat beside her. "Hey, kiddo."

"I'm sorry, Rita."

"Why are you sorry?"

"No one came to my party."

Rita let her long, reddish hair fall over her shoulder and into her lap. "There's nothing to be sorry for Reese. You tried something new. People don't like new."

"They think I'm weird, don't they."

Rita sighed. "Come with me."

Rita took Reese's hand and led her to the backyard. Reese loved her party. Or she had, before no one showed up. Rita had customized the tombstones with the names of the invitees. There were cobwebs in the trees. And she'd worn the most perfect death dress there ever was. Dark blue. A flower perched in her hair.

Reese wanted to kick the tombstones.

She wanted to tear the fake webs from the trees.

She wanted to take it all back and pretend it had never been a thought in her head.

"Sit right here," Rita said, gesturing to the stone bench she'd rented.

Reese followed.

"Dearly beloved," Rita started, collecting her breath, "we gather here today to honor our fallen friend, Reese Weller."

Reese swallowed a smile.

"As her mother, this is no easy day for me, but I have to be strong, because it's what Reese would have wanted." Rita gazed up at the sky, her hand reaching for her heart. "If it hadn't been for that banana peel... oh, God."

Flawlessly, Rita let the tears come, like she'd pulled them out of her eyes the way a magician pulls a rabbit out of a top hat.

And Reese was full-on smiling now.

Apple cheeks.

Half moon eyes.

And she remembered that she'd forgotten to remember her dad.

FORTY-SEVEN

"We've arrived," Owen announced. "Let us rage."

Vivian lugged her suitcase through the front door, trailing behind Owen, ice chest in hand.

They'd never done Mardi Gras as a group before. There had been spring breaks. There had been weekend birthday celebrations.

But Mardi Gras?

This was next level.

"Viv, you can put your stuff in my room. I'm crashing on the air mattress," Reese said.

"Are you sure? I don't want to put you out."

Vivian. All manners. All the time.

"Honestly? Just take the damn room."

"I like 'em bossy," Owen teased, winking in her direction.

"Gag me."

Vivian raised her hand to Owen. "Don't. I know you want to comment but don't."

He restrained himself.

There were more people to come. Sophie would crash with Liam, naturally. And Wendy would crash with Reese, whenever she showed. Ben would come and go as he pleased.

Simon's invite was lost in the mail. Reese had to pry it out of Owen's insistent hands, but eventually, she won that argument.

Liam was in the kitchen, wearing a stupid baseball cap and bright green croakies wrapped around the back of his neck.

He poured tequila into the empty blender.

Reese leaned over the back of the couch. "Are you making margaritas?"

He didn't answer her, because, as it happened, he wasn't talking to her. In the most mature of fashions, he'd been giving her the silent treatment since she started seeing Ben again.

"I'll take one, if you're offering," Reese said to him.

Knock on the door.

Reese leapt to her feet chanting, "*Wendy Wendy Wendy!*"

"She's here? She's here!" Viv said, shouting from the bedroom.

Reese threw open the door.

"The party has arrived," Wendy said.

Wendy looked good. The same, but in a hair-blowing-in-the-wind, day-at-the-spa sort of way. She looked like someone who'd returned home after weeks of traveling.

"You got highlights! You're here! You're here!"

Reese and Vivian tackled Wendy onto the nearest air mattress.

Wendy laughed, pure and contagious. They were together. And it felt better than a tub of ice cream, better than a trip to the beach, better than any boy could possibly measure up.

Liam stood over them, pitcher in hand. "Should I come back later?"

The girls laughed, a tangle of arms and legs and emotion.

"Liam, meet Wendy," Reese said. "Wendy, Liam made margaritas."

"We will get along just fine, then," Wendy said.

"Can we go please? There are beads to be caught! Beer to be chugged. Oh hey, Wendy."

In the hallway, Owen wore a tank top that read, "BEADS BEER BOOBS."

"That shirt—" Reese said.

"You're disgusting," Wendy said simultaneously.

Reese picked her head up, looking at Vivian. "You married that."

Vivian's eyes went dull. Like all the fight was sucked right out of them. "Liam, the margaritas. Keep them coming."

Outside, the city was alive. It was hot outside, too hot for February, but it wasn't raining, so that was an advantage.

The street was filled with characters. So much green and purple and gold. Fishnets. Face paint. Costumes of all kinds. Masks from signature shops.

Mardi Gras was the kind of place for people who wanted to feel alive, to feel the life inside them to their very core.

Reese was in her element.

They started Uptown for the day parades, with plans to head back to Lakeview before Endymion.

"Where's Ben?" Liam asked.

She wasn't even sure if it was to her at first.

Reese checked her phone. No texts.

"Where's Sophie?" she reciprocated.

Liam raised his crooked eyebrows. "She'll be here tonight, I think."

The Krewe of Iris charged across the street. Music, like rolling thunder, followed it through the crowd, while the beads and stuffed toys rained down on their heads.

"Hey," Reese called. "Throw me something!"

Liam stood at her side.

He had a habit of doing that, without even thinking about it.

"Sarah!" he yelled. "Hey, Sarah!"

"You know someone?" she asked.

He shook his head. "No. You just call out a generic name and 99% of the time, it works."

"That's cheating."

"Sarah!" he yelled again. "Hey, Sarah!"

A woman on the second level made eye contact with him from behind her mask. She paused, hoisted her bag up, and began pelting him with goods.

Bags upon bags of beads.

Fake cigars.

Brightly colored garters.

Reese held up her winnings. "You're diabolical."

"Please," he said. "You flatter me."

He was forgetting that he wasn't talking to her.

She didn't remind him.

"When did you become a Mardi Gras expert?"

He slipped a purple garter onto his arm. "Since I've lived here approximately my entire life. Honestly, your inexperience is disheartening. What do they teach you in Covington, anyway?"

He was talking to her.

She forgot how much she missed it.

He plucked a yellow garter from the bag. "Look. Same color as your wedding hair. May we never forget."

He bent down to her foot, and and she steadied herself on his shoulders, unsure.

He glanced up at her. "You're going to need to pick up your foot now."

"Yeah, right, I know. Just, uh, making you work for it," she teased.

Every inch of her stirred into existence as Liam's hands trailed up her leg. Slowly. Carefully. And the tips of his fingers just barely sailed over her skin.

But that was all it took.

The garter clung to the thick of her thigh.

And she had no idea where this was coming from.

He stood. "A perfect fit."

"Throw in a tiara and I'll be ready for the Mardi Gras ball."

"Want a beer?" he asked.

She nodded, mutely, as he left for the ice chest.

Wendy parked herself next to Reese. "Okay, what was that?"

"Oh, you know," Reese said, her eyes on the build of Liam's back, "just your everyday roommate bonding."

"No, that was straight-up groping," Wendy said. "Honestly, my temperature spiked just looking at you two."

"Shut up," Reese said.

"Beer," Liam said, handing her a cold, sweaty can.

The condensation shocked her body back into motion. "Thanks."

Her phone vibrated in her pocket.

Ben texted: "See you tonight!"

When it came to guys, Reese had a clear head. A crystal, clean-cut brain. She'd never been a whiny girl. She'd never been the type to pine or crush from the shadows.

If she liked you, you'd know it.

If she didn't? Same.

So, with Liam, she was a basket case. She chocked the situation up to leftover hormones. Proximity.

Yes, proximity.

Of course, she was attracted to him.

Of course, she felt things she didn't actually feel.

He was right there. All day. Every day.

This was science.

After the third parade, everyone returned home to crash, sprawled out through the house, waiting for the night adventures to begin.

Wendy and Reese flanked one another on the air mattress, quietly whispering.

"You like him," Wendy said. "Just admit it."

"I like that he's in the same house as me. I like that I could crawl into his bed drunk and he wouldn't say no. That's what I like."

"You're such a liar."

"I am not. I don't want a relationship. I want hookups and bar boys. Relationships aren't worth it."

She stared up at the ceiling, then let her eyes trail over to the trampoline. "Besides," she added, "I know I'm not the forever girl. I'm the pitstop to marriage. The wrong girl who occasionally pretends to be the right one."

Wendy shifted on the mattress. "You are not the wrong girl."

"Sorry," Reese said. "I'll turn down the drama."

Wendy sighed. "It's easy to say they're not worth the trouble. It's easy to throw your hands, give in, be the coldest, hardest version of yourself. That's not you, Reese. You're just scared to get hurt."

She was right and she wasn't. It wasn't a cut-and-dry diagnosis. It wasn't a psychobabble puzzle to solve. Reese didn't believe in marriage anymore. She didn't believe in *people* anymore.

Reese had herself.

She was all she needed.

But she couldn't say that to Wendy.

So, she simply said, "You're right," then rolled over and pretended to fall asleep.

The knock on the door jerked Reese awake.

It was an incessant, intrusive knocking, too demanding.

"Chill out," Reese uttered through the door, "Where's the fire?"

On the other side, the rude awakener was Sophie. Sophie, in her body glitter, from her arms to her feet, bare stomach. Sophie, in her skin tight shorts and bra top.

"I'm sorry," Reese said. "We didn't order any strippers. Try the guys next door."

Sophie laughed. "I brought tequila."

"Access granted," Reese said.

Wendy sat up from the mattress. "Sophie... how are you?"

"Wasted, and yourself?"

Sophie came in like a tornado, throwing her beads on the sofa, her purse on the kitchen counter, banging everything but—

"Liam!" Sophie squealed, barging into his room.

"Is she sluttier than I remember?" Wendy asked.

"It's Mardi Gras. Everyone's slutty at Mardi Gras."

Vivian poked her head out of the bedroom. "Hey, the married people are ready to party. Get on our level, hotter, single people!"

Reese looked to Wendy. "Round two?"

Wendy stood up and grabbed the nearest flask. "Round two."

FORTY-EIGHT

There was nothing quite as extravagant as a night parade. The entire atmosphere changed, like New Orleans evolved into light itself. Gone was the spotlight of the sun. Gone was reality.

Everything changed.

Like magic.

Bacchus was Reese's favorite parade. If Mardi Gras were a red carpet, this would be the award winner, the one reporters climbed over each other for, simply to get a closer look.

Sophie led the group to a house a block away from Reese and Liam's, where a group of her friends had taken over a porch.

She hugged the strangers, some of whom Reese recognized. With Liam on her arm, Sophie played the girlfriend role well.

"Hi so-and-so," she'd say. Hug. Kiss. "This is my boyfriend, Liam." Hug. Hand shake.

Reese and Wendy found a spot next to a pillar while Owen and Vivian made themselves a plate of food.

"I want to get drunk enough that I won't hurt when bags of beads hit my face, but not drunk enough that I get tired," Wendy said.

"Since when do you get tired?"

Wendy shrugged. "I guess I've crossed the adult threshold."

Reese's eyebrows skyrocketed. "You're crashing on an air mattress with your college roommate, day drinking."

"I retract my previous statement."

"Thank you."

The next few minutes passed slowly. Someone handed them glow sticks. Someone mistook them for the owners of the house.

And then—

"*Babe.*"

She turned her head and her lips made contact with him. She couldn't mistake those warm, confidence-killing lips.

"Oh hi," Reese told Ben.

"Let's get a drink," he told her, gripping her hand.

"I'm good right now," Reese said, struggling to get her hand back. He'd always been a little too rough.

He stroked her cheek. "Well, I'll catch up, then."

Reese spit into her cup.

She thought she could taste blood.

Ben didn't belong to her. He didn't hurt her. All the boxes were checked.

Then why do I feel like I'm drowning?

Around her, everyone else fit in their boxes, too. Owen and Vivian. Sophie and—

Liam was missing.

He was probably inside. Maybe he went walking somewhere.

For whatever reason, Reese decided to go see for herself. She walked through the house, into the backyard, and found herself staring up at the sky, wishing she was at home on her trampoline.

"What brings you to this side of the party?"

She heard his voice before she saw him.

Actually, she didn't see him at all.

"Where are you?" she asked.

A hand raised from the castle-shaped playhouse to her right.

So, apparently, we're at a family home.

She could hear the parade making its way down the street as she climbed into the playhouse with him.

"A little cramped in here," she said, tucking her knees into her chest.

Liam smiled. "Not as cramped as it is out there."

"Still not great with crowds, I see."

"Still not great with alcohol, I see."

Reese rolled her eyes. "Is anyone actually *great* with alcohol?"

The roar of the crowd started to rise.

"Sounds like the parade made it here," Reese said, turning her ear toward the street.

"You want to go back?" he asked.

The look on his face made it seem like he wasn't planning on leaving anytime soon.

And maybe, just maybe, he didn't want her to go, either.

"Do you want to go back?" she asked.

He shook his head. "No, I'm good here."

She fidgeted with her hands in her lap.

"You can stay here," he told her. "If, you know, you need a break, too."

She settled in. "Okay, then."

"I'm not so sure I'm cut out for this," he laughed, pointing outside. "Not like you."

Reese laughed. "Well, practice makes perfect."

"Do you think—" he started, then stopped himself. "Never mind."

"Oh, come on. What were you going to say?"

He smiled to himself. "Okay. Do you think it was easier, before all this?"

She had no idea what *this* was.

Living together?

Kissing each other?

Pretending nothing ever happened?

"I guess it depends on what *this* you're talking about."

He leaned back on the castle, pointing outside again. "It was better when it was just you and me."

She tried to read his face, but it wasn't giving away much.

He looked down in his lap. "I tried to stop, you know? But you're just there. All day. Every day. Being you."

Reese couldn't process what he was saying, which, as it so happened, he wasn't saying well at all.

"I'm, uh, I'm confused," she said.

"If it's not obvious that I'm in love with you yet, then I don't know when it ever will be."

Liam finally looked up in her eyes, looking for some kind of reaction.

He was right.

Things *were* easier when it was just the two of them; though, she was only just realizing that now.

And his feelings should have been obvious. They should have fit like a puzzle in her brain. But, she was scared. That much was obvious, too.

"I don't know if I'm ready for you yet," she said honestly.

He nodded. "I'm definitely not ready for you, either."

Outside, a band passed in front of the house. They were so loud and bright that Reese could hardly hear her own thoughts anymore, if she had any at all. Reese and Liam studied each other, letting the music flow over and through them, until finally, it stopped.

"So, what now?" she asked him.

He leaned over and squeezed her hand. "Nothing, now."

Liam excused himself as he returned to all the noise. Reese stayed put for a while, thinking about death. Could her own feelings kill her? Could they slice her in half, splitting her organs, leaving her heart cracked wide open?

She could die from feeling too much.

From feeling *this* much.

They survived the night, which was all they could hope for.

The air mattress felt like sheer heaven under Reese's head. It felt like clouds and swan feathers and expensive hotel sheets.

"Wake me when we're seventeen again," Wendy whispered.

"Deal," Reese groaned.

"I miss you," Wendy whispered. "I miss being home. I miss this more than physically possible. It's like... I'm only half of myself without y'all."

"Move home. We could live together. We could get a dog and name him Clooney."

Wendy laughed. "I wouldn't hate that."

"Me either," Reese said.

She realized that there was an expiration date on her living with Liam. In fact, maybe she'd already passed it. And there were the emotions again, welling up like a balloon in her chest.

"Can I just cry for a bit?" Reese asked. "This whole crying thing is new to me and I'm like a freaking faucet and I really just need to drain it all right now."

Wendy laughed. "Cry for as long as you need."

So, Reese cried even harder.

FORTY-NINE

The vegan restaurant smelled like essential oils and herbs. There were signs in the window that read, "HUG ANIMALS, NOT CONSUME THEM." The clientele was happy and boisterous, visiting each other's tables and saying hello to regulars. This was the only exclusively vegan restaurant in Covington, after all.

Rita hovered over her menu, with her mass of frizzy red hair. The waiter walked up just before Reese, and Rita pointed at her menu to say, "Tell me more about your quinoa dishes."

Reese dropped her tote bag on the floor. "Hi, Rita."

"Reese, I'm so glad that you could make it," Rita said, straightening up the table. "Did you get that article I sent you?"

"Which one?"

Rita was in the habit of emailing news articles to Reese. She sent them one at a time, up to twenty times a day, totally clogging Reese's inbox that she barely ever checked anyway. Her inbox was now a montage of animal cruelty products, vegan studies, and the occasional horoscope.

They hadn't spoken since the day that Reese barged in, but those emails kept coming. To her credit, Rita probably didn't mean anything by it. It was her idea to have lunch, after all.

Rita pushed a tuft of her hair out of her face. "The one about the peace walk this weekend. I could pick you up?"

Reese placed her napkin in her lap, though she had no intention of eating. "No."

"Alright then," Rita said, setting her hands in her lap.

Neither of them knew what to say. Rita had made the first move. Reese had made the second, by actually showing up—after several prompting phone calls from Wally. So, they were even.

"I'm a little in love with someone," Reese offered.

Rita took interest. "The boy that you live with?"

Reese nodded. "Yes, that's the one. He's dating someone, though. A great someone, actually. And I'm not great with romance."

"You don't give yourself enough credit," Rita said. "You are a great someone, too."

Reese smiled. "It's nice to hear that once in awhile, Rita. Even if it's not easy to say."

"Mom."

Rita had a peaceful look on her face as she extended her permission like an olive branch. Her eyes and her cheeks were lifted, almost like she was searching for approval from Reese. No, not approval. Acceptance.

Part of Reese wanted to tell her that it was too late. That she didn't get another chance at motherhood. But this reaction didn't sit well with her, because, if this year had proven anything, it was the magic of second and third and a hundred more chances.

"Mom," Reese repeated.

This was okay. This would all be okay.

Maybe not today.

Or tomorrow.

But eventually.

Rita leaned over the table, scooping Reese's hands up in her own. "I'm sorry."

It was simple.

It was honest.

It was a good start.

"I'm sorry, too," Reese submitted.

"Would you like some tea?" Rita asked.

"Of course," Reese said. "As long as it's just tea. No prediction."

Rita laughed meekly. "I promise."

They spent the remainder of the afternoon talking about nothing that mattered, except to them.

Reese never asked for Rita's story. She didn't need to hear it. All she needed was to know that her mother was there, always had been, and always would be.

In her unique way.

The best she knew how.

That was enough.

FIFTY

When Reese finally used up all her vacation time, she dragged herself back to work with whatever dignity she had left.

"Where you been?" Joanie asked, dropping a towel at Reese's feet. Not to be tricked, Reese picked it up before she could slip.

"Hell, how about you?"

Joanie grabbed a mug, carrying it over to the espresso machine. "I think you're going to need a few of these today."

"Good call."

She waited for Miles, but he never showed.

She told herself not to wait anymore.

Reese picked up the phone, with Joanie beside her for moral support.

"Miles," Reese started when the voicemail message ended, "It's Reese. Was hoping we could talk. I, um, I owe you an apology. Anyway, I'm back at work, so, you can catch me here whenever. Okay. Bye."

Joanie tucked a hand around Reese's shoulder. "Impeccable."

"Thank you," Reese said, not quite as sure of herself.

Walking back to the counter, Reese checked her phone.

Six missed calls.

Liam.

The car ride was a blur.

Reese drove with the intensity of a race car driver, keeping her eyes steady on the road, her foot heavy on the gas.

In the back, Cecil cried, but it wasn't his normal cry. It was an outright wail, a moan that could make anyone's skin crawl.

Liam leaned back to him the entire ride, running a hand over his back, like it would somehow make it better.

"Easy, boy," he said, over and over, like an anthem.

When they reached the emergency clinic, everything sped up.

Reese threw the car into park.

Liam opened the back door.

He carried Cecil into the clinic.

"Excuse me," he yelled. "I need help. My dog was hit."

There was a flurry of people and everything looked white. They put Cecil on a stretcher, him wailing all the while, and they pushed him through the double doors and out of sight.

Liam stood dumbfounded after him.

Reese froze.

Just like that, everything slowed down again.

A nurse, gentle and quiet, approached Liam with a clipboard of paperwork, carefully gesturing him over to the waiting room chairs.

Reese sat down beside him, without the faintest idea of what to say. Liam, deep in a state of shock, just sat staring off into space, the clipboard balancing on his thighs.

It wasn't until a few minutes later that Liam actually said anything.

"Cecil was there." He cleared his throat, trying to shove the words out of his mouth. "When my dad died, Cecil was there."

Reese listened intently, like it was the only thing she could do to contribute at all to the direness of this situation.

"If he doesn't make it..."

She waited for an end to his sentence that never came. She found her own voice. "He's going to make it."

And then, his eyes still glazed over, he reached for her hand. His hands were so strong and his clutch was sturdy. She couldn't imagine how someone so strong could stay *that* strong in a situation like this.

She imagined it must have been the same when his father had died.

"Liam," she whispered, without even realizing it.

"No," he whispered back. "You don't have to say you're sorry. I already know."

She was sorry, but that wasn't what she'd wanted to say.

She wanted to tell him that he shouldn't be with Sophie anymore.

She wanted to tell him that maybe love wasn't actually so bad, and that she'd like another turn at it.

She wanted to say she loved him, too.

"You should try to rest," she said softly. "I'll let you know if anything happens."

She expected him to fight her on this, but instead, he turned his back to her, stretching out on the bench, and passing out nearly immediately.

She hadn't laughed.

Reese realized it about twenty minutes into Liam's sleep.

Normally, she would be laughing right now, but that response was becoming less and less frequent.

Why hadn't she laughed yet?

Reese launched onto her feet and whispered to a still-asleep Liam, "I, uh, am getting coffee."

She didn't wait for a response. She just took off down the hall, raising her phone to her ear.

"I can't do this," Reese said. She stopped still and placed her back against the wall. Part of her felt like she was keeping the wall from crumbling to the ground, the whole building resting on her shoulders.

"Can't do what?" Vivian asked.

"Cecil is dying and Liam needs me and I thought I could do it, but I can't."

Breath short.

Chest tight.

She was half afraid she was in the midst of a heart attack.

"Reese," Vivian said, using her soothing, damn-near parental voice, "you can do this. Just take a deep breath and go back to Liam."

Reese inhaled hard.

Held it.

Let it out.

"I can't go back to Liam because there's nothing to go back to. I missed it. I had my chance and I missed it."

"Reese, I'm going to try and say this in the nicest way possible. Suck it up and go be there for your friend. Even if he's with someone else. Take yourself out of the equation, go back to Liam and stay with him for as long as he needs you."

Reese swallowed what tasted like her own bile.

She wasn't sure if she was more upset about the idea of going back to Liam or the idea of Vivian being right.

She pried her back away from the wall. "Okay."

"Proud of you."

Reese smiled, in spite of herself. "Thanks."

Walking back to Liam felt like walking through a war zone.

The sound of beeping from down the hall.

The smell of wet dog and dried blood in the air.

Everything looked dead or dying.

She sat down next to Liam, who was now staring at the floor, barely blinking.

She wished she could punch him in the arm, tell him to lighten up, and have everything go back to normal. But it wasn't going to happen that way.

Instead, she inched her hand over to him. She didn't know where to put it, so it hovered mid-air temporarily, before she settled it over the back of his hand.

And she didn't say anything.

Because she didn't have any of the words he needed to hear.

So she sat there, holding his hand, through the hours, past the flurry of people, until the doctor came out and gave them the news. That's when he held her. His body shaking. His tears like deep shouts into the night.

FIFTY-ONE

Nothing was the same.

The house felt empty.

Liam barely came out of his room.

Sophie visited, but always left with a mixed look of aggravation and fear splashed across her face.

Eventually, life had to go back to normal. The new normal, at least.

They went to work. They slept. They moved like life was happening to them, rather than the other way around.

"I don't know what else to do," Reese told Wendy. "He hasn't spoken a word to me since we left the animal hospital."

"Just give him time," she advised. "Be ready for the breakdown."

Reese felt like it couldn't break down more than it already had.

She'd yet to talk to Miles, too, which was a totally different story. He'd gone fishing, Joanie told her. She didn't know when he'd be back.

And then, there was Ben. Good old Ben, who hadn't called her in weeks. She had failed to initiate anything as well.

"So, what now?" she wanted to say to Liam, thinking back to that night in the playhouse. "So. What. Now."

Reese curled into her bed. "I think I need a change," she told Wendy.

"What kind of change?"

It happened on a Friday afternoon.

She packed as much as her energy would allow. Luggage bags filled with clothes and whatever she could fit into her tote bag.

Liam was in his room again, shut down and shut off.

"Liam?" she checked anyway.

He didn't say anything.

"Liam?" she repeated.

Nothing still.

"I think," she said shakily, "that it might be time for me to move out."

She waited for him to come to the door.

He didn't.

Would he think she was abandoning him?

Isn't that exactly what I'm doing?

The truth of the matter was that it hurt too much. Yes, he loved her. But, as he'd said, he had no plans to do anything about it. So, how *could* she stay?

It was time for a change of scenery.

"I'm leaving tonight," Reese continued. "I'll be back for the rest of my stuff soon."

He still didn't come to the door.

He still didn't say anything at all.

"Okay, then." She pressed her palm against the door. "I'll see you."

Her whole body felt warm with blood as she walked toward the door.

She didn't know if she'd made the right choice.

But, for now, it was the only choice.

The breakdown.

It wasn't what she expected.

It wasn't *who* she expected.

As Reese turned toward the street, there was Vivian. She had bags in her hands. Luggage bags.

Vivian and Reese were mirror images.

Lonely.

Lost.

Scared out of their minds.

"Viv—"

"I need somewhere to stay."

Be ready for the breakdown.

FIFTY-TWO

She was back where she'd started.

And yet, she was nowhere near it.

"You know," Claudia said, dragging one of Reese's luggage bags into the front room. "It's rare that an ex-college student comes back to college so late in the game. Truly. I'm impressed."

"This is temporary," Reese said.

Reese had a migraine that she could feel splitting all the way down the center of her body. She couldn't get Liam's face out of her brain. That look of total loss.

"When did you get so philosophical?" Reese asked.

The door opened again behind them. Claudia's boyfriend, Casey, dragged two big trunks in his wake. He stopped, folding over in deep, gathered breaths.

Behind him?

Vivian laughed.

Vivian, who hadn't spoken any real words about any real things.

Vivian, who may or may not be going home again.

"Reese," Casey said, "when did you get so *strong*? Seriously. Have you been swallowing egg yolks or something?"

"Every morning, every night." She flexed her puny muscles.

"Let me show you to your room," Claudia gestured, her hand trailing over the plastic-looking couch. "Cozy, right?"

It was a larger apartment than the one Reese and Wendy had shared in college. There was a large island in the center of the kitchen/living room that doubled as a beer pong table, Reese suspected.

"This is perfect, thank you," Reese said throwing herself on the couch as she watched Casey try to shove her luggage into the hall closet.

Vivian sat gracefully on the armchair. "Yes, thank you."

Claudia sat down beside her on the couch. "I'm not even going to ask."

"Ask what?" Reese said.

"Why you're here. Why *either* of you are here. I mean, it's your business, your life, whatever. I'm not going to pull a Wendy and make you tell me all your deep dark secrets."

Reese smiled, eyeing Vivian. "That's why you're my favorite Lake. Margaritas?"

"Ten steps ahead of you." Claudia grabbed the car keys and threw them at Casey. "To the bar!"

Casey gritted his teeth. "Okay, but the next time I call you at 3 a.m. asking you to help me out of the ditch that I passed out in, I want to hear no complaints."

Claudia reached up to kiss him quickly. "Deal."

Reese learned a few things as she walked into the bar:

1. She still knew the bouncers.

2. Freshman looked *way* younger than they once had.

3. College bars were no longer fun.

She pictured Liam on the couch at home, the door to her empty bedroom just standing stark and open behind him. She wondered if he ever thought about picking up the phone and calling her.

No, probably not.

She pictured Vivian, quiet and cold, back at the apartment with a head full of secrets. She wondered how it all fell apart. She wondered if they could piece it all back together.

"Hey," Claudia said, bouncing up to Reese, "you look weird. Do you need more alcohol?"

There was something sad about being the oldest person at the bar.

This wasn't her life anymore.

This didn't fit.

But, she was stuck now.

So she said, "Tequila shots."

"Now we're talking!" Claudia grabbed Reese's hand, lifting their hands into the air.

Was it an hour later?

Was it a few minutes?

Who knew where Reese was or where she was going?

Her head spun around her neck, the blur of people dancing around her. Claudia and Casey. That boy and that girl over there. That bartender with that beard.

She wasn't thinking anymore.

She wanted to not think forever.

She wanted so much but wanted to do so little in order to get it.

If she could stand right here and let the world keep rippling around her, she could be okay with that.

Until the whole thing burned down around her.

"Reese!" The voice belonged to a mouth on a head that had a blurred face.

"Who are you?"

A hand waved in front of her face. "Are you okay?"

"Are *you* okay?"

"It's Sophie."

Reese focused her eyes until the collection of parts became Sophie's face.

"Wha—"

"I know what you're thinking. I should be with Liam. I can see how you would think that considering what day it is, but before you say anything, you should know. Liam and I broke up."

Reese tried to move her feet. Every part of her felt numb. "Broke up? What... *day*... is it?"

"Yeah, we broke up," she said, using her hand as a fan against her long, swan neck. "Isn't it obvious? I'm not going to date someone who's in love with you."

The word swirled around in her head like water in a toilet bowl.

Love.

She knew.

How did she know?

"What day is it?" Reese asked again, before she could forget the question.

The question took form between them. As lifelike as the breath from her lips.

"I thought you knew..."

Reese grabbed Sophie's arms, swaying. "What *day* is it, Sophie?"

"The anniversary of his dad's death."

Reese couldn't think.

She couldn't walk either.

But she could feel herself grabbing Claudia. She could hear herself saying, "I need to go."

She could walk, crookedly, out to the car with her body leaned up against Casey.

She could tell him where to go.

And they went.

FIFTY-THREE

Reese stumbled into Delia's barefooted. She'd ditched her heels in the car ride over here. While Claudia begged her to take a nap, Reese had stayed alert the entire time, barely even pausing to blink.

She'd crafted a speech in her head.

She imagined what Wendy would say in a time like this. Wendy was always the one with the words.

And what had Vivian said?

Take yourself out of the equation. Check.

Go back to Liam. Check.

Stay with him for as long as he needs you. She'd missed the mark on that one.

There he was, at his table near the stage, the back of his head facing her. Claudia and Casey waited in the car, promising to be her getaway car, should she need it. Reese sobered up the second she walked into this bar. This secret, safe spot of his that he'd introduced to her.

She didn't wait anymore. She walked straight up in front of him, the sound of the saxophone blazing at her back.

"Reese," he said first.

She struggled to make the words happen. "If I'd known... if I'd realized what day it was... I would have been here."

"It's o—"

She held up her hand. "Here's the thing. I was wrong. I learned all of the wrong lessons. It's always just been me, alone, against everything and everybody else. And I just... I just want to... be here."

He straightened his back and opened his lips.

She held up her hand stronger. "Wait, don't say anything yet or I won't be able to say this. And I want to say this right, okay?"

He nodded. There was light in his eyes. She'd missed that.

"What I'm trying to say is," she said, feeling it fall from her mouth, "I'm sorry. Can I sit with you?"

He leaned over and gently pulled out the chair beside him, just for her.

"Thank you," she said, sitting down.

Liam smiled outright, giving it all he had. "You missed me."

"Stop laughing," she said, turning her eyes to the band. "And *you* missed *me*."

There were things to be said.

Things she should ask.

But it wasn't about her.

People belong *to people.*

No.

People belong with *people.*

And I belong with you.

They sat for a while, not saying anything.

Somewhere in the midst of the big booming jazz, it all slowed down.

The melody.

The audience.

Her heart.

Liam's hand reached for hers, and Reese followed it with her eyes. She carried the weight of it as his palm surrounded hers. And she didn't think she had ever felt so...

Wanted.

No.

Loved.

"Reese," he finally spoke, "would you like to dance?"

She'd never felt more sure of anything. "Yes. Yes, I would."

There was no dance floor in this small, hidden space, but that didn't matter. There was a floor. There was Liam. That's all that mattered.

He held her close enough that she could feel his breath on her neck. The soft skin of his shaven face pressed against hers.

There was possibility again.

Everything.

The possibility of everything.

"Liam," Reese said, tilting her head to look in his eyes, "I love you. You're my best friend. You're my *more*-than-friend. You're my family."

Liam tucked his hands underneath her hair, letting his fingers support her head. "You love me?"

"Yeah, whatever. Don't go picking out china or anything." She could only be serious for so long.

He pulled her in closer again, ignoring the lame attempt at aversion. In her ear, he whispered, "So, what now?"

"Nothing," she whispered back. "*Yet.*"

FIFTY-FOUR

Reese wore a suit.

"You sure this looks professional enough?" she'd asked Vivian.

"Would you consider a change of hair color?" Vivian prompted, pointing at the bright red hair.

Reese laughed. "Always. But not yet."

Joanie wore a suit, too.

Piercings and all, Joanie looked like she could take over the world.

"Well," Reese said, placing her hands on her hips. "you sure do clean up nicely."

Joanie crossed her legs. "Wish I could say the same for you."

"When is he getting here?" Reese asked.

"He's here." Miles' voice cracked the air behind her. Reese turned, offering him a forgiving smile.

Joanie stood, holding her hands together in front of her, nodding Reese in his direction.

"What's this all about?" Miles asked, stopping in the back doorway.

Reese closed the gap, walking toward him. "This is a business proposition."

As if the situation weren't confusing enough, this definitely was not the response Miles had been expecting. He glanced back at Joanie, then turned his attention to Reese.

"Look," he said, lowering his voice, "I don't know what you're thinking, but I'm not sure if this is the best idea."

Reese shrugged. "Honestly? Me either. But there are no rules."

"Just hear us out," Joanie chimed in from behind them.

Still, Miles hesitated. "She knows?"

"Before you, actually," Reese admitted.

Miles held his jaw in his hand, massaging his chin. "Well, damn."

"Come on," Reese said, hooking her arm through his. "You're going to want to sit down for this one."

Joanie folded her hands over the table like a poker player. "Reese, would you like to start us off?"

"I would love to," Reese said, nodding graciously. She turned to Miles. "To begin, I'd like to address the father-daughter situation that has come to light in recent weeks."—She paused.—"Well, for one of us. Here's my proposition on that new knowledge: screw the titles. I like you, Miles. I like working for you. And as far as genetics, well, we can let that work itself out."

Miles absorbed her words. "Okay," he said. "So... we take it slow?"

"Absolutely," Joanie interjected. "You two need time to adjust. Get to know each other. Let the relationship work itself out on its own, you know?"

Miles nodded at her. "Thanks for your input."

"No problem."

Still, the look of confusion didn't leave Miles' face.

"It's like this," Reese said. "I don't need to be raised anymore. I'm all whole and fixed, now. So, I'm suggesting a different sort of partnership."

"Partnership?" he asked.

Reese looked to Joanie.

Joanie straightened her back. "We'd like to propose the conversion of the coffee shop into a bar."

"For nighttime only," Reese interjected.

"And Reese and I would run it ourselves, with your guidance, of course," Joanie followed.

"With her business degree—"

"And her expansive alcohol knowledge—"

"It would be the perfect way to increase revenue and attract new customers."

They both paused, looking at each other, then, at Miles. There was nothing readable about his face. No giveaways. Nothing.

"So," Reese said, breaking the silence, "what do you think?"

Miles sighed, crossing his arms. Then, he smiled. "Let's talk numbers."

And so, they did.

They spent the rest of the afternoon talking, strategizing, and agreeing on their terms.

Reese would run the financial side of things, handling the budgets and managing their profit margins.

Joanie would take over the day-to-day operations, monitoring inventory and running all of the branding, from the new logo to the marketing push.

Miles would oversee everything, helping when needed.

"We're going to need a new name, I guess," Miles said, reluctantly.

Reese smiled. "Already got it covered."

"Introducing," Joanie said, extending her arms wide, "Bean There, Brew Dat."

Miles smiled again.

A record, by any standard.

"You've got yourselves a deal."

2017

"We are not getting hamsters."

"They're small. You won't even notice them."

"No. Hamsters."

"You know, sooner or later, you're going to have to accept one of my suggestions."

No to the chicken coop.

No to the water beds.

No to the sunrise yoga classes.

It was like Wendy was intentionally coming here to crush all of Reese's wacky, but legitimate dreams.

"I would count on later if I were you," Vivian suggested.

The three of them.

Back together again.

Family.

Reese remembered all of the things she used to love about having Wendy as her roommate.

The clean dishes.

The pancakes on Sunday mornings.

The way she'd wake Reese every time she overslept, which was basically every morning.

And now with Vivian? They could conquer the world.

"How long before we ask her what happened?" Wendy had asked Reese about Vivian.

Reese had wished for a decent answer. Instead, she'd said, "I think we have to let her come to us. We just have to be here."

So far?

Silence.

"What's in this box? Your boulder collection?" Reese asked, dropping the heaviest and last of Wendy's boxes onto the tile.

"Careful!" Wendy admonished. "Those are my paintings."

"And it's so heavy because...?"

Wendy lifted the lid. "I lined the bottom with stones so the box wouldn't flip."

"Of course. Like any sane person would."

"Here," Wendy said, handing Vivian a wrapped canvas. "A housewarming gift."

"You shouldn't have," Vivian said, as she carefully unwrapped the paper.

"Hey, where's mine?" Reese demanded.

"Calm down," Wendy said. "You have to learn how to share."

The painting was stunning. In her trademark watercolor, Wendy had painted the sun, just barely balancing over the treetops, and in the middle of the frame, was their new little house.

"Well, shit," Reese said.

"Not the reaction I was hoping for," Wendy said, laughing.

As Reese hugged Wendy, it was an automatic, knee-jerk embrace, her arms swallowing Wendy so roughly that it was a miracle any air could make it down her windpipe. Vivian, for her part, captured them both in a sweet embrace.

"You're welcome," Wendy managed to squeak out.

"I have to say one nice, serious thing to you before I go back to happy fun times, okay?"

Wendy situated herself on her knees. "Okay."

"Are you sure you're ready for this?" Reese winked at Vivian, who shook her head.

Wendy nodded. "The most ready."

Reese sucked in a deep, dramatic breath. "I told one of Simon's conquests that he had herpes. You're welcome."

Wendy's reactions went from stoic to confused to completely elated. She laughed so hard that she fell to the carpet, rolling onto her side, gripping at her waist.

"That is the greatest act of friendship you've committed for me," Wendy said.

"And the best part is," Reese added, raising her eyebrows, "it was all Vivian's idea."

Vivian shrugged. "What can I say? I'm the brains behind this operation."

Wendy's eyes grew wide. "Well, well, well. Things *have* changed around here."

"You haven't seen anything yet," Vivian answered, her head held high.

The three of them.

Back together again.

Family.

And it was like time didn't even exist anymore.

Moments became days.

Days became years.

Years became a lifetime.

THANK YOU!

A QUICK LOVE NOTE

Dear reader,

Thank you for picking up this little book of mine. (Okay, maybe not so little.) I know how many options you have, because I'm constantly faced with the sheer enormity of options in my Goodreads wish list.

What I didn't know until a few years ago was how I could support authors I loved. Then, I found out about a little thing called reviews.

Without reviews, indie books like this one have little chance of making it in the big, congested book market.

Leaving a review can be quick and painless. No need to write an essay. A single sentence can help this book find its way into the hands of readers who might like it, too.

So, if you're so inclinded, please head on over to Amazon and give this book, and any book you'd like to support, a rating.

Thank you!

Jenny

AUTHOR BIOGRAPHY

Jenny Bravo spent her childhood in Disney princess nightgowns and climbing trees barefooted. These days, she usually wears shoes. As a part-time writer, she drinks too much coffee and writes feverishly in the fringe hours. Otherwise, she blogs at www.jennybravobooks.com and plays on Twitter. She calls New Orleans home, but she also considers herself a resident of Narnia, Hogwarts and Neverland.

You can find her on social media @jennybravobooks.

For more information, visit her blog at www.jennybravobooks.com. To connect with other readers of this book, use the hashtag #TATM2 on social media.